TONY MO

SERIES HAILED AS:

"One of the best zombie novels out there."
—Horror Bound Magazine

"Fantastic … that is what you really need to know about this book above anything else. An absolute blast."
—BuyZombie.com

"Innovative and breathtaking … will reignite long lost fears and keep you up at night."
—Bryce Beattie, author of *Oasis*

"Wonderful, engaging … will continue to resonate, emotionally, long after the final page is read."
—HorrorScope

EDEN: MORIAH

A ZOMBIE NOVEL BY TONY MONCHINSKI

Permuted Press
The formula has been changed...
Shifted... Altered... *Twisted.*
www.permutedpress.com

For Garet Jax and Raymond & Andrew Garth

A PERMUTED PRESS book
published by arrangement with the author

ISBN (trade paperback): 978-1-61868-140-9
ISBN (eBook): 978-1-61868-141-6

Eden: Moriah copyright © 2013
by Tony Monchinski.
All Rights Reserved.

"I Never wanna die/ I Never wanna leave/ I'll Never say goodbye/
Forever, whatever"
—Foo Fighters, *Walk*

"How surely are the dead beyond death. Death is what the living
carry with them. A state of dread, like some uncanny foretaste of a
bitter memory. But the dead do not remember and nothingness is not
a curse. Far from it."
—Cormac McCarthy, *Suttree*

BEAR'S ARMY

Riley dragged herself out of the water, over the stones of the riverbed and into a grassy field. Exhausted and soaked through, the autumn chill left her shivering. The river, swollen from the rains, had swept her downstream. How far, she did not know. The field she crawled through was surrounded on three sides by hills carpeted with orange- and brown-leaved trees. They stretched a short distance before becoming mountains.

She had lost Anthony's beanie in the river. *That damned beanie.* She hated the thing, but her breath was catching in her throat as she considered its loss. Overcome with grief and mounting enervation, Riley did not take note of her surroundings.

She did not notice that the grass she lay in was parched. The rain had missed this area and the summer here had been extremely dry.

She did not see the upper half of the two thousand pound Mark 84 bomb jutting from the earth in the center of the mead. Riley lay among the brittle onion grass and Golden Rod, bone-weary, unaware of the explosive ordinance's proximity.

Nor did Riley see the man sitting with his back against the weapon. But he saw her.

Lowering the single lens field glasses, the man let the minocular hang from the cord around his thick neck. Now this, *this* was interesting. He had been sitting here for some time, not really expecting to see anyone, and this one was definitely *not* the one he had hoped to see. Still…

He rose to his full height, over two meters, and looked about the field. The woman was apparently alone. He had watched her pull herself out of the river to where she now sprawled. *Like something the cat had dragged in*, his father would have said. Judging by the looks of her, and the fact that she appeared unarmed, he didn't expect she was going to be able to put up much of a fight, even if she wanted to. He slung the FN FAL .63 with the chain saw mounted under the barrel over his shoulder, but left his Australian Outback Drover coat open, the butt of the .357 revolver holstered in a belly band around his midsection. Just in case.

Riley heard movement in the grass and rolled over to her hands and knees before standing unsteadily.

The man approaching her was tall and huge and cloaked in a full length sheep herders coat. His ebony hands were empty but the rubber grip of the big six shooter at his waist was obvious. He wore the strangest looking black goggles attached to a headpiece with faux dreadlocks sprouting from it. He was not a zombie. Was he a mutant?

She didn't know what he was.

When he reached her, he saw that she had been crying.

"You know you're being followed?" he asked.

The woman looked the worse for wear but she also looked ready to throw down. She was in some kind of fighting stance, one leg out in front of the other, hands open in front of her.

"Relax." He held his hands out at his sides, open palmed. "Take it easy."

"Who are you?"

"Boy…" He looked her over, thinking, *yeah*, he had been right in his assessment: Something the cat dragged in. "You look like you've been through hell."

"I said, 'Who are you?'"

As he pulled the Oakley Medusa hat and goggles off, revealing his shaved head, the man thought this woman was in no position to be making demands of him. But he didn't see how answering her would do him any harm, so he did.

"Call me Dee."

"*Dee?*"

"Yeah."

"Dee?"

"Yeah, like the fourth letter in the alphabet."

"How long have you been watching me?"

"I was just sitting, over there…" Dee turned and pointed behind him to the bomb. Riley saw it and her eyes widened in disbelief. "And I saw you get up out of the water and come over here. That's all."

"Is that what I think it is…?"

"Well, it's not a nuke, if that's what you're worried about."

"How do I know you're not with *them*?" Even as she asked it, Riley saw how this man Dee made no move to threaten her, even with the pistol in his belt and the big battle rifle slung over his back.

"How do you know I'm not with *whom*?"

"The people I—forget it." Riley waved her hand. "What do you think you're going to do to me?"

"What do I think I'm going *to do* to you?" Dee was puzzled. The way she said it…it came across as a threat. He wasn't planning on doing *anything* with her and he told her so, and after he had told her so he asked, "Why—what is it you think I was going to do with you?"

She looked him up and down, less warily though still on her guard. He was pretty damned big. Tall. Black. And bald. His eyes looked tough, but not cruel. Riley looked from him to the river, but only for a moment. "You have no idea what I've been through the last few days."

"Those people behind you have anything to do with that?"

Riley turned her back on him again, staring across the field and up the river, but she saw no one. When she turned around to tell him so he hadn't moved any closer but had extended the minocular to her.

"Take a look."

Riley relaxed her stance and lowered her hands. She took the proffered lens. When she figured out how to focus it, she saw them. The redhead was in the lead. The son, Tommy, followed, and then the brothers, David and Keith. Behind them, MacKenzie and Rodriguez and Gammon and others she didn't know the names of. *So many of them.*

"Shit," she muttered to herself.

"Maybe you should come with me." It was just a suggestion.

"Why would I do that?"

"Because I don't think you especially want those people to catch up with you, now do you?"

She did not answer right away and Dee started to wonder what he was getting himself mixed up in. Maybe it would be better to leave her here, let her deal with whatever she had gotten herself into. He did not know this woman. There might be a good reason people were after her. Maybe she had done something to deserve it.

"Just give me a gun," Riley said. "Give me that revolver you've got there."

"I can't do that."

"Why not?"

"Well, for any number of reasons."

"Like what?" Her voice nearly cracked, on the verge of hysteria.

"Listen, I don't mean to alarm you…" *Yeah*, Dee thought, he would definitely have to extricate himself from this situation. This woman wasn't right. "…but do you really think you're in a position to make demands here?" She did not answer. "And its obvious those people pursuing you are responsible for whatever it is you've gone through—and whatever *that* was, it's obvious it sure wasn't good. Am I right?"

Riley looked back over her shoulder to the river again.

"So, what am I going to do?" Dee considered aloud. "Give you *my* gun? It's got six bullets. You count how many people are coming down here after you?"

She shook her head.

"Yeah, well I have. There's more than six of them. And even if you're the best shot in the world, the way you look right now, if I hadn't walked up on you—you would have fallen asleep right there. You're done. You're not in any shape to fight today."

"You don't understand…" She looked at wit's end. "You don't understand what they did!"

"You're right, I *don't*." Dee had a change of heart. He didn't like to see women cry. Neither had his father. "So why don't you come with me and tell me about it. I give you my word: I'm not going to try and hurt you, unless you try to hurt me."

"No, you don't get it." She was shaking her head vigorously. "I have to…I have to kill them, all of them, and then I have to find *him*."

"Find who?"

"Why should I tell you?" She almost barked back.

"You're really going to persist with that crap?" Despite what his father had taught him, he was ready to turn and walk away, to leave her to her fate.

"No," she answered, distraught.

"Good."

"This is crazy."

"Damn right it is."

She blurted it out: "I have to find a man named Bear."

Dee paused and looked at her anew. "You say you're…" He wanted to make sure he had heard her right. "You're looking for someone named Bear?"

"Yes!" She nearly yelled at him. "Damn it! Give me your gun, mister, *please*."

"I can't do that. And now you *have* to come with me." Dee made to reach out and grab her arm—"Come."—but she pulled away, looking like she might bolt at any moment.

"Get away from me!" But she wasn't making to run from him. She had settled into the fighting stance again, feet shoulder width apart, a slight bend in her knees, one hand up near her face, the other down by her waist.

"No—no—no, listen to me. Okay?" Dee stepped back from her, holding his hands up. "Listen. I know this man you've come to see. *Bear*? I know Bear, okay?"

"Yeah, right." Riley shot back contemptuously. "How do you know him?"

"What I want to know…" It was the way his voice changed—like Dee was protecting someone—that sold Riley, "…is what *you* want with him."

"I have to find him."

"I heard that. *Why*?"

"That's for me to tell him."

"Uh-huh."

"Please—do you really know Bear?"

The black man in the Drover coat just continued to look at her.

"Take me to him, okay? Then I'll explain everything."

Dee considered it.

"What's your name?" he asked her.

"Riley."

Dee turned his back and walked away from her. "Let's go, Riley." She looked once towards where the hunters would be coming from before following him.

"What the hell is that?" she asked when they passed the bomb.

"It's a bomb."

"Is it dangerous?" Riley walked around it, giving it wide berth.

"Well, don't go knocking on it with a hammer, if that's what you had in mind."

As they headed towards the trees and the hills, Dee warned her. "Look, there's still a lot of Zed out here. We haven't been able to get them all yet. So let's keep it quiet, all right?"

He led her across the field and into the trees. The slope they ascended turned steeply upwards into a mountain. They had gone a couple hundred meters when they came across a green and black four-wheeled all-terrain vehicle parked in the middle of nowhere.

Dee shrugged out of the Belgian rifle and secured it on the side of the ATV. He straddled the machine and powered it up.

"Get on," he told Riley. She looked at him and the quad, then back at the field. She put one leg over it sat down behind the big man.

"Hold on," Dee told her as he gassed the four-wheeler. "Tight."

"She came up here," Red was saying, following the trail of dried, matted grass into the field. "And she stopped right there."

Gammon stood silently and let the girl do her work. She was good. The *best*. Gammon noticed how Tommy stood there, looking off into the distance. Waiting for Red to tell him which way to go.

"But she wasn't alone…" Red looked into the trees beyond the field.

"What do you mean?" Tommy asked before Gammon could.

"This set of tracks here, see?" Red knelt in the grass. "Those are a man's boots. A big man. These here? These are our woman's. They both head out over that way together…"

"Hey," Frankie called out, "look at this!"

Keith's face paled. "Is that what I think it is?"

"It's a bomb," his brother, David, averred.

Rodriguez was tapping on the bomb's casing with the butt of his HK416.

"Don't do that, you idiot," shouted Gammon. "You want to blow us all to hell?"

Rodriguez looked at him, down at the bomb, and then took a tentative step away from it.

"How do you think that got here?" Frankie was looking around the field.

Chang, his broken arm against his body in a sling, put a hand to his forehead and squinted up into the sky.

"He was sitting here…" Red knelt down next to the bomb, one hand touching it gently, respectfully. "And he got up…and he walked over there to where she was. And then the two of them got up and went…" She pointed into the trees "…that way."

Tommy was about to say, "Let's go," but no sooner had Red pointed then Tobias yelled out, "Oh, shit! Here they come!"

Three zombies were dithering their way, having emerged from the tree line ahead.

MacKenzie, Rodriguez, Tobias, Frankie and the brothers formed a firing line and immediately started to unload on them.

"3 o'clock!" Gammon yelled over the din and Red turned. Four more were coming towards them, falteringly. Red set down her N4 and drew the Stechkin APS, drawing the pistol from its wooden holster and affixing it as a shoulder stock as she broke from the group and walked off towards the gang of four.

Two of the original three zombies were already down. The third was jerking in place as bullets perforated it.

"One shot at a time," Gammon was yelling as a couple of the men fired on full-auto. "How many times I have to tell you guys?"

Five or six additional undead had joined the first three, appearing from the trees.

"Fuckers!" Rodriguez cursed. He sighted through the scope atop his HK416 and fired a short burst. The side of a zombie's head flew one way while its body fell in the other direction.

"Single shot, Rodriguez, you moron!"

"Red!" MacKenzie broke from the group and made off after Little Red. She was firing her Stechkin in three round bursts, zombies collapsing flat to the earth.

So intent was MacKenzie on reaching Red's side that he did not see the legless zombie that had dragged itself through the grass. The hideous creature wrapped its arms around MacKenzie's lower legs and brought him to the ground. No sooner had he landed on his side, the wind knocked from him and the thing bit into his exposed calf where his pants leg had ridden up over his boot.

"Shit!" MacKenzie kicked the zombie off, rolling away from the putrefactive thing.

The creature propped itself up on its palms, arms straightened. As MacKenzie watched in horror it chewed on the piece of him in its mouth.

"*Awwww*, no," he groaned.

From seemingly out of nowhere Red materialized beside the zombie and buried the business end of her throwing hatchet in the top of its skull. The creature froze in mid-chew—its mouth gone wide, MacKenzie's calf meat falling out—before splaying in the grass and dirt.

"This thing stinks." Red wrinkled her nose distastefully.

MacKenzie stood up. His leg was bleeding and hurt like hell. The firing line had succeeded in bringing down the first wave of zombies that had disgorged from the trees, but there were new moans, and MacKenzie knew more undead were coming. Many more.

"How many times do I have to tell you guys?" Gammon was chastising the others. "When you run out of ammunition, don't come crying to me."

MacKenzie looked down at his leg. *Shit.* This was *not* his day.

"Chang, you got your kit with you?" MacKenzie heard Gammon call. "Then wire that bomb up for me, all right?"

"Can I get some help here maybe? I got one arm…"

"You all right, Mac?" Red was standing next to him. She inserted a fresh magazine in her automatic pistol.

Fierce cracks rent the air as Frankie and Tobias, taking turns with their sniper rifles, drilled the zombies that blundered along out of the trees.

"Nah, Red. I'm not all right." MacKenzie held his leg out and shook it. He and Red stood next to one another, considering it. "If you ever see Janis again, Red," he nodded, "Tell her I love her and the kids." Red nodded back. MacKenzie turned away. "Make it quick, Red. Okay?"

MacKenzie was looking out over the river when Red put a three-round burst in the back of his head.

"So Mac got bit, huh?" Rodriguez stared in disbelief toward where his friend's lifeless body lay. Red had rejoined the others around the bomb. Rodriguez had seen it when the Zed grabbed his buddy. He'd known Mac got bit, and he knew the outcome of *that*. But he felt like he had to say something. MacKenzie had been his friend.

"Yeah," Little Red confirmed. "Mac got bit."

Tommy was still staring off into the woods.

"Okay," said Gammon. "From the sounds of it, we got a lot of zombies coming at us through them trees." As he spoke Frankie fired, dispatching another. "Best to get the hell out of here. How's that rig coming along, Chang?"

"Almost there."

Red looked where Tommy was looking and thought ahead. "Don't blow the bomb."

"What's that?" Gammon asked her.

"Don't blow it yet." There was conviction in her voice.

"Sounds like Red's got a plan," Keith remarked to David.

"You want me to stop?" Chang looked up from where he was running wires from the bomb to a detonator with his one good arm.

"No, finish setting it up. But I have an idea."

"*See,*" Keith told his brother.

"What's your idea?" Gammon asked the girl.

Toby fired and laid another zombie low.

"I'm done here," said Chang.

"I'll tell you about it on the way." Red had already started walking off.

"Where we going?" Gammon called after her.

"She's following the trail." Tommy walked past Gammon, after Little Red.

"She's following the trail," Gammon repeated, looking towards the trees. Red was heading into them. Tommy and the others were following Red. The tracks of the woman they had chased and whomever she was with went off into the trees. There were zombies in the trees. Probably a lot of zombies. All of them, Gammon knew, heading this way now, drawn by the gunfire.

"Shit."

Gammon thought that sometimes you just had to go along with the way events were taking you. "She's following the trail," he whispered under his breath, walking off after the others.

Riley clung to Dee's back as the quad bounced across the rugged terrain for several kilometers. They passed between two mountains, slopes carpeted with multi-colored trees on either side of them. They raced along trails she would not have noticed alone on foot.

Without warning, Dee pulled the four-wheeler over.

"Why'd we stop?" She was off the back of the quad, putting some distance between herself and the man on the all-terrain vehicle.

"What? You think I'm going to do *what* to you now?"

Dee saw the look that crossed her face before Riley clenched her jaw.

"Oh no, I'm sorry…" he said quickly. "My god—what have you been through? Look, we stopped because I have to go to the bathroom, okay? *Really.*"

"I—I'm sorry, it's just…"

"No, no, it's okay. I was insensitive. But look, I do have to go, so why don't you wait here—"

"Can't you just go right here? I won't look."

The way she asked it, something in her voice. Scared. Desperate. Dee didn't know who this woman was, or what she had experienced, but he felt for her.

"Okay, don't look."

Riley turned and looked back the way they had come. She'd left so much back there. Her brother. Troi and Ev. The guide, Krieger. Those killers. Lost in thought, she didn't need to consciously ignore the sound of Dee's urination.

"I'm good," Dee announced when he was done.

They climbed back on the quad and drove for a while longer. It was cold on the four-wheeler and Riley huddled close to the warmth and expanse of Dee's back. Her clothes, including the shirt and jacket she had stripped off the man she'd killed, were still soaked from the river, which wasn't helping.

The quad crested a rise and Dee pulled it over again, letting it idle.

"Look." He pointed, but Riley was already staring. Beneath them, perhaps two or three kilometers off, a column of men and women were marching across the terrain. Riley could see vehicles too: tanks and personnel carriers and helicopters flew over the procession.

"There's so many of them." She couldn't believe it.

"About five thousand. Roughly."

"You know them—who are they?"

"That's Bear's Army." Before she could ask, Dee told her to hold on. He gave the quad gas and Riley held fast.

★ ★ ★

They reached the first sentries fifteen minutes later. Dee slowed the quad as they hailed him—Riley noted how the man she rode with was immediately recognized—and stared at her curiously. After another ten minutes on the four-wheeler, Dee and Riley pulled into the remains of a camp. Hundreds of burned-out fires were scattered around the terrain. A dozen tents of varying sizes remained, with people moving between them.

"D.L.!"

As Dee parked the quad, a short, stocky Hispanic man of medium height greeted him. Riley thought the guy looked around her age, maybe a few years older. He wore a bandana around the side of his head and his hair was spiked up out the top of it.

"Victor. What's crackin', nephew?"

"Africa, Dee. You back just in time."

"Africa." Dee harrumphed, pushing his goggles back on top of his cap. He and Riley were standing. "Guess I *am* back just in time."

"I can think of someone who'll be glad to see you..." Riley could tell Victor was messing around with Dee, the way he smirked as he said it.

"Yeah, well, what are you going to do?"

"No, D.L, home-slice. What are *you* going to do? Hi there, pretty lady."

"Hi."

"Victor," Victor said by way of introduction, holding out his hand. Riley felt weird shaking it and telling him her name. A few short hours before she had been struggling for her life and now she was exchanging salutations.

"What'd this guy do to you, Riley?" Victor joked, alluding to her disheveled appearance.

"I think he might have saved my life. It's too early to tell."

"Yeah, well..." Before Victor could say whatever it was he was going to say, a woman's voice spoke.

"Well. Would you look at *this*." She was black, but it was difficult to tell at first because much of the skin of her face, hands and arms was blotched pink, burnt long ago. "The prodigal son returns." Thick dreadlocks hung down past her shoulders while puckered keloid scars ran up and down her face from the burns.

"I don't think that's the word you wanted to use." Riley heard the annoyance in Dee's voice. Victor stood back and watched, his smirk gone.

"You come back just in time to head to the motherland, D.L.," the woman answered. "Who's the trollop?"

"Riley, Tris." There was no enthusiasm in Dee's introduction. "Tris, Riley."

"Hello." Riley greeted the older woman, who looked her up and down. Riley tried not to stare back. Tris wore a hand grenade around her neck.

"Well, little chicken, I'm guessing you clean up okay?"

Riley didn't know what to say to that.

"D.L., you finally bring a hoochie back home and what's the matter—she can't talk?"

"Look," Riley turned to Dee, "what the hell is this woman's problem?"

"You want to keep your tongue," the black woman spoke, "hold it, girl." Riley noticed the pistols Tris wore on her hip and thigh. Two handles jutted over her shoulders from the sickles strapped on her back.

"Tris—lay off." Dee wasn't asking. "Riley's had it rough. Anyone can see that. Let's get her looked at."

"She looks like she's gonna be all right to me. You're a tough little bitch, ain't you, chickenhead?"

"Lady…" Riley looked into the other woman's burnt, scarred face, into her eyes. "Don't. Fuck. With. Me."

"*Ohhhh.*" Tris whistled. "You go, girlfriend. This one's a tart." Two other men had wandered over as Tris spoke. They were both taller than Riley, but shorter than Dee. One bore a bullet scar on either side of his neck. The other had streaks of white in his hair and dark eyes. "I think I'm going to like this one. Where'd you say you picked her up, Dee?"

"Out by the bomb. She was being chased."

"Chased?" Tris looked mildly interested. "By who?"

"That's what you're going to tell us, right, Riley?"

"Yes." Riley continued to glare at the disfigured woman.

"D.L." As she said it, Tris held Riley's gaze. "We got enough of our own shit to deal with here. Did you really have to go and adopt a stray? Yeah—*you*, freak. What'chu lookin' at?"

"Go fuck yourself, lady."

"You know what, D.L.?" Tris showed her teeth but there was no smile in her eyes. "Nah, scratch that—I'm *not* gonna like this one. Girl, something here stinks like dead fish."

"Must be you."

Victor and the two other men sniggered. Dee did not. "What the fuck are you laughing at?" Tris flared at the three. "Bruce, Kevin—shut the fuck up. You too, Victor."

"She was looking for Bear." Dee's declaration gave the others pause.

Tris looked Riley over again. "Bear, huh?"

"Yeah."

"How'd you hear about Bear?"

Riley shook her head. "Everyone's heard of Bear…"

"Is that so?" Tris did not look pleased. "What'd you hear about him?"

"I want to see him."

"You want to see Bear."

"What'd you tell her, D.L.?" the man with dark eyes, Kevin, asked.

"I didn't tell her anything."

"I said—" Tris asked a second time, none too patiently "—why do you want to see Bear?"

"Because I have something to show him."

"Show me."

Riley looked daggers at her. "Go fuck yourself."

"Gurl…you *keep* sayin' that to me…" Tris shook her head and licked her upper lip.

Bruce, the man with the bullet wounds in his neck, looked at Kevin, nodding in approval.

"Tris," Dee spoke. "You're not helping."

"This chick's tough." Bruce whispered to Kevin, his voice hoarse.

"Or fucking crazy," Kevin whispered back.

"Well," Riley demanded of Dee, "can I see Bear or not?"

"You want to see Bear?" Tris looked at Riley as though the younger woman was ignorant. She spoke to the others. "She wants to see Bear. Let her go see Bear then, D.L."

"Where is he?" Riley did not wait for Dee to direct her.

Tris pointed to a tent several yards off. Riley immediately started walking towards it.

"Riley, wait!"

"Let her go, D.L. You heard her. She wants to see Bear."

Riley entered the tent. It was lit by candles and large enough that its corners were lost in shadow. Crates stood packed atop one another, waiting to be moved. A high-backed chair was placed in the center. Something rested against it and a figure was seated in it. Riley could not see the person because the back of the chair was to her.

"Bear?" she asked hesitantly.

19

When the person did not answer, Riley walked determinedly to the chair and around it. A man was seated there, but she couldn't believe this was the Bear she had heard about. The man she looked upon was ancient and frail, his clothes hanging off him. He looked up at her as she stood there and then he looked away. A flanged mace was propped against the chair and a stuffed animal of some sort rested on his lap.

Riley looked at the man and took the photograph out of her shirt. This couldn't be Bear, could it? But it had to be…

"Are you Bear?" She asked him and when he still did not answer she asked him again, more forcefully, more desperately.

"He's not Bear." Victor and the others had come into the tent behind her.

"What happened to Bear?"

"He won't answer you," said Victor, his spikes sticking out of his bandana. "He hasn't spoken since I've known him. And I've known him all my life. Ask D.L."

The man in the chair was stroking the stuffed cat in his lap.

"It's true," Dee affirmed. Tris stood with her arms folded under the grenade on her neck, looking oddly satisfied.

Riley shook her head, feeling overwhelmed. She didn't understand any of this. *Where was Bear? Where was he?*

"I'm sorry…" She didn't want to cry, especially not in front of Tris. "There's just some things—some things I'm not getting right now."

"Go ahead," encouraged Dee.

"First," Riley sniffled and wiped a finger under her eye. "…is Dee short for something?"

"Short for D.L.," answered Victor.

"And what's D.L.?"

"Short for D.L.R.," Victor added.

"D.L.R.?"

Dee said, "David Lee Roth."

"Okay." That meant nothing to Riley. "And do you…or don't you…know Bear?"

"Of course I know him." Dee was adamant. "He's my father."

"Okay," Riley nodded. *His father.* "Now we're getting somewhere." She hoped so at least. "And where can I find your father, D.L.?"

"You won't." Tris answered before Dee could. "You can't. He dead."

"*What?*" Riley didn't believe what she'd heard.

"He's not here anymore." Dee gave Tris another cold look as he spoke, but Riley was so spent she barely noticed.

"But—but," she stammered, the information registering in her shocked, harried brain. "I came all this way...Anthony...we..." Riley put one hand out as she sunk to the ground.

"Hey, you okay?" Dee was at her side. "Victor, go get Carrie."

Riley was weeping inconsolably.

"This girl is a mess," Kevin whispered to Bruce.

"Yeah," the other rasped back. "Maybe she ain't as hard as she seems."

"I'm sorry...I'm sorry," Riley spoke through her tears. "Bear's gone. That's, that's...*great*. Then...then who's this guy?"

"He's the Bishop," Kevin said.

"Okay. *Right*. Look—again—it's me, I'm sorry..."

"You need to rest, Riley," Dee told her. "When was the last time you slept?"

"No, it's not that, it's okay...I need to go...I'll..."

"That's just crazy talk, Riley. You need a meal and a cot."

"That's a real cat in his lap, too, isn't it?"

"It is," Dee acknowledged. "I'll have to explain later."

"I brought this...to show..." Riley held the photo up and then let it fall from her fingers to the earthen floor. "I brought this to show Bear...but now..." What was the use? There was no Bear to show it to.

Dee was kneeling beside Riley, comforting her. Tris stood, arms crossed, shifting her weight from one foot to the other. Kevin looked at Bruce and Bruce looked at Kevin and when the two of them looked to Tris, she rolled her eyes in her burnt head.

The elderly man they called the Bishop had gotten out of the chair and bent gingerly to retrieve the picture. His mouth opened.

"Young lady, please..." The Bishop sunk down besides Dee, cupping Riley's face in his hands. He'd set his stuffed cat on the chair cushion. "Tell me. Where did you get this?"

Dee was staring at the Bishop, baffled. Kevin's eyes were wide and Bruce's attention was rapt. Even Tris had unfolded her arms and stood expectantly with her hands on her hips.

"A man gave it to me."

"What was his name?"

"He was crazy."

"Did he have a name?"

"Mickey. He said his name was Mickey."

The Bishop looked fixedly at Riley. The others in the tent watched him watch her. When he held the photo up in his hand, he declared, "I knew this man."

"You did—that's..." Riley didn't know how to respond or what to say. "Who—who are you?"

"Here they call me the Bishop." His voice was loud and clear—"But my Christian name is Turner."—stronger than Riley would have imagined, judging by his frail frame. "Fred Turner." The elderly man raised the photograph for all to see. "And I knew this man. In a place called Eden."

"Keep quiet," Little Red ordered Rodriguez.

"Why? They can't hear us."

In the distance below them, the tail-end of a heavily armored cavalcade of people and their vehicles disappeared into the east.

"I don't care. Hush."

Rodriguez looked at the girl. Earlier she'd killed his best friend in the world, and now she was telling *him* to shut up? *Right*. In the past, Rodriguez had deferred to Red like everyone else. He'd done so because Thomas held the little girl in such high regard. But Thomas, *well*, Thomas wasn't here now.

"Where do you think they're going?" Tommy wondered.

"To the coast," replied Gammon. The four of them were on their stomachs atop the rise where Dee and Riley had stopped an hour before.

"If she's with all those people..." Rodriguez made himself look away from Red. "...then that's it. We can't fight all them."

"Fuck that," Tommy snarled.

"She's not with them," declared Red. "See their four-wheeler's tracks? They went off north-west. Maybe they don't know those people. Maybe they were trying to avoid them. Maybe they knew them, but something else took them over there."

"What do you think, Red?" Gammon asked the girl.

"I think we keep doing what we've been doing."

"Follow their trail?"

"Follow their trail."

"Do you think she knows we're on her tail?" Rodriguez asked.

"We ought to assume she does," said Gammon. "And play it safe."

"I just want to get my hands on that—"

"There'll be time for that, Tommy," Gammon told his friend's boy. "Calmer heads need to prevail now."

The young man did not look satisfied.

They crawled back down off the rise, on their bellies, standing only when there was no chance they could be seen by the people off in the distance.

David, Keith and the others were waiting for them at the bottom of the hill.

"We got troop movements east of here," Gammon explained to the assembled hard men. "Tough to tell how many and where they're going. The bad news is there's thousands of them. The good news is they're heading away from us, over in that direction." He pointed. "The woman's trail continues over there. We're going to keep on it. Any questions?"

There were none.

"Good."

Red led them through the trees and hills. She kept one eye on the path the four-wheeled vehicle had left, her other on the foliage around them, looking for anything out of the ordinary, anything that might indicate an ambush or trap. She felt like *she* was the one playing the game now.

It wasn't an unpleasant feeling.

Red enjoyed being tested and she hadn't been tested like this in some time. In her mind she wrestled with the death of Thomas, with what she'd had to do to Mac, with the knowledge that their camp had most likely fallen to Cosmo and his ilk.

She was aware that Rodriguez was behind her, that he had that H&K HK416 in both of his hands, that he was staring holes into her back every step of the way. Rodriguez could fire from behind and cut her down, kill her whenever he wanted. She wouldn't put it past him, though she didn't think he'd go through with it in front of Gammon, in front of Tommy and the others. She knew that if Rodriguez did that, he'd die next.

"Red."

She barely paused to glance over her shoulder. "What is it, Frankie?"

"I think we're being followed." The man with the sniper rifle said it calmly.

"*We're* being followed?" Rodriguez opened his big mouth. "*We're* the ones doing the following."

"Zombies?" Chang asked, worried. Riley had broken his arm. The zombies couldn't smell that, could they?

"Not zombies."

"How long now?" Intent on the trail before them, Red had completely ignored the path behind them. Mistakes like that, she knew, could get you killed.

"For at least the last two hours. Far as I can tell."

"How many?" Red still hadn't stopped, still hadn't looked back. They had entered an especially thick copse of evergreens.

"One…" Frankie did not sound certain. "…it wasn't clear, and whoever it is, he's some way off."

"Okay. *Rodriguez.*"

"Yeah, Red?"

"You think you can stop staring at me long enough to follow this trail?" She didn't wait for him to answer, not caring for what he might say. "In one minute you're on point. All of you keep moving. Follow Rodriguez, follow the trail."

"What you gonna do, Red?" Rodriguez asked.

"Keep walking…" Red had stepped against a tree and frozen in place. Rodriguez was smart enough not to halt. He continued to follow the tracks, Frankie at his side with his sniper rifle. One by one, they passed the tree Red stood flush against. Most did not notice her.

"You okay, Red?"

"I'll catch up soon, Ed."

"Want company, Red?" She wanted to say yes to Tommy but couldn't and didn't. What she might have to do was better done alone. Tommy walked by, never turning. Chang was the last of their group to pass her tree and he whispered out of the side of his mouth—"Keep safe, Red"—as he marched by.

She placed her N4 barrel up against the tree trunk. Red wrapped her palm around the Robbins of Dudley Trench Push dagger, bent her elbow, and raised her hand to the side of her head. The five inch blade pointed straight up.

She waited.

Enough time went by that she started to wonder if maybe Frankie had been wrong. They were all a little on edge maybe, what with that army or whatever it was going off to the east. What with what had happened to Merv. Poor little Merv. And Paulson and Dalton. And the old man, Thomas. Further, Red thought, unlike herself, Frankie didn't get off the reservation very much. He probably wasn't very comfortable out here. And he'd taken a few hits from that bitch. So yeah, maybe Frankie had made a mistake.

But Red trusted her instincts. And her instincts told her that when she was ready to dismiss Frankie's concern, she should wait awhile longer, so wait she did.

A few minutes later she heard movement proceeding up the trail behind her, from the direction they'd come.

Red closed her eyes and listened. Someone or something was jostling through the trees and bushes, apparently not even bothering to suppress the racket they made. She wasn't sure, but it sounded like there was only one of whatever it was. Whatever it was. Human. Zombie. Mutant. As the noises neared she was pretty sure that, *yeah*, there was only the one.

She opened her eyes and waited. She had the Push dagger in one hand and the Stechkin APS in her other. If she fired the pistol and there were more than one of them out here, they would all know where she was. Also, Red didn't know where the girl and her ride had disappeared to—how close or how far they might be—and she couldn't tip her hat to them either. If it was just the one coming up behind her, it'd have to be the Push dagger.

The zombie passed by her tree, unaware of her presence. Its lower body and upper body were not coordinated. As it put one foot in front of the other and walked a crooked path, its arms and shoulders were jerking up and down.

Red peered around her tree, back the way the zombie had come, but did not see another. She detached herself from the trunk and fell in behind the undead thing. It was completely unaware of her presence.

She was able to walk right up to the zombie and plunge the push dagger up under the rear of its skull. The creature shuddered before sliding off her blade. Red prodded it with her boot, but the thing didn't respond. She used her foot to roll it over and studied the cadaver as she reached down and wiped the blade on its rotten shirt.

This zombie looked familiar to Red. She couldn't place it. Something...

Red gazed into the trees behind her, feeling somewhat uneasy. It was a feeling she did not like. Was she being watched? By what? *My, how the tables do turn*, Red thought. Nothing stirred back there.

She considered. It was either nothing, and her mind was playing tricks on her, which she thought was possible but unlikely...Or it was a zombie, one of the smarter ones, and it was standing there as she looked for it, but it wasn't going to make a move until she made a move. If that was the case, she could take it out as soon as it reared its ugly head.

Or it was something else entirely. *That* thought unsettled her.

And then Red realized where she had seen this zombie before and doing so she knew what was behind them. Cosmo's spawn—the one called Cleetus—had been gripping a zombie by the neck, the way a grown man might grip a puppy by its scruff. That zombie had stood in place docilely enough, its upper body herky jerky. Red remembered seeing that from the bluff, when she and Keith had helped the woman and her friends up, when Cosmo and his boys and girl had demanded they return their prey.

This was *that* zombie, dead at her feet.

Which meant Cosmo was out there somewhere, in these trees with her. So it was something else entirely.

Then, what were they waiting for? Red decided she'd rather not stick around and find out. She had to get back to Tommy and Gammon and the others. Find that damned woman. That woman was the whole reason for this, and Red knew it.

Red wasn't scared. She'd throw down with Cosmo or any of his mutant fuck kids any day. But she wasn't stupid either. It would be dark soon enough, and Cosmo and his hideous brood would have an advantage over her then. Plus, Tommy and Gammon were wandering around further ahead, unaware.

Little Red took up her N4, and as she did so, she looked the way she'd come, letting whatever might be lurking back there know *she* knew. She struck off the way the others had gone.

KNIGHTS OF FAITH

The sound of pouring water roused her. When Riley opened her eyes, she found herself on a cot, a thin blanket covering her from the neck down, a pillow under her head. She was in some kind of capacious, room-like tent. A middle-aged woman she recognized, but whose name she could not recall, had just finished emptying a bucket of steaming water into a large metal tub near the cot.

"There, all done." The woman looked over and saw that Riley was awake. "Oh, good, you're up. You've been asleep for fifteen hours."

"I have?" Riley brushed a hand across her forehead.

"Yeah, you were in some rough shape. My name is Carrie, by the way. I didn't expect you to remember that." Carrie was kind but hard-looking, a woman who had seen a lot in her lifetime. "Here, I drew you a bath."

"Oh, thank you, Carrie." Riley sat up. She felt groggy coming out of a deep sleep, but her body felt rested.

"You're welcome, Riley. You should take a bath. There's a change of clothes over there for you. Just leave yours on the floor when you're done. You've really set this camp abuzz, you know that?"

"What do you mean?"

"The Bishop? No one's heard him talk. *Ever.* And now he's talking. That's something else."

It was all coming back to Riley. Dee kneeling next to her. The photograph. The man in the chair, the Bishop. He'd said his name was Fred. He'd said he'd known the man in the picture. Other things came to mind...*Bear.* There was no Bear, not here, not anymore. She had travelled all this way with Anthony to find...Anthony. Anthony was dead.

"What's with his cat?"

"It's the Bishop's." Carrie was arranging items on the small table next to Riley's cot, packing things away. Bandages. A stethoscope. What looked like glucose meters with lancets. "That thing was his pet. He brought it with him from Eden."

"Eden?" Turner—the Bishop—had mentioned it as well.

"I don't know, twenty years ago," Carrie spoke as she worked, "a bunch of us—me, Tris, some others—we travelled into New York City to this place, some people were holed up. They'd built walls around them. We found the Bishop there, and the cat. He didn't want to leave the cat.

"When it died, there were some of us who worried it might be too much for the old guy. Someone took it and stuffed it. I don't know if he ever even noticed."

Riley thought it a bizarre tale but said nothing.

"We're all eager to hear your story. Even Tris."

"Yeah, *Tris.*" More unpleasant memories filled Riley's mind. "What's her problem anyway?"

"Ahhh, she's just got a death wish, that's all."

"The guy who talks funny?"

"Bruce."

"Why does he talk that way?"

"He got shot in the neck."

Riley asked her about the things on the table. "What's all that for?"

"While you were asleep, I tested your blood," Carrie answered her honestly. "Made sure you're not infected."

"Infected?"

"Plague. Or Zed. You're good by the way. Clean up and come on outside, okay?"

"Okay."

When Carrie had left, Riley stood and undressed. Her clothes had caked onto her body from dried sweat and dirt. She felt filthy. She stepped into the tub and shuddered. How long had it been since she'd had a bath?

She washed her body and hair and sat for some time in the tub, watching the dirt float around in the water and the soap bubbles around her. She thought back to when this whole crazy thing had begun. These people seemed decent enough. At least she didn't think they were going to hurt her. Not like Thomas and his people. Thomas. She was glad he was dead. She was glad she had killed him.

It didn't seem that Thomas' people had any ties to Bear's Army. They wouldn't have wanted to, Riley figured, not from what Thomas had said. Bear's Army was mobile, but it was also some kind of civilization. Thomas had shunned civilization.

Bear's Army. Riley had found it. And there was no Bear. She thought of the irony.

Riley was thinking she might just get to go back home one day soon. And then what? What was she going to tell her dad about Anthony? *Daddy, Anthony…*Then what? How could she look at her father and finish that sentence? How was she going to face Evan and Troi's families? Thomas was dead, but his son…and that little red-haired monster…they were all out there still, all alive. The whole thing sickened her. *Anthony*.

Lest she dwell on it, Riley rinsed her hair once more and toweled off.

* * *

When she stepped outside, all eyes turned to Riley expectantly. She wore the slacks, light sweater and boots that had been provided for her. It was nighttime.

"Riley." Dee called out to her. "Come here—*please*. You hungry?"

"I'm starving."

"We have some food for this lady?" Fred Turner asked, petting his cat. Its legs jutted out straight from its body.

"Coming."

"Please." Dee indicated a chair. "Sit down."

Riley did as he asked. Her chair was ringed by many others in which Dee and several more people had settled or were settling. Some of them she recognized, like the Bishop, Fred; like Tris and her two lackeys—Bruce and Kevin—or whatever they were; like Carrie and Victor. Other men and women she had not met before. Lights were hooked up to generators and flooded the area with illumination, banishing the shadows.

"My name is Tim," said the tall man who brought her a plate of steaming food and a two-liter bottle of water.

Riley wasn't sure what to say. "Nice to meet you, Tim."

"Pleasure to meet you too." Tim beamed.

"Dig in," invited Dee. "If it's okay with you, we'll talk while you eat. When you're done eating, we have some questions for you, okay?"

Riley nodded. She was already tearing into her meal.

"The first thing I'm going to say is that this whole situation—you showing up when you did, with that picture—it's got all of us…It's astounding."

"To say the least," Victor agreed.

"We were packing up to leave," continued Dee. "You saw the troops yesterday."

"We're taking this show on the road." Kevin had an AK-47 slung over his back.

"To Africa."

"Why Africa?" Riley asked around a mouthful of food.

"From the intelligence we've been able to gather," explained Dee, "Africa was spared any direct nuclear detonations. So, sure, there's the fallout floating around everywhere, but Africa might be the one relatively safe place left to us."

"Word to the mother." Tris sounded unimpressed.

"I hate the damned heat." Bruce huffed. "*That* kind of heat."

"Relatively safe…," continued Dee "…aside from several million zombies, but we'll deal with them. Our people here were packing up, were going to head out and meet everyone else at the ocean. Then you showed up."

Unbidden, Tim returned and handed Riley a second plate of food. She thanked him.

"And you have that picture, and now the Bishop is talking."

"Yes I am." Fred Turner smiled down at his cat. "I waited years to hear God's voice, like Elijah on Mt. Horeb."

"You ever hear it?" Tris looked suspiciously at Fred.

"Today."

"How long have you guys been out here?" asked Riley.

"Here? *This* camp?" Dee asked her by way of answering. When she nodded, he said, "A few years. The last really big zombie battles ended for us, what? Three, three and a half years ago. We've been resting up, collecting what information we can, sending scouts out, getting ready for Africa."

"Where were you before this?"

"All over the east coast and further south. Before that out west. We went where the zombies were."

"Except for the hot zones," rasped Bruce. "We stayed clear of those."

"There are five thousand of you?" The number boggled Riley's mind.

"Give or take. We've got about three hundred left here at this camp at the moment."

"We were twenty, thirty thousand once." Kevin looked sad as he said it.

"What happened? Zed?"

"Yeah," Dee confirmed. "Zed happened. But we left people behind along the way too. You clean out a city or town, you lose some people, the ones that stay behind to start repopulating it. Most people can't go on fighting forever."

"And the ones who think they can," Bruce looked at Tris as he said it, "*shouldn't.*"

"The Lord is my shield and the horn of my salvation," Fred recited from memory. "My fortress and my deliverer, my stronghold."

"Isn't that nice?" jeered Tris.

Riley had wolfed down the second helping of food.

"Want more?" Tim asked her.

"No, thank you. In a little while. It was delicious. What was it?"

"Goose."

"Goose?" Riley had never eaten goose before.

"Yeah."

"I had no idea those things tasted so good."

"Back before all of this," Bruce gestured to their world, "those goddamn geese—excuse me, Bishop—they used to be a protected species or some shit. You couldn't kill 'em, couldn't eat 'em. And all they did was shit all over the place."

"Please…" Fred fixed Riley with a gaze that radiated warmth and kindness. "Tell me the details behind this photograph. Tell us how you got here."

Riley breathed out and did so. She told them about the two men who had wandered into New Harmony; of how Evan thought her brother looked like the man in the picture; how she and Anthony had confronted their father and how he, in turn, had sent them to see a woman named Gwen.

"Gwen!" gasped Fred. "My Lord, how is she?"

"She's okay," said Riley. "I guess."

"I knew her husband, Bobby. He was a fine man, a good Christian man."

Riley continued, explaining how they had set out from New Harmony with the guide. She spoke of Krieger's fate in the mountains. She hesitated at times, as she recounted their confrontations with the mutants and Thomas' people. And she had to stop when she got to the point where she described the death of her brother.

"You think your friends made it?" Victor asked her.

She shook her head.

"What happened to this Thomas motherfucker?" Tris demanded.

"I killed him," Riley said bluntly.

Bruce cocked a thumb and forefinger and leveled it at Kevin, who nodded approvingly.

"And she got away," said Dee. "And you eventually found me, at the bomb, right?"

"That's right. You saved my life."

"Well, look at you," Tris remarked to Dee. "Super-hero homeboy."

"The bomb," Carrie was awed, "that thing is still out there?"

"No one's blown it up yet." Kevin sounded equally amazed.

"And Dee," Tris didn't ask, "you said you saw them following her."

"I did."

"You counted how many, ten?"

"At least. Hard to tell. They were still a way off."

"Well, they'd be stupid to try anything here." Tris told Riley, "Our sentries are all on alert. If these people show up anywhere near here, we'll take care of them."

"We've seen mutants like you described," noted Kevin. "Remember New Jersey? What was that place?"

"Budd Lake." Bruce whistled. "Yeah, those were some nasty fuckers up there."

Tris snickered. "They died real good though."

"Yes they did." Bruce shared a smile with Kevin and Tris.

"Is Mickey still alive?" asked Fred.

"He was when I left."

"The plague. God almighty. To live that long with it. Even Job only faced boils and the death of his family."

"*Only?*" The derision dripped off Tris' tongue.

Riley pulled out the second photograph she carried, the picture crumpled and damp.

"Who's that?" asked Victor.

"Me, my brother, Anthony, and our dad."

"Let me see that." Tris snatched the picture out of Riley's hand none too gently. She studied the photograph and as she did so she shook her head. "This your father?"

"Yes."

"Your biological?"

"No."

"This shit just keeps getting weirder. I knew this motherfucker. His name is Steve, right?"

"You know my dad?"

"Sure I knew his punk-ass." Fred Turner took the picture from Tris and looked it over as the black woman continued. "When people were leaving to go and fight and die, he was too scared to come along, the little bitch. Remember, Carrie? This motherfucker didn't want to go with us to Eden."

"Tris—" Dee tried, but she ignored him.

"Uh-huh. I can see you know what I'm talking about. Sound like your father?"

"He sure does look like Harris," Fred marveled. "Your brother. You probably have a lot of questions for us."

Riley did.

"What happened to Bear?"

"He was here one day," Bruce held out one hand, then the other, "and the next he wasn't."

"What does that mean?"

"He up and left," stated Dee.

"He must have known he was dying," said Tris. "The cancer gets everybody eventually."

"Except you, right Tris?" Bruce winked.

"Cancer won't kill me," the woman behind the scars promised.

"It wasn't cancer." Dee was shaking his head. "He was just gone one day."

"Did he leave anything?" Riley pressed. "A note?"

"He left this…" Kevin reached over and picked up a notebook. He looked at Dee, who said, "Go ahead," before he handed it to Riley.

"What is this?" She started to leaf through it.

"There was a warehouse we used to raid for supplies," explained Fred. "Every time we went there, me or John—that was my boy—we would find Bear off by himself, in what used to be a little office. He'd be reading this. Whoever had written in it was a bunch of bones behind a desk by then."

"So that's where it came from…" Dee's voice trailed off.

Riley read aloud from the notebook:

"*We had to call them something, so we came up with a variety of names…*" She looked up from the notebook. "You've all read this, I assume?"

"Yeah," confirmed Dee, but when Tris snorted he amended, "Most of us."

"And you're really the black angel?" Riley shut the book.

"The black angel *of death*," Tris corrected. She looked at Kevin and Bruce. "You hear how they're shortening my name already? And I'm not even dead yet."

"I don't know, Tris…" Kevin commiserated.

"Yeah, Tris," said Bruce. "Black angel sounds kind of bad ass enough."

"Fuck that noise. Black angel my *black* ass. Let me ask you stupid white boys a question: when you think of angels, what you think of?"

Bruce and Kevin looked at one another.

"You think of little pudgy babies," Tris told them. "That's what you think of. You think of mercy and…and *benevolence*, and other bullshit. Cherubs. Add *black* to that and what do you get? Some warm and fuzzy multicultural watered-down pussy-assed bullshit. That's what."

Dee cocked his eyebrow. "Your point being?"

"My point, likkle dread bwoy, is that the black angel *of death* negates *all* that bullshit. *Of death.* Understand?"

"Were you Bear's wife?" When Riley asked, Kevin and Bruce both sputtered while Dee groaned.

Tris looked angry. "Is that what they're saying about me? Jesus H. Christ."

"No, I just thought—"

"Don't think, chicken." Tris glared at Bruce. "And what are you laughing at?"

"Nothing, Tris." Bruce had a hand to his mouth and was trying to control himself. "Nothing."

"Better be nothing."

"Woman, you're getting meaner as you get older."

"You'll have to excuse Tris," Kevin mentioned to Riley. "She hasn't killed anything in about a week, so she's feeling kind of irritable."

"And you want me to go to Africa," Tris muttered. "Fucking Africa. For what? Rescue a bunch of jungle bunnies?"

"Tris is mad at life." There was sadness in Dee's eyes as he said it. He wasn't trying to be funny.

"You're goddamn right. Because life's a motherfucker."

* * *

"All of us here," Dee remarked to Riley, "you know what we got in common? He saved us. *Bear* saved us. Each one of us."

"More than once, too," added Kevin.

As Dee said the words he looked at Tris. "Even the ones who don't like to admit it."

"I should have died in New York City," declared the disfigured woman.

"We went down—well, I mean we were up in New York State then," Carrie offered by way of explanation. "We went down to the city twice. The first time, what I was telling you about in the tent, Bear left us."

"That's when they rescued Fred here," said Victor, "and his cat."

"Kate and Phil, Larry and Keara as well," Fred added quietly. "There weren't many of us left by then."

"I don't know how we got out of there that first time," Carrie resumed. "The place was full of those things. It was, *insane* I guess is the best word." She shook her head. "We got out of there because of you, Tris."

Tris did not answer.

"The second time we went down, Bear was leading us," Carrie resumed her story. "And we went down there in force."

"That's when they met me," said Dee.

Bruce grinned at the memory. "You were just a little nothin' back then."

"Took us six months to clear Manhattan Island alone," Kevin remembered. "We lost a lot of good people. *A lot* of good people. I thought for sure Tris was dead on Fifth Avenue."

"I should have been." Tris nearly spat. "Here's what you need to know about me," she addressed Riley directly. "When this shit all started, my husband and kids, they got bit. They turned. I killed them." As she spoke, a far-off look came to her eyes. "My husband tried to put up a fight. He was a tough man."

"But he wasn't tough enough," Bruce pointed out. "Ain't nobody as bomb as you, Tris."

"I'm not a religious woman…" The distant look went out of Tris' eyes, and she was back in the moment with them. She looked at Fred quickly as she spoke. "…but I've always hoped I'd see them again, the way they were. *Be* with them. That time in New York City—I thought that was *the* time."

Riley noticed that as Tris spoke, she fingered the grenade hanging on her neck.

"We'd gotten cut off from everybody else, outside the library on Fifth Avenue. The street was thick with them, thousands and thousands of them. You ever seen that many of them? Ever had to *smell* that many of them? No, of course you haven't…

"I climbed up on top of one of the two lion statues they had there, and I picked Zed off as he climbed up to get me. My people were dead. I was alone. A helicopter came in—one of those Apaches, AH-64. The pilot must have been a crazy flyboy to bring it down into that cavern, tight as it was. They unloaded on the dead—and I gotta admit—it was fun to watch those fuckers die like that. Fuck 'em."

"Fuck 'em!" Kevin spit and accidentally hit Bruce's boot.

"Hey!"

"Sorry."

"Something happened," Tris was telling her story, "…The pilot lost control, the helicopter bounced off a building, and the next thing you know it crashed in the street behind me and everything went up. It was like a wall of flame just, just washed over the street. All those zombies—" she snapped her fingers "—like that. And there I am, hanging on to that fucking lion in a sea of fire."

"And Death and Hades were thrown into the lake of fire," quoted Fred Turner. "…And if anyone's name was not written in the book of life, he was thrown into the lake of fire."

Tris was silent for a moment before she continued.

"I burned there. The flames were all over me. My clothes, my hair…" She reached from the grenade to her locks, but stopped her hand before touching them. "And still, there were *thousands* of them coming. Like an army of ants or something. I reached for this…" Her fingers brushed the grenade "…and my skin came off on it, I was burnt so bad.

"And that's where I should have died, on top of that lion, on fire and overrun." She looked Riley in the eye. "It would have been a righteous death, a *worthy* death."

"But you didn't," Riley surmised.

"I didn't. I don't know where he came from. I don't know how he got there. But the next thing I know, this big hand was wrapping around my wrist, pulling my hand off ..." Tris moved her hand away from the grenade. "...and there he was, this mountain of a man, this...this monster. He pulled me clear of the flames. He came out of the fire and it was like...like the flames weren't even touching him. And he was carrying this mini-gun, from the wreckage of the chopper.

"You have any idea what a mini-gun weighs?" Tris didn't wait for an answer. "He shouldn't have been able to lift that thing. He opened up on them, and all I saw was the fire comin' out of the end of it. All I heard was the shell casings on the steps, the whir of its motor. And they were falling all over the place."

"Bear was just mowing them down," enthused Bruce.

"That's where we came in," added Kevin.

"The cavalry." Bruce smiled.

"Tris was in bad shape." Kevin's tone was grave. "We didn't think you were going to make it, Tris. Bear stopped long enough to tell us to get her some help, and then he went at it again."

"And when the mini-gun was empty," Bruce remembered, "he went at them with his bare hands."

"That's the type of motherfucker he was." Tris licked her lip. "That *motherfucker*."

"But he saved you." Riley couldn't comprehend the woman's resentment.

"No, he *cheated* me!"

Bruce said, "Tris passed out from the shock," and Tris immediately replied, "No, I didn't pass out. I died." The way she said it, all of them—even Riley—knew the matter wasn't debatable.

Tris looked at Fred. "And I didn't see shit. Just black. *Nothing*." She looked away from Fred to Dee and Riley and the others. "Not my husband, not my kids. Not Saint Peter at the Pearly Gates or Lucifer at the other end. Because there's nothing." She said this to Fred, who merely smiled benevolently in return. "And the next thing I know, I'm on my back, and they're bandaging me up and the pain—like you wouldn't believe. And they wouldn't let me fight."

"We had to sedate her," remarked Kevin.

"See, woman?" raspy-voiced Bruce smirked. "You're so bad you escaped death."

"Fuck death. And fuck that big one-eyed bald-headed bastard."

"How can you talk about him like that?" Dee demanded.

"That son of a bitch..." Tris muttered almost to herself. "...Son of a bitch. I should have died...I was *supposed* to die then."

"But how can you say that?" Riley was thinking of Anthony and how she would give anything for him to be alive, how she would switch places with him if she could. And here was this bitter, scarred woman who *wanted* to be dead. "What makes you say that? What makes you think you should have died then?"

"Look at me. I ain't died since, right?"

"She's got a point," conceded Kevin.

"There was a time," Carrie had crossed her arms and was holding her shoulders, "when I thought Zed was going to get us all."

"Before Bear," noted Victor.

"Zed can't kill Tris." Bruce sounded convinced.

"Death's come knockin' a thousand times, and a thousand times I've slammed the door in its face. 'Cept that one time."

"Death can't catch you, Tris," said Bruce. "One day you'll surrender on your own terms."

"You goddamn right. Twenty-five years. Twenty-five years I fought. And now what? *This?* I'm supposed to pack it up and bring my shit to Africa? Die there? Bullshit."

"Come on, Tris..." Victor tried to soothe her.

"Don't worry." Tris fingered the grenade around her neck. "I know how I'm going out."

"A righteous death?" Dee scoffed.

"That's right." Tris' reply was curt. "And you just want to be sure you're not too close when I pull the pin."

"Tris is just angry that she never got a chance to throw down with Bear himself," said Carrie. "Aren't you, Tris?"

The black woman didn't disagree. "*He* would have been a worthy opponent." Tris looked at Riley. "But he's gone." She glanced towards Dee as she spoke. "I happen to think it was the cancer—that he knew what was about to go down. And like one of them big fucking elephants he went off, on his own, to do his thing."

Before Dee could say something to the contrary, Tris addressed him. "There's others think different on that." Victor placed his hand on Dee's shoulder. "All these years, Zed *couldn't* kill me. I mean—maybe that one time they would have if Bear hadn't…I think *he* could have. Killed me, that is." The thought didn't seem to concern her. "But he didn't, and he wouldn't.

"When it was his time—to die, or whatever the fuck some of you wishy-washy motherfuckers want to think—you know what he did?" She addressed this last part to Riley. "He went off into the woods, into the wild. Alone. Without a word to anyone. He just disappeared. The same way he showed up."

"Like he was delivered to us," said Fred.

"He ain't dead." Dee didn't sound convinced.

"Uh-huh. Sure he ain't. And every once in awhile, D.L. goes off on his own, like the good son, a good little boy, looking for him."

"I keep hoping," admitted Dee, "that he'll come back. So every year since he went away, I go out there, and I wait for him."

"Kind of sad, you ask me." Tris didn't sound sad.

"Yeah, well, look who I found this time."

"The Lord works in mysterious ways…" Fred smiled as Tris scowled at him.

"D.L. was the last one who saw Bear before he disappeared," noted Victor.

"Oh, yeah?" Riley asked Dee. "What'd he say?"

"Dee doesn't talk about that," Victor replied.

Dee shrugged.

* * *

"For almost twenty years I was silent." Fred was rubbing a stick back and forth in the dirt. "That is true." He stopped with the stick and sat up straight. "I did not speak a word, because I was listening."

"Listening?" Bruce looked at Kevin.

"That fuckin' cat of yours talk to you?" shot Tris.

"Listening to Him," replied Fred.

"And what'd he have to say?" goaded Tris.

"He didn't say anything. But don't you see? He said everything."

"What'd he say?" Bruce croaked to Kevin.

"I saw my son, John, die," Fred offered, unbidden. "And I saw him born. I was in the hospital with his mother. I was standing there by her side, next to the doctor, when she pushed and I saw the top of his…this little head." The look on Fred's face said he was seeing it all over again as clearly as when it'd happened. "And she pushed once more and there he was. He turned his head, and he looked at me…at me and the doctor, and I cried. Oh, how I cried. I'd never seen something so beautiful in all my life.

"And when he…when they killed him…Well, I've never seen anything so terrible." No one said anything, not even Tris. "I was there when he came into this world. And I was there when he left it. I witnessed the entire arc of his being."

Riley thought about Anthony.

"We've all lost people, Bishop," Carrie said. "I know how it hurts. We understand your pain. I'm sorry."

Fred looked up at the group. "I'm not talking of pain, here. I'm speaking of miracles. What else is birth? Think about it—from nothing, *something*. Have you ever watched a child born?"

"I have." Tris sounded unimpressed. "I squeezed 'em out. That shit hurts like fuck."

"A miracle brought you," Fred was looking to Riley, "brought you here to us. Do you understand how many wheels had to have been set in motion for this moment to pass? Mickey finds you, you find us. Here we are. And some would dismiss this as coincidence?"

"My brother died, horribly." Riley disagreed with him. "My friends are probably dead. I don't think it's some kind of miracle."

"But don't you see?" Fred insisted. "Their deaths meant something!"

"Oh yeah, *what?*" Dee rested a hand on Riley's arm immediately after she'd asked it.

Fred looked not the least perturbed. "I am a Knight of Faith. Have you ever heard that term before?"

"Weren't you guys the secret society that supposedly ran everything?" Bruce asked.

"No," Kevin answered him. "That was the Masons."

"Let me tell you a story," Fred stood up. "God wanted to test Abraham…" As he spoke, he used his hands to emphasize certain parts of his tale. "So He told him to go to the land of Moriah with his son, Isaac. The Lord told Abraham that he was to sacrifice Isaac. And Abraham did not question his god. He took Isaac—making the boy carry the wood for his own sacrifice—and together they journeyed for three days."

"Isaac have any idea what was going on?" asked Tris.

"None." Fred held up a finger. "Isaac even turned to his father on the way and said, 'Dad, we've got the coals and the wood, but where's the lamb for our sacrifice?' And Abraham told his son not to worry, that God would provide them with one.

"When they got where they were going, Abraham built an altar, tied Isaac up, put him on the wood, and raised his arms." Fred clasped his hands and raised his own arms. "In his hand, he held a knife, ready to kill his son. And just like that..." Fred lowered his arms and unclasped them. "...The Lord appeared and commanded Abraham not to kill Isaac. 'I know you honor and obey me, Abraham,' God told Isaac's father, 'because you have not kept back your only son from me.'"

"And then what?" Victor looked expectant.

"And then Abraham untied Isaac and they went back home."

"They went home?" Victor was disappointed. "That's it?"

"And they all lived happily ever after? *That*—" declared Tris "—is a fucked up story."

"Parents are supposed to sacrifice *themselves* for their children," Bruce pointed out, "not sacrifice their children."

"And just exactly what's the moral of your story supposed to be?" Riley looked aghast.

"Oh, it's not *my* story..." Fred looked at Riley as if she had misunderstood him.

"Just another sordid tale of child abuse from the Good Book," Tris said disdainfully. "May it rest in motherfucking pieces."

"I mean, *what* does that have to do with me, with my brother, Anthony, dying?"

"I wasn't thinking of you and your brother—may his soul rest in peace." Fred crossed himself. "I was thinking of *my* son, John. I was thinking of Soren Kierkegaard—have you heard of him? Any of you?"

None had.

"He was a Danish philosopher who lived a long time ago." As Fred spoke, Tris exhaled and looked away. "Kierkegaard wrestled with Abraham's act, and Kierkegaard argued that Abraham, in his willingness to sacrifice his only son, was transgressing the ethical."

"And that means...?" Bruce invited clarification.

"Abraham's entire life was structured along a very simple injunction. A rule. A law, if you will. That a father should love his son, the way God loved him. Like you said, Bruce. Abraham's society said the same thing: A parent should sacrifice himself for his child, never the other way around. But here he was...Abraham, asked by this very God, who he knew loved him, asked to kill his boy."

"So if a motherfucking voice in your head tells you to do it," Tris was disgusted, "then its okay?"

"Everything Abraham knew and felt," Fred continued, undaunted, "everything told him that murdering his son was wrong. But *faith* urged Abraham to ignore what he knew about human morality. Do you want to know how Kierkegaard defined faith? He said that faith is the paradox that a lone individual can be higher than the universal. Do you understand?"

No one answered. Riley wasn't sure who the question was meant for so she did. "No."

"Kierkegaard argued that Abraham could never justify killing Isaac in terms any human being would understand or agree with—"

"He got that right," Tris interjected.

"—but it's the very faith Abraham clings to that will see him through his task, that will see that his son is not taken from him. That will allow the father to transcend the universal moral norm against parents hurting their children. Abraham made a leap of faith. He went against *everything* he knew to be true, because he knew his Lord would not allow his effort to be in vain."

"There is so much wrong with that story," Tris looked up from the ground, "...and that you can't see it, Bishop, frankly *scares* me. You know Isaac wasn't Abraham's only son, right?"

"I don't expect you to understand me," Fred conceded.

"Why would an all-powerful god ask its follower to do something like that?" Tris shook her head. "If it wanted to know if Abraham was faithful, couldn't it have figured it out with some other hoodoo?"

"Hey Bishop," Bruce asked, "how'd Isaac get along with his father after that?"

"Abraham walked the narrow road of faith—as Kierkegaard put it—with no one to advise him. With no one to understand him."

"Let me tell you about another true-believing motherfucker who walked your narrow-assed road of faith." Tris did not attempt to mask her disgust. "This cat's road took him from Egypt and Germany to an Accelerated Pilot Program in Florida. From there to Logan International Airport and a first class seat on American Airlines Flight 11. Remember American Airlines Flight 11? That was the first plane to hit the World Trade Center on September Eleventh. You remember that, Bishop? Cat's name was Mohamed Atta, and the motherfucker is lucky he died that day."

"Who can forget those assholes..." Kevin muttered gruffly.

"That's the problem with faiths like Abraham's and Atta's." The look Tris gave Fred could best be described as hostile. "*Anything* is justifiable. *Everything* is justifiable. Ask any religiously-inspired suicide bomber. I really don't think we need to worship these people." Tris licked her upper teeth under her lip. "Yeah, Bishop, I liked you better when you was quiet."

"I don't know why God took my son away from me." Fred turned to Riley, "I don't know why He took all of my family from me, or your brother and your friends away from you." He addressed the larger group. "I just know I'm glad I got to be with John, with all of them, for as long as I was able to. And now, I believe I *will* be seeing them again—John, all of them—when I shrug off this mortal coil." He looked to Riley once more. "I don't know why God led you to us. But just because I don't understand it yet—or ever—that doesn't mean there is no reason."

"*Hallelujah*," muttered Tris.

"No offense, Fred," Riley said quietly. "But no god led me here. It was a guide named Krieger. And he fell off a cliff."

"I lost sight for nearly twenty years…and then today, my Damascus. How many people ever get that second chance?"

"I'd just like my brother back," Riley whispered morosely. "But that isn't going to happen."

"Think I'll go and check things out on the perimeter," announced Victor.

"You keep your little monkey ass safe," Tris told him. Victor smiled at her as he walked away.

* * *

"Hey, Bishop," Bruce's gravelly voice grated. "Let me ask you a question."

Fred looked at the other man expectantly.

"All those years you were quiet, you hear a word we were saying to you?"

"Yes."

"You heard everything?"

"I heard everything."

"Why didn't you ever say anything?"

Riley wondered if it hurt Bruce to speak. It sounded like it did.

"What was I going to say? Tell you how the zombies ate my sons? Ate my daughter? My wife and my dog?"

"They got your dog too, huh?"

"They did. By the way," Fred raised the stuffed cat. "Who's idea was Mr. Vittles here?"

"The cat? Kevin's."

"Nice touch. Very Natty Bumppo-ish."

"Natty-who?" Tris looked up.

"He wasn't talking to you," Bruce remarked off handedly. "He didn't say *nappy*."

"Oh, you too cute, froggy."

Riley would have smiled, but she was unsettled by Fred Turner.

"All those times I came and talked to you…" Bruce's scratchy voice didn't match the serious look on his face. "…You heard me?"

"Every word."

"Every word?"

"Let me ask you this, Bruce. If you didn't think I was listening, why were you talking?"

Bruce nodded, conceding the man's point. "Hey—the things I talked to you about?"

"Between you and me and God, Bruce. Don't worry."

"Thanks, Bishop."

"Well," Riley asked them, "what's next?"

"Africa," stated Kevin.

"Fuckin' Africa," Tris cursed.

"We should be going in the morning," said Carrie. "Catch up to the others."

"What about Riley?" Dee put it to the group.

"Excuse me. I'm sitting right here."

"Your skank ass want to go to Africa?" Tris was back to her nasty self.

"No."

"Then don't." Tris stood and straightened her legs. "I'm turning in. See the rest of you motherfuckers in the morning."

"Hey, Tris," Bruce winked at Kevin. "You want some company keep you warm?"

"If I want a real man to keep me company in bed," Tris said as she walked away, "maybe I'll pick me up one of those Mandingoes over in Africa."

STAND UP TO GLORY

Rodriguez, Red thought, *was a frigging idiot.* It was not the first time she had thought so.

They'd all heard the man on the quad approaching them through the trees. They'd seen his headlight cutting through the dark. Tobias had secured one end of the rope to a tree. Rodriguez could have done the same to a trunk across the path. Rodriguez should have done the same to a trunk across the path. Instead, the idiot chose to hold the rope in both hands, hiding himself behind the tree he should have tied it to.

When the man on the quad drove past, the rope caught him in the chest and knocked him off the four-wheeler. The impact of the man hitting the rope and bouncing backwards yanked Rodriguez forward off his feet. *Idiot.*

The rider landed on his back and lay there, dazed. Keith and David and Frankie and the others came out of the trees and surrounded him.

"Did he break his back?" Chang asked, his own arm broken.

"He didn't break his back," said Gammon.

"You okay, Rodriguez?" David called over to where the man was getting up, brushing himself off.

"Almost got my arms ripped out of the sockets."

"Idiot." Red didn't care that he heard what she was thinking. Gammon looked at her, though.

"Get up." Tommy gripped the man by his shirt front and put him back on his feet. The guy stood hesitantly but on his own. Keith stepped forward and pulled the man's pistol out of its holster on his side. Frankie was examining the assault rifle that had come off the man's back when he'd hit the ground.

"Take that thing off." Tommy slapped the side of the man's helmeted head. "Good thing he was wearing it," said Keith. The man reached up and unsnapped the clasp holding his helmet in place. His hair spiked up out of the bandana he wore around his head.

"You even think of yelling…" Tommy threatened the man with the barrel of his 12-gauge. They were close enough to the camp that, if the man screamed, he might be heard.

"What's your name?" Gammon asked.

"Victor."

Keith snatched the helmet out of Victor's hands.

"Victor. Listen to me, Victor. We don't want to hurt you—"

"Speak for yourself." Gammon looked at Tommy when he said it. The kid wasn't helping.

"We don't want to hurt you—" Gammon pointed a finger at Victor. "—but if we *have* to, we will."

Victor rubbed his chest with one hand. For people who didn't mean to hurt him, they'd almost killed him getting him off the quad. The four-wheeler had crashed into a tree and rolled over, its engine still running.

"We're after a woman," the older man in front of him said. "You know who I mean?"

Victor didn't see the sense in lying to these people. "Yeah. I know who you mean."

"Good. See, Tommy, I can tell already this fella is gonna help us. He's a smart one. You're a smart one, ain't you, Victor? Sure you are. Now, I don't know what that woman told you and your people—Heck, I don't know who you and your people are. But she killed some folk who were really close to us, understand?"

"She killed my dad…" Tommy was chewing on his lower lip.

"She killed Merv," Keith added, handing Victor's helmet to his brother.

"All we want is the woman, Victor. No harm will come to you unless you try to run or do something else stupid."

"You're the one making that promise, Ed." Red stood there with all her blades strapped to her body, the Noveske Diplomat with its three hundred round drum in her hands. "I'm not."

Gammon looked at her. All he needed was her *and* Tommy going off the deep end together, the two of them. "Who's got some paper and a pen or something?"

After a minute of searching their persons and packs Tobias found he had a pen and a notebook. He tore a page out of the notebook and offered it and the pen to Gammon.

"No. You write what I tell you, all right? Write this: *We have Victor.* That's your name, right? *We want the girl. Meet me at*—where should we meet them?"

"How about that field three miles back?" offered David.

"The one with the bomb?"

"No. That other one we went through."

"That's good. We'll be able to put Frankie and Tobias with their rifles somewhere where they won't see them. Write this, Toby: *One person comes with the girl, and that's it. We don't want to hurt Victor but if we have to—*"

"Wait—wait." Tobias was scribbling furiously. He had the page pressed against the notebook he'd torn it from. "You're going too fast. *One person comes...with...the...girl...*"

"*...and that's it,*" repeated Gammon. The hum of the quad's engine was annoying him. "Shut that thing off, will somebody?" Frankie turned the key in the ignition, silencing the four-wheeler. "*We don't want to hurt Victor but if we have to—*"

"We'll make him bleed." Red was staring off into the trees. She didn't like standing here like this. Victor's friends outnumbered them and were nearby. Cosmo and his crew were no doubt equally too close for comfort.

"We'll make him bleed?" Tobias looked up expectantly. Victor had blanched at Red's words.

"No, don't write that," Gammon told Tobias. "Just put that if we have to we will."

"*...have to...we...will.* There. Done."

"Print my name at the bottom."

"Shouldn't I put my name on it, Gammon? I mean, I'm writing the note and all, after all..."

"It's my note, Tobias. My name goes on it."

"Why put any name at all?" Keith wondered.

"Because we got nothing to hide," said Gammon. "Personalize it."

"You think this is funny, don't you, Victor?" Red looked at their prisoner coolly.

"Not one bit," he answered truthfully.

Red was balancing her throwing axe on her palm, letting it fall and snatching it back up by the handle before it could hit the ground. "You think we're a bunch of idiots, I bet, don't you?"

"No."

"What *do* you think, Victor?" Gammon asked.

"I think I just want to go home."

"Like I said, smart guy, this Victor guy. Good. Let's leave this somewhere where Victor's friends are sure to find it."

"Here, give me that." Red snatched the note from Tobias' hands. She strode over to the overturned quad and placed the page on the vehicle. She put a large rock on top of the note to hold it in place.

"Nice helmet," complimented David. "You don't mind if I wear it?"

"No, go ahead."

"That'll do," Gammon said to Red. "Somebody tie him up. Victor, don't take this personally, but you are our prisoner. That don't mean we can't all get along and all, it just means for the time being we're gonna have to limit your freedom somewhat. Got it?"

"Got it."

"I like this guy." Gammon smiled approvingly. "I got a good feeling about this," he remarked to the others, and he meant it. "I really do."

Red was staring off into the trees again. There was that feeling once more. As Keith and David finished tying their captive's hands behind his back, she stepped behind a tree and shuffled off a few more steps into the pines. If they noticed it, none of the men with her drew attention to her move. Only Rodriguez looked after her in the direction she'd disappeared.

"How I look, brother?" David had the visor on Victor's helmet up.

"You're looking something fierce, brother."

"What do you think, Victor? I look fierce?"

"Very."

David smiled. "You hear that, brother?"

"Okay, let's head back." Gammon said to the group. "Victor's friends are going to notice he's missing pretty soon. They're gonna come looking for him, so I want to be in place."

They moved out as a group, Rodriguez bringing up the rear, purposefully straggling behind. Chang was in front of him, but Chang wasn't paying attention to anything. After a few yards, Rodriguez stopped and stood still. When Chang disappeared into the trees, he checked the safety on his H&K, turned, and crept back towards where he'd last seen Red.

* * *

The days were growing shorter and she enjoyed her time in the night, its chilled touch on her face, a thin blanket folded on her lap lest she take cold. The glaucoma had taken her vision many years before, but she remained curiously attuned to her environment, aware of the slightest sounds from the woods around her, perceptive of the comings and goings of the raccoons and the other animals.

When Cosmo's wife had been alive, she had been his lover, the one he snuck off to visit in her cabin, a cabin he had built for her to keep her close. When Cosmo's wife had died, he continued to visit, and as Cosmo's sons grew he brought them along and she inducted them upon the path of carnal knowledge. She was already an old woman then, but she gladly served. In return, they brought her wild game and, in the winter, cords of wood to heat her one-room shanty.

She sat outside her home on a stool, her back to one of the log posts, a corn-cob pipe in her puckered mouth. She twirled a chin hair around an arthritic index finger.

She knew someone was there before they announced themselves.

"Well then who is it come to visit Maude?" she asked by way of greeting.

"Where's my father, Maude?"

Chase. She'd known the boy, his person, since his birth; known him in a different sense since the time he was ten. She knew his physical attributes and irregularities from when she'd had sight, from the touch of her hands on his body, and she did not think of them as deformities. What stood out most for her about Cosmo's son was not his distorted appearance, which she could no longer view herself, but the clarity of his thought, the lucidity of his mind. His was the sharpest and therefore most dangerous intellect among Cosmo's many children, capable of turning the white-hot rage on and off when it suited him.

"Maude," Chase repeated, "where's my father?"

He'd been away hunting, missing the events that had transpired in the past days.

"He's gone looking for some fools, Chase."

"How long?"

"Better part of a week, I figure. You been to the house?"

49

"Yeah, I been to the house. Winslow…" She wasn't sure, but she thought his voice cracked when he spoke his brother's name.

"Poor little Winslow," she murmured in sympathy. "What you thinkin' of doin', Chase?"

"I'm goin', gonna find dad, hope he ain't finished the job first before I get there."

"You leave tomorrow morning you'll catch up to 'em in a day or two I bet. Why'nt you stay and keep an old lady company?"

"I'm leaving now, Maude. I should be with my brothers."

"You ain't like them boys, Chase," she said, and it was true because he wasn't. He was less animal, and at the same time so much more dangerous. "Stay. Let 'em do whatever it is they gonna do. They be back soon enough."

But he was gone. She could tell that without seeing. She couldn't care less about the men and women Cosmo and his children pursued, though she hoped for their sakes Cosmo had taken care of business before Chase showed up.

Riley rested in the tent she'd woken up in earlier that day. She sat in a folding wooden chair at a folding wooden table. She'd slept a little more and then she was wide awake and thought it was better to be seated with her thoughts than lying down with them.

She'd couldn't get Anthony out of her mind. Her brother. Dead. It still made no sense. Anthony was the whole reason they'd come out here.

Ev and Troi. Riley wondered if they were still alive. How could they be? Could they have gotten away like she did? Maybe the red-haired girl and the others had only followed her? Maybe they'd found Thomas and the other man dead and were worked up into such a furor that they abandoned their hunt, ignoring Ev and Troi, chasing only Riley? She wanted to think so, but Riley did not.

She opened the book they had said was Bear's. It was his book, but he hadn't written in it or anything. It was some guy's depressing story of being trapped as the zombie outbreak unfolded. Riley couldn't imagine what life had been like for people at that time. Her father had lived through it, but he never spoke of it. These people she was with were intent on leaving for Africa in the next day or so. They hadn't asked her to come. Riley didn't want to go anyway. She wanted to get home, wanted to recover. And then she wanted to come back out here and find the people responsible for Anthony's death. She wanted to find them because she wanted to kill them all.

If she thought about it too much, it would drive her crazy. Instead, Riley cracked open the book and began reading.

The brain has to be destroyed, she read. *That's all there is to it...*

* * *

Rodriguez looked for Red in the trees, and when he couldn't find her, he leaned up against a trunk. He waited and listened. She was out here somewhere, he knew. They'd been out here for a few hours now, waiting for whatever Red thought was coming.

Freaky little girl. He'd heard whispered stories, third hand, how Thomas saved her when she was just a little kid from a group of men who'd been plowing her.

Rodriguez didn't want to fuck her. Skinny little runt. He only wanted to kill her.

MacKenzie was his best friend. And Red killed him. First, she'd broken him. When Mac came back from his three nights in the woods with Red, he'd told Rodriguez what had happened out there. How Red had strung him up in a barbed wire net, how she'd let Zed paw at his feet. Little cunt had probably sat there the whole time, watching everything. And what was worst of all, Rodriguez thought, was that Mac had come to believe the little psycho had done him an enormous favor.

Rodriguez knew Red was dangerous. He'd seen her fight. He knew she could handle those blades. She was five-foot-nothing, but Rodriguez knew he didn't stand a chance tangling with her hand to hand, not if she had one of her knives on her. He considered the H&K HK416 in his hands. If he could get a clear shot at her, he could take her out. She was pretty fucking fast, but she wasn't faster than a bullet.

Little Red had never really fit in the whole time Rodriguez had known her. She kept to herself, talked little, wasn't like everyone else. But no one fucked with her, because everyone knew if you fucked with Red, you were fucking with Thomas, and no one wanted to fuck with Thomas. But Thomas was gone now, so the little bitch didn't have that going for her any more.

Rodriguez knew what he'd do. If she had her back to him, he wouldn't even give her a chance. He'd just cut her runt little ass down before she knew what'd hit her. For Mac. For his friend.

It suddenly dawned on Rodriguez that someone was standing behind him. He turned to look and it was Red. She held a hand up to his mouth and a finger to her own. "Shhhh…"

He looked around, didn't see a thing. How the fuck had she done that, snuck up on him? Bitch. Rodriguez knew he was lucky that she didn't want him dead. The thought angered him more. He waited impatiently. What were they standing there for and when was she going to take her hand off his mouth?

After awhile, she removed her hand and nodded over her shoulder, indicating they should move. "You first," Red told him. Rodriguez looked at her with the N4 in her hands and he started walking, thinking to himself, again, she didn't want to kill him, because if she had, he would be dead already.

He followed the path he had last seen Chang on and wondered if he could turn fast enough and take her out. She wouldn't be expecting it, wouldn't see it coming. Well, actually, Rodriguez thought, she was walking behind him, so she *would* see it coming. But there was no way in hell she could dodge his bullets. No one was that fast.

He liked that idea. Let her last thought be that he'd lit her up. Maybe he could scream out, "This is for MacKenzie" or something as he turned. *Nah*, too many words. "For Mac," maybe. Something like that. He could put a few slugs in her and catch up to the others before noon. Yeah, *for Mac*. That's what he'd do, there was some kind of poetic justice to—

The mutant rushed out of the trees, snarling, swinging a human head on a chain.

Rodriguez reacted, raising his H&K. The head thunked on the HK416's receiver, knocking the assault rifle from him and sending Rodriguez to the dirt. He looked up, the deformed beast towering over him.

Red leaped nimbly over Rodriguez and onto the thing, burying both four-inch push daggers in its chest. It roared out in anger and tossed her from it.

Rodriguez scrambled towards his H&K and came face to face with a zombie. The mutant had not been alone. It had made its way through the trees, each of its gigantic hands around the scraggly neck of a zombie, the undead struggling futilely against it the entire way. When the mutant attacked Rodriguez and Red, it had thrust the zombies ahead of it first, propelling them onto the path.

One zombie had fallen down and was regaining its feet. The other confronted Rodriguez.

Red had left her push daggers buried in the mutant's chest. She came at it again, thrusting with the Robbins of Dudley dagger in her left hand. The mutant took the blow in its meaty forearm, the five-inch dagger disappearing in its forelimb. Undeterred, the beast rushed forward into Red. She yanked the dagger from its forearm and cracked the monster across the face with the dagger's steel knuckles. If it noticed the blow, it gave no indication. The thing's right hand reached out and wrapped itself around Red's throat, crushing down on her windpipe like a vise, simultaneously lifting her from her feet.

Rodriguez couldn't wield a blade like Red, but he could hold his own. He whipped his boot dagger from its sheath and buried it in the decaying head of the zombie facing him in one fluid motion. Rodriguez dodged to the side, expecting the second zombie to attack. It stood there on the path, stinking and moaning, looking from him to Red and the mutant choking the life out of the girl.

Hanging from its outstretched arm, Red thrust the trench dagger into the monster's head. It grunted when the blade entered the side of its head and still, somehow, the thrust didn't kill it. Worse yet, Red's dagger was lodged there. With the oxygen cut off to her lungs and brain, Red let the Robbins of Dudley push dagger go, her right hand yanking one of the four-inch daggers from mutant's chest, stabbing down with it, her left hand coming up with the doubled edged fifteen-inch weapon. She flicked her wrist as she wielded the blade, slicing ragged trenches through the thing's face, blinding it in one eye.

Still it refused to release her.

Rodriguez looked from his rifle on the ground to the zombie before him. The beast hissed at him but turned and staggered towards Red and her assailant.

Another flourish of the doubled-edged blade destroyed the mutant's remaining eye, and it finally dropped her, grasping at its own face, roaring out in anger. Red gasped air through her damaged throat and did not relent. Her right arm came around with the throwing hatchet, burying it in the creature's knee. The mutant's leg went out from under it and it went down on one leg.

Red hacked at its other thigh until that one collapsed underneath the beast as well. Cosmo's son took its hands off its face and reached out blindly for Red, looking to grab her and draw her in close where it could destroy her, but the little red-head was already in close, the karambit gouging flesh from its face and neck.

Rodriguez tore his eyes from the spectacle and made for his automatic rifle.

The mutant lashed out wildly, its blow pushing Red back three feet. She stumbled into the zombie that was coming for her, its arms outstretched. Before its teeth could sink into her flesh, Red twisted and punched it in the face, her knuckles cracking it in the mouth. The zombie staggered back a step, stunned. It was just regaining whatever limited senses it had when Red's throwing hatchet buried itself in its head. The handle jutting from its skull, the undead sprawled bonelessly.

Red glanced down at her hand and moved in on the blinded beast kneeling there, hooking it under the chin with the karambit. With a grunt and a heave, she took its throat out in a spray of blood.

The force she put into ripping out the creature's neck turned her around, and before Red's mind fully registered that Rodriguez had taken up his H&K and leveled it at her she was already diving away from the mutant. Rodriguez's automatic rifle chattered, blood erupting from the mutant's dying chest. Red's hand flicked up, steel flashing as it covered the distance between herself and Rodriguez.

Staggering back, Rodriguez's arms flailed, the barrel of his H&K whip-sawing towards the trees. The handle of one of Red's push daggers was stuck in the middle of his chest. Somewhere it registered for Rodriguez that this meant the blade itself was inside him. *Aw shit.* He hadn't even seen her pull the dagger out of the mutant. She *was* that fast. Mortally wounded, Rodriguez steadied himself and caught Red's eye.

She had landed flat on her palms and the balls of her feet and pushed herself up to a crouch.

Rodriguez knew he was done. First Mac, now him. The thought flashed through his mind in less than a second and then he was swinging his arm wildly, attempting with the last of his strength and control to bring the barrel of his H&K around at Red.

She rolled and came out of the tumble with her Noveske N4, the assault rifle rattling as she unloaded on Rodriguez with the three hundred round drum magazine. Red put half the drum in him before letting her finger up off the trigger.

There was a death rattle behind her from the mutant on the ground.

She shook her head in disgust. The path was silent again. Rodriguez had kind of surprised her. Not that he had tried to kill her. She figured he'd have gotten around to that eventually. But that he'd tried here, now. It didn't surprise her he had failed. *Idiot.*

Red held her hand up and looked at it.

She was the idiot.

She'd cut the skin of her knuckles on the teeth of the zombie she'd punched in the mouth. She knew what that meant, the same way MacKenzie had known what it'd meant when he'd been bitten.

Dammit.

Red wouldn't allow that.

She let the N4 drop to the ground and drew her 9mm Stechkin. How ironic, she thought. But how right. Red thought about Thomas and how good he had been to her and Tommy. She swallowed and before she could change her mind she rolled her head back, pressed the barrel of the pistol to her chin and pulled the trigger.

Nothing happened.

Red looked at the Stechkin again. It hadn't fired. She could have cried, and as she cleared the jam, preparing to complete what she'd begun, the thought occurred to her that maybe it wasn't a coincidence that the gun hadn't fired.

Tommy and Gammon were going to trade that Victor guy for the woman. This wasn't over yet. Infected or not, Red had to see it through. She had a few hours at least, maybe half a day at most. She could do this.

Putting the pistol away, Red bent to pick up the N4. She shouldn't have tossed it down onto the ground like that, she thought. Red looked from Rodriguez's body with the push dagger's handle sticking out of his chest, to her blades buried in the mutant, to her throwing axe in the head of the zombie. She did not look forward to retrieving the blades and cleaning them off.

"Riley, you awake?"

She couldn't see him, backlit by the daylight in the tent flap, but the deep baritone was unmistakably Dee's.

"Yeah."

"Can I come in? Talk to you?"

"Yeah."

She'd been lying there thinking about Anthony for some time.

Dee had a Coleman lamp, the flame extinguished. After Riley had turned in, several of the others had stayed up and talked. He found the folding chair and sat down in it, placing the lamp on the floor near his feet.

Riley was sitting on the bed. "I can't sleep."

"Yeah, me neither. You thinking about your brother?"

"Yes." She didn't know Dee well but she felt she could talk to him.

"I'm sorry that happened to him...to you. I'm sorry about what Tris said last night, about your father."

"No, she had his number. She knows him, all right."

"I wonder if my dad knew your dad. I'd think he must have."

"You miss him a lot still, don't you?"

"Every day. It's hard to talk to people about. See, to all of them, he was almost... it was like he was more than human. It's like talking to someone about a god, to the Bishop—to Fred—about his god. It's hard to convey to them what he meant to me, as a boy, as a man."

"And Tris doesn't help there either."

"I do love Tris. And I know she loves me. And I know she loved dad, too, as much as she talks ill about him. She's just got issues."

"That story she told about having to kill her husband and children..."

"Yeah. I guess it doesn't get much worse than that. I mean..." Dee thought about Riley's situation with her brother and decided not to address it. "You were born after—you don't remember the outbreak, do you?"

"None of it."

"Yeah, well, I was a little boy. I remember some things. I remember it as clear as yesterday when I met Bear and Bruce and Kevin and all. Tris too. You know, they all had families, all of them. And then they didn't. They don't talk much about it."

"What was Bear like, as a person?"

"He was quiet most of the time. He taught me how to fight, how to survive. Whatever he didn't know, he had others teach me. Tris and Bruce...others that aren't around anymore. You know, he's been gone long enough, and I'm old enough now—got some distance between those days—I can say this about him: my father was extremely driven. I don't want to couch it in religious language like the Bishop, like Fred, but it really was like he was answering some calling."

"We learned about the zombie wars in school," Riley told him. "It was never a given that human beings were going to win."

"I don't think I ever realized how bleak it was, even as a little kid. I mean, I've seen Bear and Tris and the army go at it with millions of those things. Millions. And *win*. And after every battle there was another one looming. I guess, if I had been old enough, it might have crossed my mind that the battles were never ceasing, that as soon as one had been won, there were dozens more, right? I know it was hopeless for a lot of people. We had so many casualties, and they weren't all at Zed's teeth. But I was a kid. What did I know?"

"Well, our side won, right?"

"Pretty much. There's still pockets of them here and there. Those trees and mountains where I met you? Out by the bomb? A few hundred of them up in there."

"And Africa?"

"Africa should be pretty hairy."

"You guys have come this far, you'll make it."

"You know, Tris wants to find those people that were following you."

Riley had been thinking about them too. "So do I."

"Most everybody else, though, they understand the importance of getting this show on the road. We have to meet the others at the coast. When they get there, they're not going to wait forever."

"I know, Dee. I don't expect anyone to help me. I mean, you've helped me so much already. I'm safe here. I'm finally safe."

"What will you do?"

"I guess I'll find my way back to New Harmony. And I'll tell them what happened. I don't know what I'll tell my dad. I'll get some people together, and we'll go and find Tommy and the girl. And we'll kill them."

"That's the thing that always bothered me about this," admitted Dee. "Like Zed wasn't enough for all of us to worry about. You'd think, if something was going to have the power to band us together—Zed would have been it, wouldn't it?"

"But it did, Dee. For the most part. I don't know if you've seen that, out here, on the move all this time. In New Harmony it's different. The only other people you're going to come across out here are the ones that don't want to be a part of any society, the ones that were thrown out."

"Yeah, you're right about that."

"Bear never wanted to settle down?"

"I don't know, maybe…" Dee said, reflecting. "But I don't know if he could. She was wrong, you know."

Somehow Riley knew Dee was referring to Tris. "How do you mean?"

"We spoke, the night before he went away." Dee meant himself and Bear.

"What'd he say?"

"We talked about the difference between remorse and regret, and you know what he said? He said remorse was regret for something you'd done in your life. And regret was, well regret was regret that you *hadn't* done something in your life. He told me he had no remorse, for any of it. But he said he did have a regret."

"Which was?"

"He told me—and you've got to understand how weird this was, coming from him…I mean, he was larger than life, yes? He said he regretted he never got married. He said he regretted the fact that he never loved anyone the way a man was made to love, was made to love another, to love a woman."

"Well, judging by the stories, it sounds like he was too busy killing."

"That's just it. And here's the thing. The difference between him and Tris? He recognized it, and it bothered him. Tris doesn't. Bear felt that what he had done all those years, fighting like that, that it had left him incapable of love."

"What'd you say to him?"

"I told him that me—" Dee touched his chest to emphasize the words "—my person—my existence—that I gave lie to that claim."

"How'd he respond to that?"

"He smiled. He was so…big. I know you're probably thinking to yourself, why does that matter? But this is the thing about Bear. I've heard other people say, when they were kids, how their dads or moms or whoever seemed so big to them, and then when they—the kids—get older, they get bigger than their dads and moms. But Bear? As I got older and grew, he got bigger. And I don't just mean physically."

"You were living with a myth," remarked Riley, thinking back to a conversation in a bar with a drunken tracker.

"And that's why—when he talked to me about how he wished he'd gotten married? That sounds so mundane, doesn't it? I'd never seen him that vulnerable. I don't know. Part of me didn't like seeing him like that. You have to understand. He was more than human to me."

"I do understand, Dee."

"Thanks."

"He was your dad."

Dee rubbed his mouth with his hand.

"And that was it? You never saw him again?"

"Never."

"Do you have anything to remember him by?"

"He left behind some of his weapons. He'd given me this a long time before." Dee drew the .357 magnum from its holster. "Be careful. It's loaded."

Riley made sure to keep the barrel aimed away at the floor as she hefted the revolver in her hand.

"This is nice." After studying it from several angles, she handed it back to him. "Well, you're not going to ask me to marry you, are you?"

Dee laughed, taken aback. "*No.*"

"Listen—"

There was a commotion outside.

"Come on," Dee didn't bother to holster the Colt Python. He rose, grabbing up the lantern. Riley followed him, wrapping the blanket around her shoulders against the day's chill.

As soon as they'd stepped outside, Kevin came running up to them. "Dee!" he yelled. "They got Victor!" Men and women were moving around the camp, preparing for something.

"What happened, Kev?"

"Command tent," Kevin called as he trotted past, "now."

Inside the tent, Tris was sharpening the blades of her sickles on a whet stone. She had a determined look on her ruined face. She wore black-grey camouflage pants and a black tactical assault vest brimming with flap pouches. The dozen other men and women present looked up as Dee and Riley entered.

"This is her fault," someone said, pointing at Riley.

"Shut up." The anger in Dee's voice was unmistakable. "Shut up! You know what? Get out of here. Get your ass out of here now. You hear me?"

The man left sheepishly.

"What happened?" Dee asked Tris.

"Whoever those people were, chasing Riley?" Tris didn't take her eyes from her work. "They snatched Victor."

"What? How do we—"

"They left a note." Fred Turner held his cat. "They said they were willing to trade. Her—" he indicated Riley, "—for him."

"I'll go," Riley stated.

"They can't be serious."

"They're serious," stated Bruce. He and Kevin wore black vests that matched Tris'.

"I'll go."

"They'd better not touch a hair on Victor's head."

"They won't," Riley mentioned quietly.

"What?" asked Kevin. "How do you know?"

"I just know. They're not like that. If they told you they'd trade him for me, that's what they'll do. And I'll go."

"So what are we going to do?" Carrie wondered.

"I'll go to them. This wasn't right. It *was* my fault this happened. If I wasn't here—"

"Riley, be quiet."

"No, Dee," said Tris. "Let's hear her."

"Just give me a gun or something." Riley pointed to the grenade around Tris' neck. "Just me one of those."

"This girl got moxie, huh?" Tris held her sickles up to the light in the tent, admiring the shine of the blades.

"No good, Riley," said Dee. "We'll take care of this."

"We'll take care of this *together*." Tris twirled the sickles in her hands before replacing them on her back. "Including you." She looked at Riley. "Dee, get her a gun. Bruce, Kevin. Grab your rifles. Carrie, you get ready too. We're out of here in fifteen."

"I'm coming," Fred invited himself along.

"Do whatever you want, bishop."

* * *

When Alex came to visit him that morning, Steve was playing cards with Brent. He'd heard about the double suicide in the hospital, known who they'd been. He found himself looking out the window often, but the corner across from his house was empty. It was reassuring to have Brent, his old friend, around.

A bottle stood unopened on the table between them. It'd been there since last night when Brent had brought it over.

"Hello, Alex." Brent greeted the younger man who came into his house, Riley's ex-boyfriend.

"I'm glad you're up," Alex said to Steve. "I wasn't sure…" Alex knew from having dated Riley that there were nights Steve and Riley's uncle Brent drank so much they didn't move much before noon the following day. "I was hoping I could talk to you."

Steve gestured to an empty seat at the kitchen nook. "Let's talk."

Alex settled down. "I'm going out there, to find Riley."

Steve, Brent, and Alex filled the three seats where Steve usually sat with his son and daughter, both of whom had been gone for nearly two weeks, gone into the Outlands.

"That's a bad idea," Brent responded. "You don't even know where they went."

"I know where they were put down," Alex forged ahead, intrepidly. "I talked to the helicopter pilot. Grimaldi's going to take me."

"That was a week ago, over a week ago," Brent shook his head. "They could be…" he looked at Steve. "They could be anywhere now."

"So what'd you want to come and talk to me about?" Steve asked Alex.

Alex looked at him, disappointed. "I don't know." He inhaled and puffed out the air. "I thought maybe you'd want to go with me."

"Riley and Anthony are grown up now, Alex," Steve reminded him.

"Which means, *what*? They can look after themselves?"

"They can make their own decisions. And believe me, this wasn't one I agreed with."

"Maybe coming here wasn't…" Alex looked down at the table. "I don't know what I was thinking."

"You two broke up, didn't you?" asked Brent.

"She broke up with me. But so what?"

"So," Steve put it to him plainly, "maybe you shouldn't concern yourself—"

"See, that's funny, because here I was thinking—seeing how Riley is *your* daughter—that maybe *you* should."

Brent watched the look come and go across his old friend's face, knew how close Alex had come to getting hit.

"Alex," Steve said, "You're a good guy. I wouldn't want to see anything happen to you."

"I'm not worried about me. I'm worried about Riley."

"What about your parents, Alex?" asked Brent. "How would they feel if you went out there and something happened to you?"

"Like Steve said," Alex gazed out at the man from the corners of his eyes. "I'm all grown up now, too."

"I had to prepare myself," Steve said quietly. "When they left, I had to prepare myself that maybe I'd never see them again. You know how hard that is? Any idea?"

"So, *what*, we're just going to sit around—"

"Alex—" Brent attempted to interrupt.

"I'm hoping they'll be back," Steve remarked almost to himself, "I hope to God they are."

Alex was breathing heavy, as if he were barely containing himself. Steve and Brent didn't know if the young man was close to crying or screaming. When he could speak, he did. "I'll be at the helipad, if you change your mind. Tomorrow morning, first light."

He pushed himself away from the table and got out of his chair.

"Hey, Alex," Brent called after him as he made for the door. "Be careful out there." His comment went unacknowledged.

Sometime after Alex had left, the bottle on the table remained untouched. Steve sighed and laid his cards down. "My head isn't in this."

Brent looked at him. "Whatever you decide," he told Steve, "I'm in."

"Thanks, Brent."

Steve parted the slats of the window blinds with his thumb and index finger and looked out onto an empty street and the dark night.

"Dee." The man with the thick mustache behind the table in the armory tent smiled warmly at Dee and Riley. "New lady."

"Jerry. We need to outfit Riley here." Dee turned to her. "Well…" Dee wasn't very happy that Tris demanded that Riley accompany them, and that Riley *wanted* to. "What do you want?"

"What's this one?"

"Pick it up."

Riley raised a black, mean-looking rifle in both hands.

"Heavy?" Jerry asked her.

"No, it feels good. It's got some heft to it."

"CETME semi-automatic battle rifle," Jerry explained as Riley sighted down the barrel. "Chambered in 7.62 NATO. Big recoil on that sucker."

"Can it mess someone up?" she asked him.

"It'll ruin their day."

"I think I can handle it."

"That one's got a fixed stock. We've got another here with a folding stock."

"This will do. Thank you—Jerry, right?"

"That's right." Jerry looked seriously at Dee. "They have Victor, huh?"

"Yeah," Dee answered glumly, then told Riley, "You'll need a handgun."

"Hey, Sharon," Jerry called back further in the tent to someone unseen. "Could you bring up some seven-sixty-two NATO and whatever twenty round magazines we have for the CETME's? Thanks, honey."

Jerry turned his attention back to Riley and Dee. "My wife." He smiled at Riley. "May I recommend this?"

Riley took the revolver Jerry handed her.

"Taurus Model 4510." Jerry ran down the specs as Riley popped the cylinder, squinted down the barrel and felt the weapon in her hand. "Chambered for .45 Colt ammunition. Five rounds. Fixed rear sight, fiber optic front sight. Ribber—not rubber—grips. Nice little piece. Decent range for a hand gun what with those .45s, too."

"I'll take it."

"Tris asked for a ballistic shield." Dee relayed the request to Jerry.

"Now what's she got in mind?"

"Who knows."

"I think we've got something. Hey, Sharon, hon? Could you bring up that riot shield too, please?" Jerry lowered his voice and spoke seriously to Dee and Riley. "You all go and bring Victor back."

"That's the plan," acknowledged Dee.

"Okay, Frankie, I want you a few hundred yards behind me, over there," Gammon pointed. "And Toby, you're over there."

Frankie and Tobias looked towards the woods where Gammon indicated. They'd have the trees behind them and the grass to cover them, but Gammon was going to be sitting here exposed.

"Now, when they show up," Gammon instructed them, "ya'll don't go doin' anything stupid. Don't show your hand until you have to is what I'm sayin'. Stay where you are, let me get the girl and cover us on our way out. These people got no trouble with us, they just want their Victor back."

"What if they try and kill you once you tell them where they can find their Victor?"

"Well, see Toby, I'm kind of counting on that *not* happening. But if it does, that's when you two step in. But both of you wait for my signal."

"Which is…?"

"Which is what, Toby?"

"What's the signal, Ed?"

"Well, it's not like I have one worked out. But if you see me hollerin' and shootin', that's a sure good sign right there. Any other questions? No. Good. Get yourselves out there now."

"Ed?" Frankie asked. Toby, gripping his scoped rifle, trudged off through the grass.

"What's on your mind, Frankie?"

"Red."

"What about her?"

"Rodriguez ain't happy about Red."

"Yeah, I know that…"

"No," Frankie warned, "you better keep an eye on him."

"I'm hearing you, Frankie." Gammon looked out at the night. "We get this girl, we get back to the others, the both of us can keep tabs on Rodriguez, all right?"

Frankie nodded. "See you later, Ed."

"Yeah, I'll be seeing you, Frankie."

✳ ✳ ✳

"Here," Tris tossed a hand grenade to Dee. He caught it but yelled at her, "Tris—for Christ's sake!"

"Don't worry, they're smoke." Tris gave Riley the once over. "Give your rifle to Dee." Riley figured it was better not to ask. "Okay, let me see your sidearm." Riley handed Tris the Taurus 4510. "Revolver.

Nice." Tris stuffed the Taurus in her own web belt. "Here, hold this," she handed the riot shield to Riley, "and this." Riley looked down at the roll of duct tape Tris had placed in her other hand.

"What's the shield for?" Dee asked Tris.

"In case we need it."

"Hey, what about my guns?" Riley demanded.

"It's all part of the plan," said Tris. "You trust me?"

"No."

"Good." The corners of Tris' mouth lifted, sending ripples up her scarred face. "You found a smart one, Dee."

"Where's your AR, Tris?" Bruce was feeding cartridges into the internal magazine of an M24 SWS bolt-action sniper rifle.

"AR's my zombie-killing gun."

"Then what's that?" Riley indicated the submachine gun Tris held in one hand, a folding-stock Calico M960A fitted with a hundred round magazine.

"This is my man-killin' gun."

"Wait a minute." Riley looked confused. "I don't get a gun?"

"We don't have time for this." Tris sounded annoyed. "I'm going to give you back your pistol on one condition. When I ask for it again, you give it to me, and you do everything I say. *Everything.*"

Dee looked at Riley. His expression read, *Don't do it.*

"Okay." Riley consented.

"Now that's what I like to hear." Tris handed the Taurus back to Riley, butt-first. "Dee, you keep hanging out with her. You might learn something."

∗ ∗ ∗

"They all think I'm crazy." Fred Turner looked pleased as they marched. He didn't carry a gun, but he carried a Bible under one arm and his stuffed cat under the other.

"You've been through a lot." Bruce was generous.

"Nah," said Tris, "the Bishop is just crazy."

Fred laughed. "What do you think, Riley?"

"I don't think the cat helps."

"Mr. Vittles, my old friend." Fred asked Riley, "Where you come from, are there Christians?"

"A few. There's some religious groups, but they're spaced out."

"That's what I'm sayin'," commented Tris.

"I mean geographically."

Kevin and Dee were ahead, leading the group from their quads to their destination.

"So," inquired Fred, "what do people believe?"

"What do you mean?"

"What do people think happens when they die?"

"Well…" Riley herself harbored no beliefs in any afterlife or deities. "I can't speak for everybody. But I think when you die…I don't know, that's it. You're dead."

"And where do you think we came from?" There was a spring in Fred's step. He looked completely different from the skeleton of a man Riley had first set eyes on the previous day. Some animating force was present in him now. He'd shaved. "Why do you think we're here?"

"I don't know." Riley thought Tris might be right about the man, especially after his leap-of-faith story. "About fourteen million years ago the universe expanded and cooled and now we're here. Look, I'm no scientist."

"That sounds plausible to you?"

"You know, Fred. I've been thinking a lot…especially since my brother died. Maybe the important questions aren't how we got here and why. Maybe we should be thinking of the future, about where we're going."

"A couple more clicks," said Tris.

"I couldn't agree more." Fred understood Riley's point.

"And I'm thinking, whatever unites us and helps us live together, peaceably—is that a word?—that those are things we should be encouraging. Everything else…"

"Everything else," Bruce rasped, "is pretty much just bullshit."

"Pretty much," Riley agreed. "We don't have a lot of time. Any of us, individually I mean. But I've seen things, getting here. I think maybe human beings will continue on, different maybe than what we've been used to. I don't think humanity is going to just disappear. So it all goes back to what you said, right? About having a second chance?"

"That's why He came here," Fred nodded his head in agreement.

Riley thought he meant Bear.

"Hey, Tris," said Bruce. "You look happy."

"I'm going to get a chance to kill someone soon. Riley, tell me more about this red-headed bitch."

THIS MORTAL COIL

Gammon waited in the field, the grass up to his knees. He looked up into the sky behind him and squinted. The sun was going down. If they'd gotten the note…

He didn't like this one bit. He drew his .45, racked back the slide, checked the round chambered there, and holstered the pistol. No, he didn't like this, not at all. A few moments later he drew the M1911 again and stuffed it in the front of his pants, within easy reach, within sight of anyone approaching him.

There were cicadas stirring up a racket, unseen around him. He was surprised the insects were still above ground, what with the autumn chill upon them.

Frankie and Tobias were off behind him, in the tree line. Waiting, like him. He knew they were good shots. It didn't make him feel much better.

Gammon was here for Thomas, and to keep Tommy safe. Thomas had always been there for him, and he'd be there for his friend, even if his friend wasn't here anymore, even if Gammon himself didn't like how this was playing out.

He thought about camp and the people there. He'd see them soon enough, he hoped. Exchange the girl for this guy, Victor, then haul ass back home. Be there in three, four days. Tommy would kill the girl, Gammon knew. It was wrong, in a way, but he wouldn't stop the kid. She *had* killed Thomas, after all. Merv too. That didn't sit right with Gammon, how Merv had died.

Some big, lazy bug was flying slow loops in front of him.

Gammon saw them then, two figures, coming across the field towards him. The girl with a black woman behind her. He touched the butt of his pistol before forcing his hand down to his side. Frankie and Toby were there, somewhere behind him, drawing down on the women as he watched them come.

Looked like the black woman was pushing the girl ahead of her. Sure. The kid had arrived at those people's camp, uninvited, and look at the whole world of trouble she'd brought with her. They'd want to get their Victor back, that group. They wouldn't want to fight—not human against human. Too many people would get killed, and all for what?

Yeah, the black woman was definitely pushing the girl ahead, Gammon noted as they got closer, cutting the distance between himself and them. It looked like the girl had her hands secured behind her back, too. Looked like the black woman wasn't armed. And boy did she look mad, real mad.

Gammon shifted his weight from one leg to the other. Okay then…

"Hey," he called out when he judged they were within hearing. "I just want you to know, I don't like this any more than you do." His words were intended for the black woman. That look on her face. Mad as hell and determined. Heck, thought Gammon, she must be. This girl shows up and everything goes to hell.

"I'm going to reach down to my pistol here…" Gammon did so, grasping the butt with his fingertips, slipping the weapon out of his belt, holding it up for the black woman to see. She didn't stop walking, and she was still giving the girl a push ahead. She was close enough now that Gammon could see how messed up her face was under the dreads, like she'd been burned.

"I'm putting this down…" Gammon bent at the knee, placing the .45 in the grass and dirt, "…because I can see you did what the note said. You came here without a weapon, in good faith." He stood back up. "And in the end, that's what we all gotta do, right? Trust one another?"

That look on the woman's face…Gammon didn't like it. Sure, if he were in her shoes, he'd be pissed all to hell too, but…The way she kept coming, like she wasn't gonna stop. Toby and Frankie were out there, behind him, unseen, ready, fingers on triggers.

"He ain't dead." Gammon thought his words might reassure her. "And we don't mean to kill him."

They kept coming.

"So let me tell you how this is gonna be," Gammon started to say when the women were less than ten meters from him. Two cracks followed one upon the other in such quick succession that they sounded like a single shot. They had come from *in front* of Gammon, not behind him.

Frankie and Toby.

"Awww, damn," Gammon muttered, the realization dawning on him. The girl brought her hands out from behind her and they weren't bound. She'd just had them back there to fool him, and she held them down at her sides now, fists balled. It looked like the black woman went to shove the girl once more, but instead she reached up and tore the sickle she had duct taped to the girl's back free and cocked her arm back, all in one motion.

It registered in Gammon's mind too late. Yeah, the woman was angry, madder than hell, but not with the girl.

Five meters away, Tris let the sickle fly.

She had aimed for his stomach, but Gammon was squatting down, reaching for his pistol. His hand closed on the cold steel butt at the same moment that the sickle—a blur across the grass—buried itself in his chest beneath his neck.

Riley covered the remaining distance in a sprint, reaching the felled man. Tris didn't break her stride, walking at the same determined pace.

"You son of a bitch!" Riley cursed Gammon, standing above him.

He lay there, both hands grasping at the blade, the handle jutting out of his body. This was it. He could feel the blood staining his shirt. He knew he was dying, here in this field. Wasn't right. *Thomas. Merv.*

That big, lazy bug circled overhead.

Tommy

Tris reached the downed man and Riley. She bent over and retrieved the guy's .45. "No," Tris said as she pulled back the slide, the bullet already chambered there flying off into the grass, "Let *me* tell *you* how this is going to be." She pointed the gun down at the man's face. "I'm going to kill you, and then I'm going to go and find all your fuck friends, and I'm going to kill all of them too. Got it?"

Red.

Gammon managed to gargle something before Tris fired a single round into his forehead. He lay there, eyes open, staring up at the sky.

"Son of a bitch," Riley spat again. "This son of a bitch."

The others were loping through the grass, past them to the felled snipers. It had been Bruce and Kevin who'd detected the two men in the tree line and taken them out.

"Yeah, that's right," snapped Tris. "A *real* son of a bitch."

"What now?" asked Riley.

"Like I told him," Tris said matter-of-factly. "I'm going to go and find his friends. Kill them. Get Victor back."

"I'm going with you."

"No, you're not." Dee had reached them, along with Fred Turner and Carrie.

"Excuse me?" Riley demanded.

"This ain't over, Riley. There's gonna be a lot more killing. You could get hurt."

Riley dismissed the comment with a wave of her hand. "I'm not worried about that, Dee."

"I got your stuff here, Tris." Carrie dumped Tris' ruck on the ground.

"Thanks." There was a wet sound as Tris yanked the sickle out of the dead man's chest. The fly that had landed on his forehead circled away, bothered.

"You can't get hurt," Dee tried to persuade Riley. "Not you. You gotta live. You've got to live to finish what your brother started—to go back to your father and tell him what happened. Let him know what happened to your brother."

Riley looked at him incredulously. Tris indelicately wiped the blade of the sickle clean on the dead man's pants.

From the tree line, one of their party called to them.

"What's that?"

"They got a live one." Fred Turner stroked his cat's back as he looked down on the old dead man.

Tris, clutching the .45 she had picked up and the sickle, stalked off for the trees.

"Riley. You've got to listen to me, okay?"

"No, Dee. It's not okay. They killed my friends. They killed my brother. I want to kill them. I'm going with Tris."

"Riley, these aren't zombies. These are people. And a lot of people are going to die before this is over—them and us."

"Looks like they're doing most of the dying so far." Carrie looked down on Gammon.

"Fred, help me out here." Dee looked to him. "You can't go, honey. You gotta stay."

"*Honey*? Don't patronize me, Dee."

"No," Fred Turner disagreed. "She's gotta go."

"*What?*"

"You've got to see this through." Fred told Riley. "You go, yeah, you might die. But if you don't go, you'll regret that all your life."

"Fred, you gotta be—"

"Let her go, Dee. It's for her to do."

"Shit!"

Riley looked at Fred and the look said *Thank you.*

There was a gunshot from the trees.

"Shit." Dee smacked his head. "Tris killed him. Tris fucking killed him." He yelled out to the others, "You killed him, didn't you, Tris?"

Tris was walking back to them. She looked contemptuously at the .45 in her hand and tossed it away into the grass. She didn't speak until she reached them.

"Well." She looked at Riley. "You coming or what?"

"I'm in." There was steel in Riley's voice.

"Did he talk?" Carrie asked Tris.

"Yeah, he talked."

"They always talk," Carrie offered as an aside to Riley. "You had to kill him, Tris?" asked Dee, and the way he said it, it sounded like he thought she didn't have to.

"No," Tris confirmed. "I didn't *have* to kill him. But I did." She looked at Riley. "Let's go."

"You're going to allow this?" Dee looked at Fred Turner.

"*Allow* it?" Fred asked Dee, then spoke to Riley. "You've got my blessing. Go and find those people, and exact your vengeance." He made the sign of the cross in the air between them. "God is with you, whether you recognize His presence or not."

Dee exhaled, but Tris and Riley were already walking away. "Go home, Bishop," Tris called back to Fred. "My shit's about to get biblical."

Dee and Fred hurried along to keep up with them.

"Hey, Tris," Kevin was asking her. "How'd you know Bruce was only going to wound the one? And how'd you know the dude was going to talk?"

"I didn't."

"Tris can be so bad-ass sometimes," Carrie remarked.

"You know my steez."

"Oh, man," Bruce remarked to Kevin, purposefully loud enough that Tris would hear it. "I love when she talks black."

"Bruce." Tris eyeballed him over her shoulder as she walked. "Shut the fuck up before I cut your dick off and pickle it."

"Well, not to brag, Tris, but you better make sure you have yourself a big enough jar."

"For what, your little tinky winky?"

"Wasn't Tinky Winky a Teletubby?" Kevin asked Carrie.

"Yeah. I think he was the gay one."

"Tris," Bruce continued, "I ain't braggin' sweetheart, but—"

"I seen worms in the bottom of Tequila bottles would put you to shame." Tris put a scowl on her face, but she seemed to enjoy the give and take. "Now quit."

"Ouch." Kevin winced. He and Bruce had taken the sniper rifles from the dead men.

"He takes his life in his hands every time he talks to her like that," noted Carrie.

"Nah," replied Kevin. "Tris wouldn't hurt him too much. In her own way, she loves us all. Don't you Tris?"

"Keep foolin' yourself."

"I don't like this, Tris," said Dee. "And it's got nothing to do with me. Using Riley as bait—"

"It worked, right?"

"Yeah, but—"

"And, no, I'm not done using her as bait either."

"What are you talking about, Tris?" Dee demanded.

Tris stopped and turned to face Riley. "You want to get close enough to these motherfuckers, close enough to kill 'em, right?"

Riley nodded her head vigorously. "Right."

"Good." Tris clasped the woman on the shoulder and resumed walking. "Because I got a plan."

"This should be good," Bruce said to Kevin.

"Bishop," Tris stopped walking and turned to face Fred. "I'm serious. This is where you turn back. Go back to the quads. You can wait for us there. We be back in the morning. Rest of you sorry-assed motherfuckers, come with me."

Without another word, Tris walked away, Bruce and Kevin falling in behind her. The others stood around staring at one another for a moment.

"Well, then." Fred blessed Dee, Riley and Carrie. "Go with god."

* * *

He'd been walking for a half hour, heading back to where they'd left their quads, when Fred realized he was not alone.

"Dee?" He called back to the trees. "Carrie?"

Had they followed him?

"Bruce?"

The animals and insects in the trees were silent in the early evening. Fred felt like eyes were upon him. He looked down at the bible in his hand, at the cat under his arm, and he breathed in.

Though I walk through the valley of the shadow of death... He banished the thought from his head.

Fred continued along the way he'd been going. He thought about running. He was old, but maybe, if he had to, he could sprint a short distance. He decided not to. Something in these woods might be watching him, but Fred knew something more powerful than anything he might encounter on this earth had charted his path and was guiding him now. The thought gave him some comfort.

"John," Fred said, thinking of his dead son.

A club or something—Fred only caught a glance of it—came flying out of the air and cracked him in the leg, crippling the limb. He flopped down face first, dropping his bible and cat.

His eyes squeezed shut...the pain in his leg. As he lay there grimacing, Fred was vaguely aware of shadows detaching themselves from the trees about him, forms that moved in to surround him.

When he looked up, he was almost taken aback by the collection of visages gathered around. They were like creatures from some other planet, vaguely human, yet terribly deformed. Bodies outsized and misproportioned, hunchbacked and dysmorphic. Flesh marred with welts and scaly crusts. One with its head at a ninety degree angle to its upper torso.

All God's children, he hastened to remind himself. *All God's children.*

"I was wondering when you'd show yourselves." Fred pushed up onto his palms and one good foot, taking up his bible, leaving the cat stiff legged on its back where it was. They watched him as he struggled and finally managed to rise unsteadily, keeping the weight off his damaged leg.

"That…" Fred grimaced in pain and indicated his crippled leg. "That was unnecessary."

These were unlike any beings he had ever seen. They towered over him, gargantuan and odiferous. Their eyes shone with malicious intent. It was true, Fred realized, that old saying that the Lord spoke in mysterious ways. But his god had spoken to him—with Riley's appearance, with news of Mickey and the picture of Harris—and Fred had understood. His god was speaking to him now.

Fred Turner smiled at the fiends, his face mirroring the succor he found in his conviction.

"What are you smiling about?" one of them asked, its voice heavily impeded because its mouth was bent and twisted, teeth growing out of its gums in a seemingly random pattern, its lips curled up into a permanent snarl.

Fred merely nodded at it. He was convinced this would all be over soon.

"Who are you, mister?" The man who asked was the only conventional-looking one among the bunch. He was an older man, like Fred, and Fred assumed he was the patriarch of this tribe.

"I was a father…" Fred looked from disfigured face to disfigured face. "…who thought he had lost a son. But now, I'm a son, who realized he's found his father."

"Is that it?"

Fred glanced down at the cat. "Just don't hurt the cat, please?"

"We won't," Cosmo vowed. "Bothar."

A grunt, a swing and a body on the ground. Bothar lowered his club, Fred Turner's blood dripping from the rusty, bent nails studding it.

"There's more of 'em up that way." Cosmo indicated Fred's path. "We gotta get goin'. Your brothers are gonna start the fires soon."

One of his boys held the cat up. "Can I fuck it, paw?"

"No, Titus. You heard what I told that man. Give it here," Cosmo snatched the stuffed animal from his son's massive hand.

"Ain't no pictures in this book, dad." Having set the Hawk MM1 grenade launcher on the ground, Mergatroid was leafing through Fred's bible. "Cans I keep it?"

"Nah. Give me that. I gotta take me a shit."

* * *

Tommy was dreaming. He was a kid again. The smoke from the fire where his mother was cooking a hog wafted through the cabin. His father was outdoors chopping wood and Merv was playing with his homemade toys on the floor.

"Tommy, get up."

"No, mah…" he protested groggily, until Little Red shook him violently.

"Wake up, Tommy—*Now!*"

"What? What's going on?" He sat up among the trees. Red had come back to them in the middle of the night, minus Rodriguez. Rodriguez. He'd drawn on her and she'd taken him out. That was Red's story and Tommy believed it.

He'd dreamed of smoke, and now, awake, he could still smell it. "What's that?" he scrunched up his nose.

Red answered matter-of-factly. "They're burning the forest."

Around them the others were packing up, strapping on their weapons and packs, making ready to decamp. It was nearly dawn.

"They're burning the forest?" he asked incredulously.

"They want to drive us out of the trees."

"Shit." Tommy stood and looked over to their captive, Victor, who sat quietly. The guy probably thought they were going to kill him now. And maybe they should, Tommy thought. Gammon, Frankie and Toby hadn't come back. He didn't kid himself about what that meant. They wouldn't have allowed themselves to be taken alive. "Don't you go getting any ideas," he said to the man in the bandana.

Keith and David had struck off into the trees.

"Hurry up, Tommy," Red called, slinging her Noveske Diplomat over her shoulder. "Chang. Grab him."

"I got one functional arm here!" Chang protested but walked over to their captive.

Victor thought Red looked agitated and, more so, worried. When she'd come back, her hand had been tied up with a strip of cloth. Victor had heard her tell her friends she'd cut herself fighting the Rodriguez guy. She hadn't let anyone look at her hand and Victor wondered if something more wasn't going on there.

"Get up." Chang reached down, a knife in the hand of his unbroken arm, cutting the ropes binding Victor's legs. "On your feet. Time to walk again."

* * *

Dawn had broken a half hour past.

Riley waited in the clearing, watching the smoke rise from the trees on three sides of the meadow. That worried her for a number of reasons. One, none of those with her had set it; neither did it make sense that the people holding Victor would burn their own cover. So, she wondered, if not us or them, then who?

Secondly, Riley reasoned, the fire would drive whatever zombies remained in these hills and mountains down into the clearing…where she was. And hadn't Dee said these hills were full of the undead?

She sat against the bomb and waited. Its casing was cold and slick with morning dew. One of the men who pursued her had wired it, and the detonator rested on her leg. She didn't know why they had primed it to explode, nor could she understand why they hadn't detonated it already. All she would need to do, she'd been told, was push the red button on it and *boom*. Dee said it was a two thousand pound bomb, enough to destroy everything in this clearing and leave a crater a meter or more deep in this spot where she sat.

Riley did not like this situation. She hadn't liked how Tris had taken out Gammon either, propelling her across the field with the sickle duct taped to her back. Gammon just waiting there, thinking they were going to talk, Tris planning to kill him the whole time. Not that she wanted Gammon to live, but she'd had some questions for him first. Questions she hadn't been able to ask.

She sat there and felt uncomfortable, because she was the vulnerable one again. There was a good chance they would see her and just shoot her.

Thick plumes of black smoke were roiling off the mountainsides. Whoever had set that fire was going to burn the whole forest down.

She didn't want to die here. Riley looked down at the riot shield resting in the knee-high grass. She looked down to her other side, at the CETME rifle. She wanted to kill that guy, Tommy, the son of that old man. The redhead, too. Riley wanted to end this family tree right here and now.

They'd be coming soon, she thought. She picked up the detonator and held it where anyone in the trees could see her holding it. She wouldn't get a chance to kill Tommy if one of the men and or the woman with him killed her first. It was personal for Riley. And she knew it was personal for them too, which made her doubt any of them would want to snipe her from the trees. Little Red especially would want to get in close, the way she'd been coming for her on the rocks above the river, the better to see the look on Riley's face.

Riley couldn't wait to see the look on *her* face.

"She's alone," reported Chang.

"She ain't alone." David was still wearing Victor's safety helmet.

"Don't see no one else."

"Doesn't mean she's alone."

They crouched in the trees, looking out into the field where Riley sat a few hundred yards away, the river beyond her. Keith had the barrel of his pistol pressed to Victor's head. "Don't even think of saying anything," he whispered to the captive.

"You think it's a trap?" Tommy asked.

"Sure it's a trap," answered Little Red.

"She's sitting on that bomb," observed David. He had to smile at how crazy that was. "Maybe we shouldn't have left it wired."

"She wants to lure us out of these trees," surmised Chang. "That's why they set this fire."

Smoke was rising above the treetops around them.

"She didn't set this fire." Little Red shook her head. "People with her didn't set this fire."

Tommy looked at Red. "Then who did?"

"She wants to lure us out of these trees," Chang repeated.

"Of course she does," Red ignored Tommy. "It's a trap."

"She's gonna get us all out there in the open," said Chang, "and then she's going to detonate that bomb and kill all of us."

"No, she won't."

"How do you know, Red?" Tommy asked.

"Because she doesn't want to die."

"See?" David remonstrated with Chang. "You overthink shit."

Tommy did not take his eyes off Red. "And what makes you say that?"

Little Red ignored him again.

"I can take her from here." David sighted down the barrel of his rifle.

"Don't you dare." Tommy turned his attention to the helmeted man. "She's mine."

"Come on, let's think here," Chang pled. "We *know* we're walking into a trap, right? We're giving them *exactly* what they want."

"You got any other ideas?" asked Keith.

"Yeah, let David make the shot. Nail that little bitch. If she blows herself up, so what? All we lose is a bunch of grass. Then we wait for her friends to show themselves and we knock them off too."

"Sounds like a plan," said Red. "Except in about five minutes this place is going to be swarming with zombies."

White smoke billowed out of the forest, filling the air.

"Sounds like a plan," echoed Tommy. "Except she's *mine*."

"Come on." Little Red rose.

"What?"

"Let's go. Give me him." Red walked over to Keith and grabbed Victor by the arm. She looked him in the eye. "Listen to me good. I don't give two shits about you, right? So whether you live or die—it's all the same to me. You understand what that means?" Victor nodded. "You do what I say and maybe you'll live."

"You want to go out there?" David really looked like he'd rather take the shot.

"We've got to get out of these trees." Chang had changed his tune. "Zombies are coming."

"He's right," affirmed Keith.

"Okay, well then—"

"Shit, Red!" Tommy spat because Little Red had already left the cover of the trees, her bandaged hand around Victor's arm, walking towards the woman on the bomb.

"The shooting starts," she promised Victor, "and the first thing you're going to feel is my steel."

"What do we do, Tommy?" asked David.

"Let's go. Spread out."

* * *

"You know what this is?" Riley called out when Little Red and Victor were within earshot. She raised the detonator higher than she'd had it before, made sure they could see it.

Riley wondered what she would do if the woman pulled a Tris and didn't stop walking. Little Red had a pistol with a wooden stock in the hand that wasn't propelling Victor forward, but the barrel was aimed at the ground. She also had her assault rifle and all sorts of sharp edges strapped tight to her body.

Riley knew she wasn't alone. She knew Bruce was on the ridge behind her, across the river, sighting through the scope of his M24 or one of the M40s they'd taken off the dead men. She hoped he was centering the redhead's forehead, under the chopsticks. Riley knew where the others were too, but she dared not look less she unwittingly reveal their positions.

Still, she fretted. She wanted the guy, Tommy. Not this little red-haired psycho. The girl, however, seemed fixated on her.

"You know this man?" Red called back, meaning Victor.

"I don't know him at all."

Red abruptly stopped in her tracks, halting Victor with her. Riley focused on the woman and her captive but was aware of the four other men fanning out behind Red in the field. The barrels of their weapons were not aimed at the ground. Tommy was there, his shotgun leveled at Riley.

"So," yelled Red. "It doesn't matter to you if he lives or dies?"

"I could care less." Riley shrugged. "No offense," she called out to Victor. "I want your friend," she yelled back at Red. "Tommy."

"Well, you're not going to get him." Red placed the Stechkin pistol in the grass at her feet as Riley eyed her warily across the distance. "You're gonna get me." Red produced a knife and cut the ropes binding Victor's wrists. Victor looked surprised and flexed his hands, getting blood back into them. "Go," Red gave him a push as she sheathed the blade. Victor glanced at the bandaged hand she'd pushed him with and Red saw him look. As he walked away, she stooped to pick up her pistol.

"That's not acceptable," Riley yelled to her.

Red looked across the distance separating her from the other woman. "Not acceptable?"

Victor fought the urge to run as he placed one foot in front of the other, moving away from the redheaded girl and towards the woman at the bomb.

"You heard me."

"Here I am, asshole!" Though Red and the three others were stationary, Tommy continued walking towards Riley. "You wanted me? Well, here I am."

Little Red held up her hand and Tommy hesitated where he was, looking unsure.

"Yeah, I heard you." Red called to Riley. "Let me ask you a question before I kill you. Why'd your people set the fire?"

Riley told the truth. "We didn't set the fire."

"Well then," Tommy demanded, "who did?"

As if on cue, the mutant broke from the tree line, roaring a battle cry, swinging a thigh bone over its head. It had what looked like half of a foot growing out of its skull.

"Shit!" screamed Chang.

"Fuck!" Tommy's eyes went wide.

Victor broke into a sprint, away from the bomb, towards the river.

"Now!" Tris stood, waist deep in the ground, tossing the spider hole's lid—camouflaged with tufts of dried grass and soil—aside, firing her Calico M960A in one hand.

Across the river, Bruce fired, but Red had already tucked and rolled, the bullet snapping the air above her head.

Riley threw herself backwards towards the bomb, landing in the grass behind it, twisting flat on her stomach, bullets raising plumes of soil around her. She ditched the detonator none too gently and came up with the Taurus, firing the .45 as quickly as she could pull the trigger.

The covers of three other spider holes were tossed off and Dee, Carrie and Kevin popped up, opening fire immediately. Chang yelped, his good arm outstretched, lifted off his feet in the barrage of automatic fire.

Red came out of her roll, flicking her wrist, the blade spinning end over end, catching Victor in the back of his shoulder. He went down with an *Oomph!*

The mutant screamed—a bullet plowed a hole through its side—but the thing did not slow as it barreled across the grass towards the nearest people.

Keith and David, on the ground, were firing back at the four men and women in the earth. In tandem, the brothers rolled onto their sides and shifted their fire to the mutant. Blood erupted from a dozen wounds on its torso and the thing pitched headfirst to the ground. The brothers turned back to their original positions and resumed firing at the people in the spider holes.

Red fired her pistol out at Riley and then started in with the N4, ragged bursts of 5.56mm lead sending geysers of dirt skyward around the bomb.

A dozen zombies broke from the tree line and started to run towards the humans who were trying to kill one another. Behind them, at least twice as many staggered out of the foliage. One of the slower ones had been an obese woman. It spotted a flash of red hair and stumbled mindlessly towards Red.

Having emptied her revolver, Riley pressed herself flat to the ground as bullets from Red's Noveske pinged and ricocheted off the bomb in front of her.

David and Keith were prone in the grass, the brothers firing side by side.

"Fuck this, D.L.," Dee muttered to himself, ducking down inside his hole in the ground, bullets zipping by overhead. Maybe the spider holes *hadn't* been such a good idea.

"Screw this!" Riley tucked her arms in close to her body and rolled on her side to the riot shield, snatching it up, drawing her legs up behind it and covering herself. No sooner had she done so than the opaque ballistic shield began to shake in her grasp as small arms fire impacted it. "Shit!" Riley struggled to reload her pistol and keep the shield in place.

Victor couldn't reach around far enough to grab the handle of the hatchet that jutted from his back. His adrenaline was pumping and he didn't know how bad the wound was. He gave up attempting to dislodge the weapon and instead scampered across the field, wanting to get away from his captors and the undead coming up behind them.

Tris popped up and fired at Keith and David with her Calico, forcing the brothers to duck their heads down in the grass. Red turned her fire from Riley to the dreadlocked woman, driving Tris back into the earth.

* * *

"You!" Tommy yelled at Riley, walking across the field, oblivious to the automatic weapons fire erupting around him. He fired his shotgun as he came, pumped, fired, pumped and fired. The shield rocked violently in Riley's grasp as the buckshot connected with it. It sounded like a handful of gravel was being thrown against it each time Tommy's 12-gauge boomed.

Carrie fired on the redheaded girl until a burst of fire from Keith sent her ducking back into her spider hole.

The fifteen-inch, double-edged weapon blurred through the air like a Frisbee, burying itself in Victor's leg. He cried out, reached for it and collapsed. Red knew she was good with a blade but even she chalked that one up to some degree of luck.

As Keith kept up his fire on the men and the women in the spider holes, David turned his aim to the zombies that were sprinting at them.

The lead booker's head snapped back and its body slid through the grass.

Riley gave up on the pistol and gripped the body bunker shield with two hands. She was taking fire from Tommy and Red. She watched Tommy come towards her, pumping his shotgun, bringing it to his shoulder. He was yelling at her, but she couldn't make out his words over the din. Suddenly Tommy was knocked off his feet, shot down by Bruce across the river. Riley silently thanked Bruce and grabbed up her pistol again.

Tris was pinned down in her spider hole. "Smoke!" she yelled at the top of her lungs as she tossed the first of the three smoke grenades she carried into the field. Tris pulled the pins on the second and third and lobbed those too. Dee, Carrie, and Kevin followed suit.

Flat on his back, Tommy lay in the grass. He'd been hit. Sniper. *Fuck*. He extended the shotgun in the direction of the shooter and fired, knowing the buckshot had no chance of reaching the gunman, much less the river. He just wanted to let the fuck know he was still in this game. Tommy let the shotgun go and drew his pistols.

A score of zombies were staggering across the field towards the firefight. They moaned and walked with arms outstretched, seeing food before them and smelling blood. The obese one watched little Red's head bob up and down in the grass and made for its intended meal.

Victor pulled the doubled edged weapon from his leg. "Damn it." He threw the thing away from himself in disgust. Reaching up—his back and shoulder screaming at him—he undid the bandana he wore. He bound the cloth as best he could above the wound in his leg. He still had the hatchet in his back. He could feel it there.

Red had watched Tommy go down—"*Tommy!*"—and turned her fire on Bruce across the river. She fired the N4 and missed, the rounds kicking up dirt two feet from Bruce.

"Whoa!" Bruce twitched involuntarily and adjusted his own aim, finding Red through his sights. He fired and watched through the telescopic sight as his own round went wide.

"Okay-okay-okay…" Bruce kept Red in his scope as he worked the bolt on the M40 A3, preparing his next shot, determined not to miss on this one, the ground around him churning up in a maelstrom of dirt and dust.

"Yes!" Red saw blood mist as Bruce went down.

The mutant with the foot on its head sat up in the grass and growled, a low moan of pain and anger. Three of the bookers abruptly tackled it, flattening it.

Tommy signaled to Red that he was okay. He pointed behind Red to the enormous female zombie trundling her way. Red looked over her shoulder, relieved Tommy was okay. She ignored the zombie, knowing it wouldn't bite her because of her own wound.

"Oh, shit!" A bullet careened off David's helmeted head. He reached up and touched the helmet he'd taken from Victor. "Oh, shit," he repeated, relieved.

As black smoke ballooned from the tree line—driving more zombies before it—the grey smoke from the hand grenades wafted across the field.

Riley had scrabbled over to her CETME on the soles of her feet and a palm, doing her best to keep the shield in place with one hand. Incoming fire continued to spark off the casing of the bomb in front of her. She took up the semi-automatic rifle but had difficulty bracing it with one hand.

The obese zombie reached Red and bent down over her. She hadn't expected it to get so close but just as suddenly it lost interest and stood, beginning to lumber off.

"Wait!" Red sprang up, onto the rotund creature's back. She was small and the zombie was elephantine. Its ass jutted out behind it like a shelf, and Red found her footing there as she sank the curved edge of the karambit deep between its shoulder blades, right where its neck met its clavicle.

The zombie tried futilely to reach around to the diminutive redhead on its back. Red jammed the barrel of the Noveske Diplomat N4 under the zombie's right arm. She leaned over the undead's meaty limb, peering through the smoke and haze, and fired the N4 with one hand, the other gripping the karambit like a pommel.

"Down!" Tris screamed.

The earth in front of Dee churned up in a spray of soil and grass and he barely had time to fling himself to the side, a 5.56 mm round catching him in his boot.

"Shhiii—Sugar!" Dee lay on his side, cringing at the pain in his foot.

Tris—out of her hole and stalking through the smoke—fired the Calico at the zombie on which Red perched. The undead absorbed the 9mm rounds, its torso shivering with the impact, fat rolls jiggling. Red swiveled the barrel of the N4 and sent a stream of lead at Tris, but the black woman had already found cover in an abandoned spider hole.

"Tris!" Carrie crouched in the grass and fired her submachine gun. Red's zombie turned towards her, the barrel of the N4 pinned between its arm and torso tracking her movement as well. Carrie went flat as the bullets from the Diplomat sheared the grass above her.

Tris hopped up and fired out what remained of the Calico's 100-round box magazine. As the zombie shifted in place from one foot to the other, disintegrating under the hail of lead, Red appeared over its left shoulder, her left arm hooked around the beast's arm, her hand filled with the Stechkin APS, the 9mm cracking.

Carrie and Riley fired on the heavyset zombie as one, heavy booms from Riley's CETME punctuating the chatter of Carrie's SMG. Tris dove to her left—out of Red's limited field of fire—and came up with her 9mms in both hands, discharging them. No sooner had she done so than she spied muzzle flashes through the smoke and haze and dropped, the brothers firing on her.

The obese zombie shuddered, driven back a step as it absorbed rounds, and collapsed onto its knees. Red flung herself from its back at the same time that a 7.62mm round caught it between the eyes. The creature flopped to the dirt, unmoving.

The mutant with the foot in its head stood up in the smoke. Pocked with bullet wounds and bleeding from numerous bites, it had a vacant look in its eyes. In one hand it still gripped the thigh bone.

"Tommy!" Red's voice was nearly drowned out in the bedlam. "Stay down!" Tommy had pulled back the slides on both pistols as he lay in the grass and waited for his chance. When he thought he'd found it, he rolled onto his side and stood, ignoring the pain in his side where the sniper had got him.

"Damned smoke," David said to his brother. "Can't see the black woman."

"She's there." Keith swapped magazines in his AR. "She'll pop up again."

"Brother, you know this helmet saved my life?"

"That's good, then."

Another mutant broke from the trees, racing across the field. Its hair hung down to its waist and it waved a nail gun as it ran.

Riley spied Tommy through the small, armored sight window of her shield. He was walking across the flatlands towards her once more, firing a pistol in each hand, his bullets and those of others bouncing off the ballistic shield. He was screaming at her as he came, and she still couldn't make out whatever it was he was saying. Riley huddled under her cover and watched Tommy die.

Dee fired and a gush of blood spouted from Tommy's thigh. Tommy turned one pistol on D.L. and managed to fire it a few times until a round from Kevin's AK shattered his forearm.

"Tommy!" Red screamed as she and David lit Kevin up in a withering crossfire, the dark eyed man knocked down into the grass.

Thomas' son dropped the pistol in his crippled arm and staggered towards Riley and her shield, straight-arming his remaining pistol, firing it, determined that he would kill her before he died. When the slide of his pistol locked open on an empty chamber, Tommy looked down at it in disgust and threw it away. He continued walking towards the bomb and the woman, pointing at her, screaming, then balling his fist, ready to finish her with his one good hand.

Riley let the shield fall to one side and fired the CETME from her back. Her first round caught Tommy in the stomach and would have doubled him over except that a full-auto 9mm rip from Tris' Calico zippered up his back at the same time, causing him to stand ramrod straight. Riley fired and hit him again, but he was already dead before he hit the ground.

Red's mouth dropped open as she watched Tommy fall.

When Keith and David turned their fire on Tris, she disappeared, seeking meager concealment in the grass. The combined smoke from the grenades and the forest fire obscured the battlefield.

Dee heard a bellow and felt a pain in his shoulder as a nail stuck him there. The mutant with long hair and the nail gun was bearing down on him as he triggered the FN-FAL. Nothing happened. The thirty -ound magazine was empty.

"My luck." Dee dropped the rifle, his hands filling with the Colt Python. He fired the revolver and it kicked back in his hand, the .357 round blasting a hole out of the mutant's back. Dee doubled-actioned the Colt three more times, each bullet tearing through the creature, the thing still firing its nail gun. Dee's fifth shot caved in its face and it went down.

Red stared in disbelief at the scene before her. Tommy was dead. *Tommy.* Thomas. Merv. All the others, her friends, her people—the closest she'd ever had to a family. All gone. She howled in anger and pain and fired her Noveske out in Riley's direction, forcing the woman back under the safety of her shield. Red raced across the distance that separated her from Tommy, sinking to her knees in the grass beside him.

"Tommy-Tommy-Tommy."

She pressed her head to his bloodied chest and held him, unaware of the bullets whipping through the air about her and the moaning zombies shambling past.

Keith and David were firing at where they had last seen Tris when the mutant zombie wailed. The brothers rolled away from one another, each into a seated position, facing one another, looking for a target.

Keith saw the monstrosity looming behind David. "David!" His brother's eyes flashed at him through the helmet, not comprehending. The mutant brought the femur down with both hands, crushing the helmet and David's head like egg shells. Red splashed against the inside of the visor, which had been knocked into place by the death blow.

"No!" The AR-15 in Keith's hands fired, pulverizing the mutant's face and head. Keith got as low as he could, scrambling to his fallen brother. "Ah, no…"

"Wanna play?!" Dee had fired out his Python and was standing, facing the zombies that were upon him with bare fists. He punched the closest one in the nose and it clenched its eyes shut, addled. "How's that, huh?!" The zombie opened its eyes and growled.

When Keith looked up from his fallen brother, Tris was next to him. She hadn't known he was there and was reloading her Calico on one knee. "You…" he muttered.

Tris turned her head to look at him. The barrel of Keith's AR was pointing right at her. If she was surprised or worried it didn't show on her burnt face.

"You gonna shoot me?" she asked, continuing to reload the submachine gun. "Then *what?* You gonna kill them all by yourself?" Keith looked where she indicated. Dozens of zombies milled about them, driven before the thick, dark smoke that ballooned out of the trees.

"You gonna shoot me, shoot me," Tris cranked the Calico. "Otherwise let's fuck these fools up." Still on her knee, Tris fired into the advancing horde. Keith swallowed what he felt in his throat and joined her, rising to his feet, sighting down the AR's barrel at the nearest zombie, squeezing the trigger—"This is for you, David!"—watching part of its skull lift off.

For the first time in what seemed to her like forever, no one was firing at Riley. She looked through the armored sight window of her shield but much of the meadow was lost to her in smoke. There was still plenty of gunfire, but none of it was coming her way.

She got off her back and rose to a crouch, covering herself behind the ballistic shield. And still no one fired on her. Riley walked the few feet to the bomb and propped the shield against it, facing towards the direction from which the gunfire originated. She backed slowly towards the river, eyeing the smoke in front of her with suspicion. There were zombies in that smoke.

"I'm out," Keith called to Tris. She had just reloaded her Calico and was firing it one handed, the unique design of the gun placing its center of gravity over her wrist. Keith reloaded his assault rifle and pulled back the bolt, chambering a fresh shell. He brought the stock back up into his shoulder and—"That's for my brother!"—resumed firing, shell casings ejecting from the AR's side port.

Tris fired out the last hundred round helical magazine for her Calico and abandoned the weapon. "I'm out!" she yelled to him as she unholstered her Sigs. Tris extended the P238, saying to Keith, "You're out, too." When he turned to see what the dreadlocked woman was talking about, she put two in his chest—"Say hi to your brother"—and one in the center of his forehead.

* * *

Little Red stepped from the smoke and confusion. She glared across the space that separated her from Riley and started in her direction. A zombie stumbled between them and Red struck, driving her Robbins of Dudley Trench Push dagger through the side of its head.

"Riley!" Dee called, spotting the diminutive redhead with her knives drawn and clear intent in her eye. Dee balanced himself on his FN-FAL, using its barrel and the chainsaw blade attached to it as a crutch. He hopped on one foot to intervene, but knew he wouldn't get there fast enough.

Riley shot and killed a zombie, unaware that Red was approaching her.

Little Red was fuming as she neared Riley. The bitch had killed Thomas. She'd killed Tommy. Because of her, Mac was dead. Gammon was dead, everyone… Because of her, Red was bit. Red decided she was going to open the woman up, open her up and leave her for the zombies to finish off.

Carrie interposed herself between Riley and Little Red, straight-arming her pistol, firing, but Red had already dropped and rolled forward, coming up in a crouch under Carrie's outstretched arms, thrusting with the Trench Push dagger, slashing with the karambit, sticking and slicing Carrie's torso repeatedly.

Carrie tripped backwards, multiple puncture wounds perforating her torso, a look of shock and a lack of comprehension washing over her face.

"Carrie!" Kevin swatted at Little Red with the butt of his AK-47. If he hadn't been wearing his body armor, he would have been dead when Red and David unloaded on him earlier. And if he hadn't just yelled, Red wouldn't have heard him and wouldn't have been able to react as she did. The butt of Kevin's AK connected with the five-inch Trench Push dagger in Red's right hand, knocking it from her grasp.

"Die!" Kevin swatted at Red's head but she had already ducked and weaved, coming up around and behind him and his half-assed swing, gouging the karambit in her left hand through his side, under the vest he wore.

"Fuck!" Kevin cried, grasping her wrist before she could dislodge the blade and jam it through him again.

"Kevin!" Dee grabbed Red from behind, lifting her off the ground, away from Kevin. She let the blade go and kicked back with her foot, catching Dee below the knee of his wounded leg.

"Shit!" Dee dropped her, his leg wobbling beneath him. Red twisted and shot her foot out again. Something in Dee's leg gave and he collapsed, grunting in pain.

Red dodged as Kevin came back at her, wielding her own karambit, which he had dug out of his side. She hit him in the face with the palm of her hand and he dropped, dead or unconscious. She couldn't tell which. She didn't care.

The undead had fallen upon Carrie and Dee was fighting to get them off.

Little Red turned back in the direction she'd been heading, back towards Riley. The girl was staring down the barrel of her battle rifle at Red. And the bitch wasn't alone. The black woman was at her side.

"No, chicken," Tris pushed Riley's CETME aside. "This one's mine."

"*No!*" Riley said.

Red stopped where she was and calmly reached to her left forearm with her right hand, drawing the push dagger from its wrist holster. Then she repeated the movement with her left hand, drawing the identical push dagger from the other wrist holster. "Get out of my way," she warned Tris.

"This girl don't stand a chance against you," Tris stated matter-of-factly. "And you know it." Tris placed her Sig Sauer pistols on the ground. "Try mixing it up with me."

"Tris!" Dee yelled at her, above an unresponsive Carrie. What the fuck was Tris doing?

"Let's dance, grandma," Red told Tris.

Tris smiled at her and Little Red smiled back.

Tris' hands went behind her and returned with two sickles. Red still didn't look worried. She nodded at Tris and the Tris returned the gesture.

"Tris!" They both ignored Riley.

Red and Tris covered the few yards between them in a silent dash and met with a clash of steel on steel. Each moved at whirlwind speed, a flurry of arms and edged weapons.

The forest surrounding the clearing ablaze, the smoke pouring in from the burning trees was oppressive.

Victor coughed and found a pistol on the ground. When the zombie came out of the smoke he sighted, held his breath, and squeezed the trigger. The zombie dropped, head shot, and Victor pushed off on his elbow and his one good leg, Red's hatchet protruding from his back. He propelled himself foot by painful foot across the field in the direction he thought the river must be, his vision limited by the haze.

The chainsaw underneath Dee's FN-FAL revved as it cleaved a zombie's head in two. It had come for Dee as he sat there, wounded and vulnerable. Another zombie moved in out of the smoke, a tribal tattoo taking up much of one side of its face. The thing growled at Dee where he sat, his rifle with the under-barrel chainsaw keeping it at bay.

Apparently changing its mind, the tattooed thing slinked away into the mist.

"Dee, oh no—are you okay?" Riley was at his side. She was dragging a bleeding, confused-looking Kevin with her.

"Ahhh, Carrie," Kevin looked down on the partially eaten dead woman.

"Help me up!" Dee's foot was shot and his leg felt broken. Riley bent down and he reached around over her other shoulder, latching onto Kevin. "Now, let's get out of here."

Carrie sat up, a dull look in her eyes. Riley shot the zombie in the head.

Amid the whirling smoke, the crackle of flame, and the moans of the undead, two women faced each other in battle. Tris swung one of her sickles, a blow that would have lopped Red's head from her shoulders if the shorter woman hadn't ducked. Tris grunted as Red jabbed her in the shoulder with a blade, but she managed to come around with her elbow, catching Red in the side of her skull.

Little Red stumbled, blinking her eyes and shaking her head.

Victor reached the bomb and sat down. "Oh, man…" He thought he'd crawled farther than that. He knew he wasn't doing well. He was bleeding out. There was a cord attached to the bomb. Victor pulled the cord over to himself. It was a detonator.

Tris and Red stepped away from one another. Both were breathing heavily, each bleeding from various slash and stab wounds. They eyed one another warily.

"I can't tell you," Tris remarked, "how long I've been waiting for this."

"Waiting to die?"

Tris smiled. "Yes."

Red spied Riley getting away with the two wounded men.

"No!" She screamed, snapping her wrist, sending a blade through the air at Tris' head, seeking to end this fight so she could get to Riley. Tris raised a sickle and Red's blade deflected off it with a clang. Red had snapped her other wrist, but Tris crouched, the handle of the second blade bouncing harmlessly off her shoulder.

Tris rose to her full height and looked down at the redhead. "What else you got, shorty?"

Victor sat with his back to the bomb. Zed was closing in. He could make out their shadows through the smoke. The smoke. Victor coughed. It was filling his lungs. He held the detonator in one hand and his pistol in the other.

The women met in a tangle of limbs, flesh on flesh and steel on steel. They pirouetted as one, seemingly stuck together, each grunting and gasping. When they parted, Red was bleeding profusely from half a dozen deep wounds in her upper body and thigh, one hand impaled through the palm. But the handles of her blades were sticking out of Tris.

"That…" Tris panted, "that it? That…all you got?"

Red cried out in hatred and rage, thrusting the Robbins of Dudley Trench dagger into Tris repeatedly, her teeth barred, spittle flecking her lips.

Tris punched Red square in the face, breaking the girl's nose. Red's eyes clenched shut automatically and she felt Tris grab her by her head. Tris snatched one of Red's own sharpened chopsticks out of her hair and Red forced her eyes open in time to watch the stick plunge into her shoulder.

"Bitch!" Red cursed Tris, but Tris had already stolen the second chop stick from Red's hair and made to ram it through the girl's eye socket. Little Red's speed nearly defied physics. With her wounded hand, she palmed the elbow of the hand Tris gripped the chopstick in, pushing it up and towards the black woman. At the same time, she cupped Tris's hand with her good palm, driving the chopstick through the black woman's throat.

Tris blinked, shocked, the chopstick run through her neck. Her hand was still clasped around the instrument.

"That's it, grandma."

✶ ✶ ✶

Victor was out of bullets. He didn't want to be eaten by Zed. He had the bomb. He'd blow them all sky high. He wondered if anyone had gotten away. He hoped so. They'd come back to get him, to free him from his captors. They'd come back for him. Tris hadn't left him out here. He was thankful for that.

Where was the detonator? He looked. There was a pistol he didn't recognize in his hand. Where had he gotten it? Its slide was locked open. Victor knew that meant something but he couldn't remember what. He felt sluggish. Somewhere close by, a zombie moaned. There was a pistol in his hand. Hadn't he just noticed that? There was a box in his other hand. The detonator. He knew it was the detonator.

Victor told his thumb to close over the button and push it, but Victor's body wasn't listening to him anymore. He closed his eyes, thinking he'd open them and try it one more time, but once he closed them they did not open again.

* * *

"That's it, grandma."

Red stared into Tris' eyes and grinned triumphantly, her teeth bloody. This woman was finished. She brushed Tris' hand off the chopstick and gripped the utensil herself. "You're done, bitch." Red pulled the chopstick from Tris' neck and a jet of blood squirted out. "Done. You hear me?"

Red wasn't prepared for Tris' next move. The dreadlocked woman snatched the chop stick out of Red's hand and thrust it back into place, skewering her throat through the already-opened wound, choking off the squirting crimson.

Red stared at the woman in disbelief and incomprehension. *This* was one crazy burnt bitch.

A hand gripped her shoulder and Red shrugged it off as she turned, facing the zombie that had come up behind her.

"You don't want me," she told it, feeling woozy.

Dozens of zombies had gathered around them.

The sickle blade caught Red in the clavicle from behind, sinking six inches into her upper chest. She screamed in shock and agony as Tris yanked on the handle, spinning the girl around to face her.

The zombies groaned about them.

Tris's face was burnt and scarred but her eyes were clear. She grabbed Red with her free hand, pulling the girl close, hugging her to her own body.

"You..." Red tried to speak.

When Tris opened her mouth to respond, blood poured out.

One of Red's arms was free but it hung at her side, useless, her palm run through. As Red watched, Tris reached up to her mouth, her bloodied teeth clenching down on the cotter pin of the grenade she wore around her neck. Tris yanked the pin free with her teeth and spit it away with the last of her strength as the handle flipped off.

Red felt the fingers of a zombie brush against her hair.

As Tris' legs gave out, the two women went to the earth as one, the undead piling on top of them.

Their bodies muffled the grenade blast.

* * *

They found some shallows and crossed the river, Riley and Kevin on either side of Dee. When their feet touched firm ground they continued their awkward five-legged walk several meters, until, finally overcome by their wounds and exhaustion, the three of them slumped together on the ground, breathing heavily.

"What should we do?" Riley asked.

"I think I'm going to lay here and bleed," Kevin answered.

Across the river, hidden from them in the smoke, a zombie stumbled out of the fumes and stooped above Victor's body and the bomb. It had scented Victor's blood from a distance and worked its way through the haze and growing heat. The creature looked down on the human being and was disappointed. This man was dead.

"Well, look who we got here…"

Riley and Dee sat up. Five meters from their position, Cosmo and four of his children stood in a line, one of the most disturbing sights either Riley or Dee had ever seen.

"I don't want to see this," Kevin lay where he was, an arm over his eyes. "Do I?"

"…only question, now," Cosmo continued, petting Fred Turner's stuffed cat, "…is who we gonna kill first?"

One of Cosmo's kids started to laugh and shake uncontrollably as it did so. The man-thing clutched a machete and had a sizable fluid-filled lump growing on its back.

The zombie across the river reached down and touched Victor's body, prodding it. The man was definitely dead. There would be no eating this one. In its own way, the creature was disappointed. It pried the detonator out of Victor's hand, curious.

"Yeah," Kevin had sat up with Dee and Riley and was staring, eyes wide. "I don't want to see this."

"Can we fuck 'em first, dad?" a mutant with a spiked club asked.

"Yeah, I think we can do that."

One of the mutants tittered and clapped its hands in anticipation while another began unbuckling its pants.

"Eeeny…meeny…miney…moe," Cosmo had taken his hand from the stuffed cat, moving his finger from Dee to Riley to Kevin and back. "Grab a piggy…by the…toe…"

The zombie stared down at the detonator in its hand. It was a square box with a cord running out of the bottom. The undead had no idea what the contraption was. But the bright red button in the center of the detonator interested it.

"Hey, anybody seen my sister Mergatroid?" The mutant with the spiked club glanced around. "She was standing over here a minute ago…"

"…if he hollers…let him go…my mother said…to pick this one…"

A whistle sounded off to the side. The mutants, their father, and the human beings seated on the ground turned as one.

Bruce stepped from behind a tree. His upper arm and shoulder were heavily bandaged, the gauze stained red. In both his hands he held the MM1 multi-barrel grenade launcher.

"And *you're* it, bitches!" He cried, firing the HAWK. Dee flung himself back, his outstretched arm driving Riley to the dirt with him.

The buckshot rounds pulverized flesh and bone and severed limbs from torsos. A few quick yelps were cut off abruptly as projectile rounds hit their targets. Remains showered down from the sky in a red vapor. The more solid pieces thumped to the earth, streaming bits of bloodied flesh and clothing. The stuffed cat was thrown clear, head over tail.

When Bruce stopped firing, Dee and Riley sat back up. Kevin had remained in a seated position the entire time and blinked through the mutant viscera and body fluids that drenched him.

Something struggled to right itself amid the scattered body parts and ruptured torsos. Something that had survived.

Dee pushed himself off the ground with the barrel of his FN-FAL, standing unsteadily on his one good leg. He cranked up the chain saw mounted under the barrel of his rifle and hopped forward to the quivering mass. His jaw clenched, he plunged the whirling blade into whatever was moving. It squealed in agony as blood jetted, Dee sawing into the misshaped heap.

When he was satisfied that nothing else stirred, Dee silenced the chain saw.

"That was…" Kevin, sitting there, was at a loss for words.

"Hey," asked Bruce. "Anybody seen Tris?"

The concussion from the bomb's detonation knocked those standing flat.

DEATH LANDS

There was a ringing in Riley's ears. She stared into an autumn sky clear and blue.

When she could, she sat up. She put a hand to her head and groaned. That had not been pleasant. Around her, Dee, Kevin and Bruce were righting themselves, rising.

"Think that was Tris?" Kevin asked Bruce. He yelled because he could not hear himself very well.

"What?" Bruce rasped back.

Across the river from them, a smoking hole was all that was left where the bomb had been. Pieces of zombies littered a meadow scoured of all life. The force of the blast had knocked down trees and blown out the advancing flames.

Dee slung the FN-FAL across his back and checked the load on his Python. His foot and leg hurt like hell. He could feel blood pooling around his toes. He half sat, half fell back on his butt, and got to work removing his boot.

"Let me help you." Riley unknotted the laces and started to pull them from the eyelets.

"Thanks."

"You think that's it?"

"Yeah, Riley. I think that's it."

In the scorched grassland past the river, a head lay smoking amid the ruins. A stub of vertebra jutted from its neck. The eyes were open and darting about, lucid and aware. The head opened its mouth and moved its jaws, but no sound emerged. Though it was burned from the explosion, the tattoo that covered almost half of its face remained clearly visible. The head waited there, amidst the singed and blackened grasses, beneath the azure skies.

"Oh, man." Kevin touched at his side where Red's karambit had bit into him. "We're all fucked up."

"What?" Bruce yelled back at him.

"We're all fucked up."

"Say that again?"

"You're deaf."

"What?"

"The explosion!" Kevin raised both hands, mimicking an eruption. He pointed to his ear. "You're deaf!"

"You can't hear me?"

"My foot is…" Dee stared down at the mess at the end of his leg. Riley had removed his boot and cut off his sock. The bottom half of Dee's foot was a busted, bloodied mess.

"Bruce." Riley called to the deafened man who stared without blinking around them. "*Bruce!*" When he didn't acknowledge her, she turned back to Dee. "I'm going to go down to the river and get some water to clean these wounds." She motioned from Dee's foot to Kevin and Bruce and their assorted injuries. She raised Dee's foot by the ankle and placed it on a rucksack. "Keep it elevated and wait here."

"I'm not going anywhere," Dee promised. "Can you see if you can find my jacket? I left it in my spider hole." He watched her go. "Hey, Kevin." His friend was soaked from head to toe with blood and bits and pieces of things. "You okay?"

"I'll be okay, I think." When he shook the body armor he'd stripped from his torso, small gobs of lead dropped from it. "Look at that. Damn." He tossed the armor away. "Bruce got hit in the shoulder pretty good. And he's deaf."

"What?" Bruce looked puzzled.

"Just ignore him," Kevin counseled. "I've got to get down to the water, wash this crap off me. I'm covered in…" He looked over at the pile of steaming entrails and flesh.

Dee studied the bloody wreck at the end of his ankle before laying his head back in the grass. He watched the sky while Bruce sat nearby with a blank look on his face. A cotton-like cloud had just entered his field of vision when Riley returned, wet and lugging an assortment of equipment.

She washed his foot and cleaned it as best as she could. "If my friend Troi was here, she'd know what to do." There were no bones coming through Dee's skin, and Riley thought this was a good sign. "She worked in a hospital." When they were kids, Anthony had broken two toes and the doctor had sent him home as he was, explaining that a toe would basically set itself so long as you didn't go out of your way to aggravate it. She wondered if feet were the same way. Riley packed Dee's foot with gauze and bound it with elastic wrap. His leg was another matter. She couldn't tell if it was truly broken without x-rays.

"You're next," she motioned to Bruce. When he asked her *what*, she waved him over.

Kevin returned with a couple of rifles and two overstuffed packs over his shoulders. He was wet and clean, his skin red where he'd scrubbed it. "Here." He set his load down. "I gathered what antibiotics and all I could."

Riley told him, "This is good," and looked at a package of medication she had never seen before. "What's this?"

Dee looked at the label. "An anti-inflammatory."

"You'll need some of these. Where did you guys get them, anyway?"

"There's places out there," answered Kevin. "Societies and cities like where you're from. They're producing things. Think we got those out west."

Riley nodded, filing this information away for later. She'd spent her entire life in New Harmony. Of course she was aware of the existence of other civilizations but she had never visited any or met anyone who had. Perhaps, she corrected herself, Krieger had, though the guide hadn't been too communicative during his time with them. No, that wasn't true either. Krieger had spoken at length with Troi a couple of times that Riley knew of.

"Riley?" Dee touched her shoulder, his tone gentle, concerned. "You okay?"

She wiped away the tears she hadn't realized were there and nodded. "I wish we had ice." She turned her attention back to the men and their wounds.

"I think I'm deaf," yelled Bruce.

Riley nodded back at him.

Concern passed over Kevin's face as he consulted his dosimeter. "Radiation levels are higher around here now."

"Who knows what that bomb blew up into the atmosphere." Dee bared his teeth as Riley applied pressure to his leg. "Those zombies and mutants."

"We don't want to stay here forever."

"Dee." Riley heeded Kevin's warning. "I'm going to take your boot down to the water and wash it out. You're going to put it back on and we're going to lace it up tight, keep pressure on that foot." He nodded. "We're going to need to splint your leg with something, just in case." She looked around for a suitable splint. "And then I'm going back to my brother's body and I'm going to…I'm going to…"

"I understand." Dee gave her a look that said he did. "We'll go together. On the quads. We'll get there faster that way. That okay with you guys?"

"Sure," replied Kevin.

Bruce appeared baffled. "What?"

$$\star\,\star\,\star$$

He had his leg sticking straight out, over the running board, splinted with a disassembled rifle barrel. The wind whipped against the bug-eyed goggles of Dee's Oakley Medusa, the cape of his oilskin drover trailing behind him, Riley ducking within its folds, clinging to his back on the four wheeler. Dee watched the terrain ahead and around him, cognizant of the rise and fall of the open country, the grass-covered flatlands, the afternoon sun shining bright above. The quad's tires took the terrain well, yet periodically his boot made contact with the running board, new pains coursing up Dee's foot and leg. He would grimace beneath his goggles. Despite the jolts of fresh agony, part of Dee's mind dwelt on his father.

Bear, just gone like that one day. Dee suspected Tris was right, that Bear knew he was dying. Weighted with such knowledge, his father had sought isolation, better to be alone. His father, Dee knew, was a man among men, but he was also a man who had walked alone much of his life, even when among men. Too much. Dee, on the other hand, didn't think he would want to be alone when his time came. He'd rather be surrounded by people he cared about, people who cared about him. Unfortunately, that circle had constricted radically since daybreak.

It was amazing he had survived the battle. Amazing any of them had.

Tris, Carrie and Victor. Even the Bishop. Gone, all of them. Just like that. But now there was Riley. *You're not going to ask me to marry you.* That's what she'd said to him back in the tent, this woman at his back. That'd been a good one.

She was special, Riley was. Dee recognized this. Special in general, in her own right, and—Dee could admit it to himself—special to himself. More so with every passing hour. The way she'd handled herself out on the battlefield. She'd gone for the redhead and was not pleased when Tris wouldn't let her have her. The way she'd helped Dee out of there before the bomb went off. Riley was tough enough to survive out here, when all her friends had fallen. Tough enough to avenge her brother. She'd even stood up to Tris and never backed down. Like she'd stood up to him when they'd first met. He thought about that stance she'd assumed, how he could tell in her mind she was going to mess him up if she had to.

When those people had chased her—the little redhead and her friends, the ones who'd taken Victor—Riley had stood her ground. When forced, she'd retreated, but she'd done so to fight again. She'd escaped with every intention of bringing the fight back to the ones who had it coming to them. Dee smiled under his goggles, thinking about the first time he'd seen her: Riley pulling herself out of the river and across the field, in the shirt and jacket of a man she'd killed, looking like she'd been to hell and back. Because she had.

Dee had gone out alone, as he did each year. He'd gone out hoping to find his father, but also hoping he would not. The thing he was most afraid of, each year when he set out, was finding his father's remains, bones stacked like some ancient cairn. Worse to find his father alive, emaciated and rawboned, wasted and alone. Instead, he'd found Riley. Or she'd found him. Or, Dee granted, some combination of the two.

If he had to die one day, and Dee knew they were all going to die one day, he wanted to die with someone like Riley at his side. Someone like Riley. Friends like Bruce and Kevin. If that was how he checked out, Dee thought, he'd probably be able to go peacefully enough, not fighting it. He liked to think he'd be satisfied.

The front wheels of the quad dipped in a rut and Riley tightened her grip around his waist. Dee gripped the handlebars tightly until they came up out of it and thumbed the accelerator, roaring along on their way, his leg and foot screaming at him. Kevin and Bruce followed on their respective four-wheelers.

* * *

They'd arrived to find a sacrilege.

"What do you think she's thinking?" Kevin tossed a branch down into the fire they had going in the pit.

Riley sat on the ground, her arms crossed on knees drawn up to her chin. She stared straight ahead, her eyes occasionally blinking, deep in thought. She was aware of the three men busying themselves around her, Kevin and Dee collecting the remains that were collectable, Bruce scanning the earth for clues.

"She's sad," pronounced Dee. "Sad and mad."

Reaching the place where Riley's brother had died, they'd found nothing recognizable as her sibling. Dismembered human parts were strewn around the area, most in chunks and pieces so miniscule to be unidentifiable. The sheer amount of dismantled human material and the grounds they covered spoke to more than one body.

Riley had told them about Thomas in the pit, but all that was in the pit were two zombies, each headshot. Even more puzzling was the intact male body that lay off to the side, naked from the waist up. Its face and head were crushed, and its torso was split where natural gases had built up and burst, but aside from this it appeared unmolested.

"This is the one she killed," Dee remarked of Dalton's body, recalling Riley's story. He looked down on the body, oddly fascinated. She'd done that to the man's face. Yeah, Riley was tough enough all right.

She was aware of their conversing about her, but Riley did not comprehend their words. She remembered mornings at the kitchen nook with her brother, each of them getting ready for work, he to school, she to the *dojang*, both sipping their juice. She recalled camping trips when they were kids, their dad taking them to parts of New Harmony that felt as foreign and desolate as she'd then imagined the Outlands. Now she knew better.

"Someone came back." Bruce was down on one knee above an imprint in the earth. "Someone came back and did this."

Dee looked up from gathering remains. Bruce was speaking of the mutilation of Riley's brother and what must have been Thomas' body. Whoever had torn these bodies apart had thrown the pieces far and wide, into the trees and bushes, out of sight.

"I'm no Tris..." A look of consternation gripped Bruce's face. "...but these tracks look fresh."

"How fresh?"

Bruce shook his head. He had an idea that he wasn't sharing, and it was apparently an idea he didn't like. "I don't know." When he answered, he spoke too loudly because of his hearing. "Someone got here before we did."

When she'd lost the second baby—the *second* for goodness' sake, a part of Riley's mind beseeched her and she immediately felt guilty for it. Other women Riley knew had lost so many more than two. When she'd lost the second one, she'd gone to the wall, staring into the Outlands, pondering not so much on what the barren wastelands held as on the contents of her own body. Why did that seem so long in the past?

Riley couldn't kid herself; she'd known coming out here wasn't a good idea. She couldn't revise the past, even if it was less than two weeks gone. She'd come along because she didn't want Anthony to go alone, yes, but also because she'd felt she needed to get away.

"It doesn't make sense." Kevin was genuinely perplexed.

"Who'd have done this to either of them?" Dee picked up what might have been part of a lower leg. "And not to him?" Dalton's body lay where it had for days.

"Something doesn't sit right with me about this." Bruce thought he was mumbling when in fact he was loud and clear.

"Imagine how she feels." Kevin threw something that was recognizable as part of a hand into the flames.

Camping. They'd been planning on going camping like when they'd been kids. Before Mickey and Gary wandered into their lives. What if the autistic man and the plague victim hadn't walked right up to Evan? Evan of all people. What if they hadn't had the picture on them or if Anthony hadn't looked *exactly* like his father, exactly like the man Mickey had known? What if Gary hadn't been there to communicate, to translate, for his rotting friend? So many *what if's.*

"Talk to us, Bruce."

"Okay, follow me on this." Bruce laid it out as he saw it. "I'm a munt, what's my motivation?"

"Your motivation?" asked Kevin. "You're pissed."

"Huh?"

"You're pissed," Kevin nearly shouted.

"I'm more than pissed. Remember what Riley told us. When those people 'rescued' her and her friends from them, they were effectively declaring war on the munts. So if I'm a munt, and I come across this scene, I drag the old man's body out of the pit—sure it's chewed up good from Zed, but there's still something left for me to take my anger out on, and I do."

"The old man's body, okay." Dee could see it. "But what about her brother's?"

"Yeah, I know. So our munt leaves, but it's going to come back later to do the same thing."

Growing up in New Harmony, you knew you had to be wary of those from the Outlands. Krieger, for one, Riley thought. He'd been damaged worse than any of them could imagine. She didn't think the old tracker had purposefully sent them astray. In fact, Riley was fairly certain they'd misunderstood his directions, blindly wandering into the territory of that savage family. The mutants. *Has anybody seen my sister Mergatroid?* one of them had asked when they'd lined up on the river bank, looking to deliver the coup de grace to Riley, Dee and Kevin. Mergatroid had been the name of the female.

Which reminded Riley of something Gary had said in passing in the hospital. *Gotta watch out for Mergatroid.* Gary said it when she and Anthony were standing over Mickey's bed. *You don't want to meet Mergatroid.* She'd thought it was just Gary rambling, trading old movie or television lines back and forth with his rotting friend. But no, now she understood that Gary and Mickey must have had some kind of contact with the mutants in their journeys. For some reason, the munts hadn't harmed the two, or, if they had, the evidence of such hadn't been obvious.

"Why would it come back?" Kevin had one hand resting on top of his AK's barrel. "Why would it do this to Riley's brother?"

"Can you say that again?" Bruce touched his ear. Kevin repeated his questions, louder.

"Maybe it saw what we did to its brothers and sister." Bruce thought about the way the mutant's bodies had flown apart when he'd laid into them with the Hawk MM-1. "To its father."

"That still doesn't tell us why it would come back here."

"Yes it does if *you're* listening to me, Dee. I think *it* was *listening* to us. I think it was close enough to hear us."

"What?" Kevin started in disbelief. "We would have—"

"No, we wouldn't have."

"He's right." Dee didn't want to sound spooked, though he eyed the woods about them warily. "Remember the dosimeter."

Not for the first time in several days, Riley wished Mickey and Gary had never come to New Harmony, that Evan had not been on the wall when they did. She wished that Anthony hadn't gotten it into his head to come out here and look for whatever he thought he was going to find. That her father had forbidden them to go, that he had physically disallowed their exit. That she hadn't been so foolish as to accompany and encourage Anthony. She'd lost his beanie in the river and that, for some inexplicable reason, bothered her more than a lot of the other stuff. The fact of its loss irritated her and her irritation brought her back to their present reality.

"Bruce, if you're right…" Kevin checked the dosimeter as they spoke. If Bruce was right, the mutant might still be around. The radiation detector read normal now. "It's not."

"It could be watching us," Bruce ventured.

Dee agreed. "It could be."

"We *are* being watched." Riley had spoken. "It's watching us." They turned to her and she was standing, brushing the dirt and twigs from her legs and backside. "I can *feel* it. I felt this way when we destroyed their house. Their barn."

Kevin took his hand from the top of his AK's barrel and wrapped it around the foregrip.

"If it was going to attack us," she continued, "it would have already."

"How do we know there's only the one?"

"More than one, it would have attacked us," wagered Dee. "You saw the ones on the battlefield."

"Yeah, I did." Kevin didn't look reassured. "Did that one really have a foot growing out of the side of its head?"

"What?"

"It did," Riley declared.

"Nothing," Kevin told Bruce.

"I can't imagine it can keep up with us on the quads," said Dee.

"I'm telling you, I think it got here before we did." Bruce scanned the surrounding countryside through the scope mounted on the M40A3 he'd appropriated. "It's got to have some kind of transportation."

"Wouldn't we have heard it?"

Kevin answered. "We didn't know to listen, Dee."

"Yeah, well," Riley stared into the trees about them, "now we do."

"Isn't it possible…" Bruce had the side of his face pressed to the saddle-type cheek piece. "…that there's another explanation for this?"

"It's possible."

"Something we're not thinking of?" Bruce said it but he didn't sound like he bought it.

"Something."

"I'm spooked." Bruce lowered the sniper rifle. "I'm shot." He tapped his chest beneath the bandages taped to his shoulder, under his shirt and vest. "My imagination could be running away with me."

"Could be."

"I'm a little deaf, too. What'd you say?"

"She said it could be," Kevin repeated.

"Oh." Bruce nodded, understanding. "Could be, right?"

"But it's not," stated Riley.

"Well, that isn't good."

Dee looked at the woman. "We stick together. We stay alert. We're okay."

"We're a week away from New Harmony, at least."

"I was that thing," Dee speculated. "This isn't over…"

"This—" Kevin referred to the remains afire in the pit, to the blood stained earth around them "—was just the warm-up."

"It is," Riley confirmed.

"…I'd be watching us now," Dee finished his thought.

"It is."

"Riley's right." Bruce made a conscious effort to lower his voice. "But if it was going to attack us, it would have already."

"That's what Riley said before."

"What, Kev?"

"It'll wait for night," Dee speculated. "Wait until we're not on our guard."

"We're forgetting one thing," Riley reminded them.

"Which is?"

"It doesn't know we know about it."

"It could be hearing our every word…"

"It's not." Kevin referred to the dosimeter. "Unless it's got hearing none of us can imagine. I think it's watching us, but it can't hear what we're saying. Even you," he remarked to Bruce. "It doesn't know we know."

"So we have some kind of advantage?"

"Maybe, Dee."

"What do we do now?" Kevin looked down at the fire in the pit.

"The coast is three, maybe four days on the quads," Dee offered.

"We have enough gas for that?" Riley didn't know much about the four-wheelers and had no idea how far the fuel in the red metal cans strapped to the chassis would take them.

"They'd have left resupply points." Dee spoke of army. "Best idea," he looked at Riley, urging, "we stick together."

"Let's get to the coast," she consented, " and put this thing—whatever it is—behind us. Then I can get back to New Harmony. Get—"

"To Africa." Dee's tone lacked luster.

"Out of here," Riley amended.

Dee let Riley drive their quad. She was hesitant on the handlebars, learning her way, but they were in no particular rush. They rolled through foothills long reclaimed by nature, low, rolling hills gone to russet with autumn. The hillocks they crested and dipped were all that was left of ancient mountain chains, worn and weathered. Sticking to the open grasses, they skirted pine and hickory forests, the soil beneath their four-wheeler a brown sandy loam.

"What's that?" Riley called back to Dee, her head nodding towards a field overgrown with wild, dark-leaved flowers.

"Tobacco."

They went by a train stalled on tracks covered over with grasses, a skein of long abandoned railcars, now no more than empty rectangles, civilization quitclaim. They passed what had been a pig farm, the piggery long untouched by trotters. Fresh, green growth sprouted from its former waste lagoon. The plateau region let out onto flat, low-lying lands, a vast coastal plain. Beneath their feet, igneous rocks yielded to sedimentary.

Kevin wore the dosimeter but Dee rarely called a halt to consult the device, this terrain familiar to the three men. A relatively narrow strait of land was open to them, free of the worst excesses of radiation.

About them, the signs of a congregation's pilgrimage, the land and grasses trod under by many feet. Bear's Army had passed this way. As now did these wayfarers, hosting injuries bodily and emotional, limbs bound and forced inflexible with jerry-rigged splints, their spirits contuse.

They stopped for the evening at what remained of a cache left for them by their comrades. Freeze-dried provisions, ammunition, and medicines were scattered and pilfered, torn open and pawed through by hands human or humanoid, impossible to tell.

"Who would have done this?" Riley asked. They spread out, cautiously watchful, gathering what was salvageable.

"We always had stragglers." Bruce thumbed through some medications. His hearing was returning and he spoke in a more normal tone. "Groups of people would follow us." He meant the army. "Never wanted to do the fighting, but they were always there for the clean up."

"Human hyenas," Dee added disdainfully, settling himself to the ground.

"Why'd they leave any ammo?"

"Lot of it is useless to them." Kevin held up a round. "Us too." He tossed it aside, puffing his cheeks and exhaling.

"They took most of the food," Bruce mentioned, to which Kevin interjected "All of the gas" before Bruce finished, "But we've still got some. And they left these." He held up freeze-dried packages that had not been tampered with.

"Do you think they'll be back?" Riley scanned the horizon about them.

"No," Dee pronounced with finality.

"We should have a fire," said Kevin. "Got to get some wood. Something that will burn."

"I'll go," Riley volunteered. They looked at her. "I'm the most able-bodied. Look at you." The three men looked each other over, an assortment of lacerations and bullet punctures, their bodies testament to her words.

"Don't go far," Bruce cautioned.

The CTME destroyed in the bomb blast, Riley held up an AR-15 she had taken. "You hear this," she looked at Dee, "you come hopping." She wandered off from them, clearly visible to their eyes as she went about her foraging, this cool day ebbing unto a chill evening. The three men sat together and considered the packages they had reclaimed.

"How you two feeling?" Kevin asked his friends.

"Foot hurts like hell."

"I think my shoulder is infected." Bruce pressed his chin to his chest, trying to look at the wound. "It's starting to stink."

"I can't believe they're all gone." Dee paid little attention to the food package in his hands, his gaze drawn instead to Riley amid the grasses.

Bruce sighed. "Tris…"

"I don't think I ever really thought *she'd* check out," admitted Kevin.

"You loved her, didn't you, Bruce?"

"Yeah, Dee, I loved her. But it wasn't like I was actually *in love* with her. I mean, I didn't think we were ever going to settle down and make a family or anything like that."

Kevin laughed at some image this brought to mind.

"I just always had a…she was so *bad*, and so *good* at it. I could appreciate her, that's all."

"How about you, Kev?" Dee never took his eyes off Riley. "You ever been in love?"

"Yes, I've been in love."

"What was her name?" Bruce smirked, learning something about an old friend he had never known.

"Nadjia."

"That's a pretty name."

"She was a pretty lady, Dee."

"She your wife?" Bruce inquired. "Before this?" He referred to the entirety of their lives this past quarter century.

"No." Kevin looked at Dee. "Met her when I met your dad," he said. Glancing back to Bruce, "before I met you."

"What happened to her?"

"Well, Dee, she said to me once—she said fighting zombies the way she and Bear were fighting them, she said it had a way of taking a toll on you, that it wears you down. Said she couldn't go on fighting forever. And she was right. It wore her down."

Bruce and Dee looked at one another.

"Well," ventured Bruce. "What happened?"

"What do you mean what happened?"

"Did she," Dee tried to think of some delicate way of putting it. "Did she, you know?"

"No. Not that I know about. She just stopped fighting one day. Settled down."

"And you didn't settle down with her?" Bruce looked at his friend.

"I was still fighting."

"Did she know you were in love with her?"

"Yeah, Dee, I'm pretty sure she knew."

"And?"

"*And* what?"

"And you never did anything about it?"

"What was I going to do?" Kevin asked them and then repeated the question, as if to himself. "What was I going to do?" He looked at his friends. "You remember those days, Bruce—you remember too, Dee. Zed everywhere." He looked away again. "All those Zed."

"How'd you know?"

"How'd I know *what*, Dee?"

"How'd you know you were in love?"

"Aw, shit. It's one of those things. You just know when you know."

"You're in love with Riley," Bruce had wised up, "aren't you, Dee?"

"What? No, I—"

"Come on, Dee. You don't have to act like that around us. We're practically family."

"Act like what?"

"Like a shy child."

"I'm no shy child."

"Like an embarrassed kid."

"I'm not embarrassed."

"Don't worry, Dee," Kevin assured him. "We're not going to say anything."

"Dee. You gonna talk to her?"

"I talk to her, Bruce."

"No, I mean are you going to *talk* to her. Let her know how you're feeling?"

"I don't know. Maybe. Eventually."

"In the words of a very wise man," Bruce quoted, "*tell her about it.*"

"*Tell her everything you feel,*" Kevin pointed a finger at Dee, smiling at Bruce.

"*Give her every reason to accept*—" Bruce gave Kevin a thumbs up "—*that you're for real.*" The two older men reached out to one another—"*Tell her all your crazy dreams*"—and high fived one another.

"Yeah," Kevin sighed, satisfied.

"Whatever-whatever-whatever." Bruce had forgotten the words.

"Well," Dee acknowledged, "you guys just shared some kind of moment."

"Billy Joel, my friend," explained Bruce. "And you'd be wise to heed his advice."

"Yeah, maybe I'll get around to it."

"Good rock 'n roll never stops being good rock 'n roll, does it?" Kevin remarked.

"Too old to rock 'n roll, too young to die."

"I hear that, Bruce."

Riley returned and they kindled a fire with the thin limbs and brambles she'd gathered. They ate from the packages and sat around the fire as the day's afterglow made way for the nightfall. Stars appeared in the purple sky like pinpricks granting access to the illume of an otherworld beyond the overhang of their own blackened dome.

"What if you were right about that other part?" Kevin asked Bruce the last question of the evening. "What if we're being paranoid here and it isn't the way we imagine it?"

"Then we've got nothing to lose."

A watch was kept through the night.

* * *

In its wake, the night brought with it the uncertainty and mystery of the dark. Alex's apprehension had ratcheted up another several notches, though the actual pain from his ankle had subsided to a dull, ever present throb. He'd propped his leg up and refused to move the ankle, which he knew was broken. He was alone and wounded, in the Outlands, in the night.

Among the items he could resort to for personal defense was his Model 7. He had six magazines of ammunition for it in addition to the full magazine already housed in the well. He'd stacked three of the magazines within easy reach next to where he lay. The remaining three rested in their tactical pouch beside the exposed magazines. There were things out there in the dark of the night, and if any of them came too close, Alex was ready for them.

Or so he told himself. In all honesty, he'd never felt so alone. Never had the night seemed so ominous.

He'd hurt himself in the full light of day. The rise had not been very steep, but he'd lost his footing and slid, the stones and earth going out underneath him, a minor rockslide. The ankle had caught on something and snapped and he'd yelled out loud, rolling down the slope until he'd come to a rest in the grass. He'd lain there and gasped. Seemingly every move he'd made, even those not directly connected to his ankle, brought pain from it.

It had take him some time to get his boot off. He'd wasted no time on delicacy, cutting away the sock. His ankle hadn't looked good then and it didn't look any better now, several hours later. The last time he'd checked on it with the flashlight, it was swollen and discolored.

After he'd initially checked and made sure his injury was not life threatening, Alex had lain there in disbelief. It hadn't even been a full day out of New Harmony. Grimaldi had dropped him off in the Outlands that morning. Alex had had the helicopter pilot set him down in nearly the exact spot as Riley and her brother and friends had set off from. Grimaldi had thought Alex was crazy, what he was doing, and the pilot volunteered as much. He told Alex he'd thought Evan and his friends were just as crazy when he'd brought them out here nearly a fortnight past, but Alex made no reply.

Grimaldi, Alex couldn't help thinking now, was right. Alex carried a radio, but he was two hundred kilometers into the Outlands and out of New Harmony's range. He'd set off his distress beacon as soon as he'd thought to do so. Anyone tuned to its frequency would pick it up, but they'd have to be out here in the Outlands with him to pick it up.

Now it was dark and it was night and there was something out there with him.

Alex could hear it. He had a flashlight riding the rail of his Model 7. The last time he'd turned it on had been to take a look at his ankle. He fought the urge—and it was a very powerful urge—to shine the light and see what was out there with him. If he turned on the light, he might get a look at whatever it was out there, but it'd also be like shining a search beacon on his exact location for whatever lurked there.

It was some kind of animal, Alex told himself. Had to be. Zed couldn't be this close in, could he? *This close in*, Alex corrected himself, *I'm two hundred kilometers in.* He checked his Geiger meter again. If it was Zed out there, it hadn't wandered in from a radiated zone. Or if it had, it wasn't close enough to set off the device yet.

Before the sun had retreated, he'd tried to set himself in a defensible position. Standing for any length of time was nearly impossible, but he'd gotten up on his one good leg and looked around as best he could. Having settled back to the earth, Alex worked his way forward on his hands and the knee of his good leg. He tried to keep the leg of his bad ankle straight out behind him, but it occasionally brushed the earth as he scampered and later crawled forward, and he grit his teeth and sweated out the discomfort.

He'd worked his way through the grass, towards his goal. When he reached the section of chain link fence he'd breathed a sigh of relief, knowing he was near. The fence's top section was angled. Other portions slumped in the grass. Alex figured further parts were long buried under the soil. He crawled past the fence, under the steel pole that rose into the sky, atop which rested a bank of lights and anodized reflectors. He worked his way towards the small, collapsed structure, long ago given to rot. Before he reached it, Alex's hand chanced upon something in the grass and he dug it free.

A five-sided slab of whitened rubber. He'd found home plate. Alex was on a baseball field. Looking out across the uninterrupted sea of grass and wildflowers that had engulfed the soil, he'd thought this a strange place for a former baseball field, out in the middle of nowhere. Nowhere now, sure, except this used to be somewhere.

Alex dragged himself the remaining meters to the dugout. Its walls and roof had partially collapsed inwards and moss covered the wood. When he'd realized what it was, he'd thought he could hole up and spend the night inside. Reaching it, he found stagnant water pooled within. He'd consulted his Geiger meter at that point and found a higher reading coming off the water than from the surrounding area and atmosphere. He chalked it up to toxic rain and crawled away from the dugout. Couldn't sleep there tonight.

Half crawling, half rolling himself back to home plate, Alex settled down, waiting for the night, stacking his ammunition.

Grimaldi. The flyboy had been right. Alex was crazy to come out here. What had been going through his head? He wanted to find Riley. Okay. He was going to find Riley and then what? She was going to throw her arms around him, *Oh, Alex, you cared so much, thank you, I never want to be apart from you again.* No. He didn't expect that. They'd seen each other at the party two weeks ago. She was with her brother and her friend Troi. She'd said hi to him and he'd said hi to her and they'd spoken. Everything had been cool, cordial, not unfriendly. But not like it had once been.

No, Alex hadn't thought Riley was going to be overwhelmed with emotion when she saw him. But, just as he should never have come out here, neither should she have. Her father didn't stop her and shame on him that he hadn't, letting both his children go. And Evan. What had Evan been thinking? Alex knew Evan from their time in the Defense Forces together. Evan had been stoned out of his skull at the party, dancing with his shirt off. Evan had come out here with Riley and Anthony and Troi. Evan, at least, would be happy to see Alex. Surprised? Sure. But happy.

I came out here to protect her, Alex admitted to himself. Because he had. He nearly laughed aloud. Who had he been kidding? Protect Riley. Rescue *her* from danger? Riley could take care of herself, probably better than Alex could take care of himself. Considering his broken ankle resting atop his backpack, Alex figured wherever Riley was at the moment, chances were she was doing better than he was. It was Alex who needed rescuing. He'd come out here to play some kind of hero, and now he was the one in want of a hero.

A rustle in the grass, and the thing came closer, whatever it was. Alex stared out into the dark but it gave him nothing in return.

It had to be some kind of animal. Had to be. Alex tried to be logical, rational. The bone had not broken from the skin; his ankle hadn't bled. If it had, the scent of his blood would have attracted any zombies for kilometers.

Which—if he was being completely rational, he knew he had to grant—didn't mean the thing out there with him *wasn't* Zed. It could be. Zombies were out here, wandering around. They even still occasionally found themselves outside New Harmony's walls. Hadn't two just shown up recently? Of course there was some story that those weren't actually zombies, or maybe one of them was or wasn't or whatever, but—

A chortle sounded, a raspy sound like sand paper being drawn across timber.

Alex raised his head and shoulders, his finger moving from the M-7's trigger guard to the trigger itself. His other hand supported the barrel. He waited. He could hear it clearly now. It was coming towards him.

Two circles shone in the night before him and Alex gasped. He came within a hair's breadth of firing the M-7 when the reasoning part of his brain halted him, reassuring him. They were corneas out there, light reflecting off the tapeta.

The hand on the M-7's barrel went to the flashlight and thumbed it on.

The thing screeched and Alex beheld long front claws, muscled legs, an elongated body covered in black hair. The feet, which had been digging in the ground for grubs and insects, were stomping, the hair on the creature's body standing up, two white stripes along its back, its tail high. It hissed at Alex before turning—

"No, don't!"

—and loosing its anal scent glands at him. Alex managed to shut his eyes before the skunk doused him. He groaned and yelled at it, frustrated, indignity added to injury. He would have shot at it, but firing his M-7 out here was not a good idea. He heard a rustle as the polecat retreated into the night.

"You little son of a bitch!" Alex yelled after it, wiping at his face. The stench was unbelievable, like rotten eggs and burnt rubber. "Son of a bitch!"

His eyes closed, Alex rummaged through his pack until he found the package of wipes. He dabbed at his eyes—it hadn't gotten in his eyes—and rubbed his face. Son of a bitch. Little son of a bitch. He used half a pack of the wipes before he conceded that the stench was not going anywhere. Frustrated, he discarded the wipes and threw his upper body back down into the grass.

A skunk. A frigging skunk.

When he had calmed down, Alex checked his Geiger meter. Nothing to worry about. He lay in the dark on what had been a baseball field, a foe the size of a house cat somewhere out there in the night with him, either long gone or waiting him out, awaiting his departure. *Yeah, you might be waiting a long while, you little son of a bitch.*

At least, Alex tried to console himself, it hadn't been Zed. Where were the zombies? He lay there, exhausted and injured, reeking of skunk, and when his ears first heard the motorized reverberations in the distance, Alex thought it was his mind playing tricks on him.

As though the cosmos sought to make amends for the scenes from the prior day, Riley woke with the dawn to find herself face to face with a sight of exquisite beauty. An equine eye blinked at her, its owner a mere meter from her sleeping body. Despite herself, she drew her breath in shortly and sat up, her sudden action startling the feral horse. Whickering—Riley got a good glimpse of its sorrel coat, the fine hairs on its fetlocks whipping through the air—it joined its band, five of them galloping away across the grasslands.

The horses' abrupt departure woke Kevin and Bruce.

"What was that?" Kevin sat up with the barrel of his AK-47, searching for a target.

"Wild horses." Dee had been on watch. "They wandered over in the night. Curious about us."

"Look at them go…" Bruce had stood and watched the receding horses grow smaller on the horizon. He reached up and touched at his wound.

"How's your shoulder?" asked Riley.

"Okay."

They left their slumber behind for the day, rising and busying themselves. Dee had spent the night with his boot off to let the air get to the wound and Riley helped him clean and re-bandage his foot. Kevin dug around in his pack until he found a roll of toilet paper and walked off, away from the others, the bathroom tissue in one hand, his AK in the other.

"I'm going to go and see if I can find us something to eat for breakfast." Bruce slung the sniper rifle over his shoulder.

"Don't shoot a horse."

"Lot of good meat on a horse, Dee. But don't worry, I'll bring you back a raccoon or something."

Dee noticed the way Riley looked pained when Bruce mentioned a raccoon. He waited until the others were out of earshot before asking her if she was okay.

"What? Yeah."

"You looked kind of…far away there."

"I was. Come on, help me put on your boot."

"I got it. You were thinking about your brother."

She nodded.

It had only been a few days since he'd found Riley, but between that first day at the river and this morning it felt like an eternity had passed. Dee didn't know why and couldn't explain it, but he felt like he had known her for a much longer time.

"He was a good guy, wasn't he?"

"Yes."

Dee winced as they pulled his boot back up over his foot. "What'd you say he did?"

"He was a teacher."

"He liked it?"

"He loved it."

"I'm sorry you had to, had to watch him…"

"He died in my arms. I was holding him."

"I'm sorry, Riley."

"Me too."

He gritted his teeth and hissed as Riley pulled his bootlaces tight.

"Do you know what he said to me?" She remembered clearly. "He kept thanking me."

"Thanking you?"

"For going with him." Riley was standing and Dee looked up at her, the woman's curly, brownish hair against the bluing sky. "For coming with him, out here." Her pretty, honest face. "He thought—I guess *we* thought—we'd find Bear, maybe Bear would have some answers for him." The blue of her eyes would do any sky an injustice.

Dee looked away from her. "He loved you very much."

"And I loved him so much, *so, so* much."

"He knew that."

"Yeah, I know he did." Riley crossed her arms and rubbed them with her hands, the air chill. "You know, I was going to tell him," she touched at her stomach, "I was going to tell him something and I never got the chance."

"What were you going to tell him?"

"Just how happy I was to have gone with him. Outside of New Harmony. Not happy about how things turned out, obviously…" Images—of Thomas, the mutants, of Evan and Troi walking away from them—flashed through her mind before she banished them "…but happy I was there with him, that he was there with me."

"Why are you holding your stomach when you say that? Your belly hurt?"

"No, it's not that."

"There was something else you were going to tell him, wasn't there?"

"How do you…?"

"Call me perceptive. So what was it?"

"I was pregnant."

"Was?"

"I lost the baby."

"Oh, that's terrible." Dee plucked a blade of grass from beside where he lay. "I'm sorry. Who's was it?"

"A guy I was seeing."

Dee nodded at this. "You were going to tell Anthony because he was your brother and you could tell your brother anything, right?"

"Exactly." Riley looked for the horses but they had long disappeared from sight. "I miss him so much, Dee. I can't believe he's gone."

"I know."

"I feel so selfish, saying all this to you…" Riley looked down on the bald-headed man in his oilskin Drover. His chin was beginning to shadow with stubble. "You've lost everybody in the last few days."

"Not everybody." Dee held the blade of grass up and looked at it. "I've still got Bruce and Kevin." *I've got you*, he thought but didn't say it.

"I just feel like it's all my fault. If I hadn't shown up…"

"I get why you feel that way," Dee put the grass down. "But you know none of us feel that way. They took Victor. We went and got Victor back."

"But Tris—"

"Tris went out just the way she always wanted to. You heard her yourself. A 'worthy' death. She'd outlived her expiration date."

"It doesn't upset you? Their dying?"

"Sure it upsets me." Dee was silent for a moment. "Its upsets me terribly. I've been out here my whole life, Riley. You know how I hooked up with them? Bruce found me when I was this little kid, roaming around all by myself. I'd had people, sure, there were people taking care of me."

"What happened to them? Zombies?"

"There's shit happened before that I just don't remember well." Uncertainty painted Dee's face. "Don't know how I made it that far by myself. I know there were people who looked out for me, and then they were gone. And I know they didn't die nice. But the details I can't remember. Maybe that's a good thing."

Still some way off, Kevin was approaching them, a tail of toilet paper trailing from the roll he carried.

"My point is," Dee continued, "this is all I've known. People I care about dying around me. It hasn't been as bad as it was earlier on, but man, it hasn't been easy."

"Are you afraid of dying?"

"No, I don't think I am. I don't want to die, but I hope when it comes…I hope I handle it well. I hope I'm with people I know and care about, people who know and care about me."

"Well," she smiled at him, "there's still Bruce and Kevin."

He smiled back at her. "There's almost another five thousand of them up ahead somewhere, if we ever catch up to them."

Riley waved to Kevin and he bore his AK aloft.

"Yeah, Dee, but Africa? Really?"

"I don't know what we were thinking."

* * *

In the afternoon they spied apartment towers on the horizon and rode to them. Long relinquished to ruin and decay, they stood lonely sentinel, dilapidated eyesores. Where a trio had once risen, there were now only two, the third reduced to a jagged massif of rubble and rebar. The remaining buildings stood twelve stories each, chambered by blackened, gaping holes, as if pummeled by a furious god. Concrete walls were scorched black above vacant windows. They had stood there through it all: through the rise of the dead and the fall of the living; through the end of the world in which they had been built.

"If a lot of people lived here," Riley speculated, "shouldn't there be more cars?"

Only two dozen decrepit hulks dotted the former parking lot, sun-bleached and rusted out. They'd dismounted in the shadow of the towers and strode among the foot of a building, their approach rousing no interested parties.

"When it happened," Kevin remembered, "everyone was trying to get out of places like this."

They chose the more stable looking of the two buildings. A beer truck was sunk a close walk from its entrance, trays of bottles and cans scattered. Propped against it, a skeleton's mouth was locked around the tattered remains of a cigar.

Shrouded in dust and gloom, the lobby yielded before their flashlights. Walls of tarnished mailboxes stood untouched, the layer of dust thick and undisturbed on the floor. Only one elevator was open. It gave onto a yawning shaft, at the bottom of which a skull sat atop a pile of bones.

"That makes for a good murder hole."

Riley looked up where Dee's light illuminated a ragged opening in the ceiling, near the door to a stairwell. *Murder hole?* It was the first time she'd heard the term but she immediately understood what it meant. Whoever commanded the view from above could fire down on anyone where she and Dee stood. The second stairwell they had found was clogged with furniture, impassable. Anyone seeking access to the upper stories—themselves included—would need to pass beneath this opening to reach the stairs.

Kevin and Bruce took turns driving the quads into the lobby, turning them around to face outside before cutting the ignitions. Together they explored the stairwell, finding it deserted. The door to the

118

second floor opened onto a desolate hallway, a section of the floor yawning open above the lobby. The third and fourth floors were barred and blocked, sealed shut. When they cracked the door to the fifth floor corridor, a rushing in the dark brought their flashlight beams down upon the refuse-strewn floor.

Six months at most when it'd changed, a baby zombie skulked towards the door on hands and knees. A keening wail issued from it as it came. The flesh of its knees had been worn away while blackened, varicose veins spider webbed its skin.

They shut themselves in on the stairwell, leaving the thing where it was, whining against the stairwell door.

The sixth floor was as quiet as the second. The landing on the seventh floor was obstructed with furniture and junk, cutting off the rest of the building from them and they from it. Aiding Dee on the stairs had them sweating and they chose an apartment on the sixth floor. The corridor was bare except for sheaves of paper scattered about the dusty floor. The apartment itself was mostly empty, the majority of its furniture gone, conceivably lugged to a stairwell to bar entry.

"How's it going, Bruce?"

"I think I can smell myself, Dee."

"We could all use a bath."

"No. I mean I think my wound is infected."

"I don't smell anything. Kev, you smell anything?"

"No."

A balcony overlooked the beer truck and the other tower. They made camp on the floor of the room just inside the patio doors. After they'd eaten, Riley stood on the balcony watching the day fade. Bruce came out and stood with her.

"Zombies going to come tonight," he rasped matter-of-factly. They looked out on the land abutting the apartment complex, a mass of trees broken only by a fragmented road, the same road they had come in on. "We're safe for the night. Getting out in the morning will be fun."

Riley drew the final watch. The sky was greying when she relieved Kevin on the patio. He handed her Dee's minocular. For an hour or more there was little to see or hear. At one point she thought she detected a cry in the far distance. Soon thereafter the birds started talking to one another. In the dawn's light she saw something scurrying below, between the cars. A rabbit? She tried to track it with the minocular but lost it at the beer truck.

There were forms shambling along on the road, zombies. Riley knew that as long as she remained quiet, the undead would remain ignorant of her presence six stories above. She watched the beer truck closely. Where had the rabbit gone? She didn't want to imagine it down on the ground with those things coming close. As the men started to wake, Riley excused herself and listened before she stepped into the hall. The dust on the floor was disturbed only where she and the others had unsettled in the night before. It carpeted the remaining length of the hallway floor, untrodden.

She walked down the stairs, eyeing the door on the fifth floor landing. Wherever the baby was in there, she couldn't hear it.

Outside, a chill gripped the morning. Riley crossed to the beer truck, intent on the rabbit. The zombies on the road were clear to her, the sky above lighter. She moved in the shadows between the building and the truck, lost to their eyes. At this distance, their moans and protestations were faint but unmistakable. It sounded like there were more of them up there than she would ever like to meet.

Broken glass bottles, cans and kegs had spilled from the truck. Riley took care not to step on or kick any of them. Because Dee, Kevin and Bruce were wounded, the zombies were in their vicinity. Riley bore no open wounds, so the only way they would detect her would be if they saw or heard her. The cargo bays were deep and high. She shone her light into one, empty. The rabbit could be hiding anywhere inside.

"Yeah," Riley said to the skeleton sitting there, the cigar stub clenched in its jaw. "How you doing?"

Behind her, the shadow of the beer truck was cast on the apartment building as a vehicle's headlights pinned it from the road. Riley crouched down and risked a glance around the side of the truck.

She did not like what she saw.

"We've got company," Bruce announced on the balcony. A dozen pick-up trucks and two flat beds turned in from the road. A Howitzer rested on one of the flat beds. A delta tricycle—one wheel in front, two in the rear—weaved in and out between the pick-ups.

"Who are they?" Dee had limped over on his own, doing his best to conceal himself inside the apartment while gazing out onto the scene shaping up below.

"What warlords are near here?" Kevin squatted next to Bruce on the concrete balcony, peering over the railing.

"Tolman?" Bruce sounded doubtful.

"Nah, he doesn't come this far north."

"Fucking look at them."

They passed the monocular between them. The marauders had halted their vehicles at a distance from the other side of the beer truck. Men and women clambered out of the trucks and off the flatbeds. Most of them wore dark eye shadow, their hair dyed black with auburn and blonde streaks, fingernails painted black. One man wore a Viking motorcycle helmet with black horns. A woman in black parachute pants and a bikini top was painted yellow with black spots on her arms and shoulders, lending her a leopard-like appearance. There were fifty or sixty of them on the ground and they were loud, the motorcycle tricycle the only vehicle still moving, circling the area.

"It's the fucking Village People," Bruce observed.

"Now that guy—" Kevin spoke of a man whose fat, hairy belly parted his leather vest, the man's face made up in black and white corpse paint "—is pretty scary looking,"

"I'm not seeing a lot of guns," Dee whispered from the balcony door. And aside from a dozen shotguns and a few pistols, the marauders' weapons appeared primitive in the light: baseball bats and cudgels, clubs and knives. Despite the apparent dearth of modern weapons, there was no shortage of fishnet stockings, black leather thigh boots, and dark eyeliner.

"You get a load of that cannon?" Kevin remarked. The Howitzer's barrel aimed away from them, back at the road. "That's all they need."

"They have no clue we're here." There was optimism in Bruce's gravelly inflection.

"Hey," Dee asked from the balcony door. "Where's Riley?"

They stole away from the others, two of them seeking privacy. One had a Harajuku girl look going, dark make up over a white painted face, knee-length black skirt over knee-high stockings of the same color. The other wore a miniskirt and her face was made up to resemble a fox, whiskers painted on her cheeks, her hair cut short in a bob. They laughed at something the one said and couldn't keep their hands off each another as they approached the beer truck.

They laughed again at the skeleton with its back to the truck. The cigar had come dislodged and rested in its lap.

The cargo bay door screeched as it rolled up and open. The girl with the fox getup bent over, bracing herself on the lip of the bay door. Her companion lifted the fox's skirt over her hips and proceeded to go down on her from behind. Fox girl was starting to gasp when she looked into the dark of the truck bay and saw—

Riley's foot snapped out of the dark and caught her in the head, knocking the fox nose rubber banded to her face askance. The girl's companion, startled, stood up, staring down the barrel of the revolver in Riley's hand.

"Not a word," Riley warned, but the gothic Lolita screamed, her voice surprisingly deep. Riley shut her up with the side of her hand to the face. The cry had been drowned out in the roar of the motorcycle and the bustle of people. Zombies were staggering in off the road and the marauders were dealing with them, toying with them, laughing and gleefully ducking outstretched arms. A shotgun blast sounded as one zombie got too close.

"Get up," Riley told fox girl. "The both of you—" she moved the revolver from one to the other "—we're going to walk back to that building. If you try and run or yell for help—" she glowered at the Harajuku girl "—I'll shoot you both. Come on!"

They were almost to the apartment building when the companions of Riley's two hostages noticed what was going on. A hue and cry went up and excitement turned from the zombies trickling into their midst to the drama unfolding.

"Move!" Riley urged, walking backwards now, the .45 revolver pressed to the back of the GothLoli, her free hand pulling the fox girl along. She kept them between herself and the other men and women. "Faster!"

"Kitty!" someone cried out clearly. "She got Kitty!"

A giant broke from the pack, uttering a high-pitched streak. His ratty beard was forked and rubber banded, his meaty arms jangling out of his furry vest as he raced towards them. He wore studded leather forearm vambraces and hefted a war hammer, which he looked eager to use.

The ground in front of the brute boiled up as the cracks of a rifle sounded from on high. The man stopped where he was and looked up to the sixth floor balcony. He gave another shriek—its pitch incongruous with his size—and repeatedly smashed the ground with his maul, venting his frustration on the earth.

"Don't shoot me!" Riley called up to the ceiling in the lobby. "It's me! I've got two of them." A flashlight beam shone down on her and her prisoners.

Dee's voice growled back from the aperture, "Get upstairs, Riley."

* * *

"Did you search these guys for weapons?"

"No." Riley told Bruce. She stood against the wall, her heart only beginning to slow. Kevin had slapped plastic cuffs on the two women and knelt between them, searching them. "Bruce, keep an eye on that cannon."

The marauders were milling about outside, trying to figure out what to do. Shotguns boomed intermittently, dispatching zombies. As they procrastinated, more undead poured in, drawn by the clamor. The Howitzer continued to face away from the building.

"Garden shears?" Kevin looked at their Goth detainee. "What were you going to do with these? Trim our hedges?" He threw the shears away across the room.

"Where was she hiding those?" Bruce croaked.

When he was satisfied that they were disarmed, Kevin stood.

"Who are you?" Neither answered him.

"You with Tolman?" rasped Bruce. A look passed on the fox girl's face. She'd affixed her canid nose back in place, her own nose and mouth bloody where Riley had kicked her. "Didn't think so."

A shotgun discharged outside.

"Man," Bruce remarked, regarding the Harajuku girl. "You know, you're a real rough looking broad."

"She's not a woman," said Riley.

"What?"

"Look."

Kevin lifted the woman's black dress with the muzzle of his AK. "She's not wearing underwear," he told Bruce. "And she's got testicles."

Bruce uttered a *damn*. "Let me try talking to them. Riley, keep an eye on things down there."

He came in and squatted down in front of them. "Hey, Raggedy Ann, you going to talk?" The cross-dresser looked away. "Didn't think so. How about you? You're not going to talk either, are you?"

"Do you think she can talk?" asked Kevin.

"Let's take a look." Bruce gripped her jaw in his hand and tried to pry her mouth open with his index finger. She snapped at him, nearly biting him.

"Get off me!"

"She can talk." Bruce eyed the girl with impatience.

"She can talk," Kevin agreed.

"You know," Bruce told the girl, "you'd be a lot scarier if you weren't dressed up like a fox."

"She's not going to tell you a thing," the other hostage said defiantly.

"So you going to talk then?"

"I'll tell you you've bitten off more than you can chew, man. Do you know who you're fucking with?"

"No. Why don't you tell us who we're fucking with."

"You're fucking with Burning Man Tribe."

"Whoa, Kev. You hear that? Burning Man Tribe." Bruce did not sound impressed. "And you don't know who *we* are, do you?"

The man dressed like a woman didn't take the bait.

"We're Bear's Army."

"Yeah, right."

"Guys, look at this."

Bruce and Kevin joined Riley on the balcony. Below, the brigands had secured a zombie to a ladder, its arms bound at its sides, its legs together. A dozen costumed and painted men and women danced around the thing, dousing it with fluid.

"We know you're in there!" Speakers mounted in the trucks and on the flat bed came to life. A paunchy little man stood with a microphone. "Come out now—" He wore a white powdered wig, gold-tasseled epaulettes on a purple smoking jacket, and a pistol in a chest holster "—or you'll wish you did." The PA system howled with feedback.

They lifted the ladder and secured it in place. The zombie looked down on them, not comprehending. The fat man with the leather vest came forward with a torch and tossed it on the ladder. With a *whoosh*, the zombie went up in flame. Men and women began dancing around the pyre, frolicking to the undead's distressed wails.

"Black Rock retards." Bruce sighted through the scope affixed to his M-40. The rifle cracked and the cries from the fire ceased.

"Now you done it, man," said the guy dressed in former Japanese alternative fashion.

"Yeah, looks like I done it."

The short man looked up towards them before saying something to a man in a camisole and codpiece with a leather studded choker.

"I always wondered what happened to Alice Cooper." Bruce worked the bolt on the M40, chambering a fresh round.

"Tris would have loved these guys." Kevin took the other side of the balcony, readying his rifle. The people besieging them made no move to storm the apartment building. A volley of shotgun fire dropped half a dozen zombies.

"No, she wouldn't. These fucks are fucking with me on the wrong day. I feel like shit."

Kevin crouched back down in front of the two prisoners. Riley stood behind him. "Are you Kitty?" she asked the fox girl.

"I'm Kitty." It was the man who answered.

"You're Kitty…" Kevin looked to the girl, who was visibly frightened. "Look, your sense of fashion and company aside, you're not a dumb girl. You can't be to be alive out here. You can see we're outnumbered. But you can also tell we've got better guns than your side. And your guys can't seem to get their act together. You know it's true, right? Sure you do."

"Don't listen to him, 'chelle. They're not Bear's Army."

"Who are you?" Riley glared at the man. "Her father?"

"'*chelle?*'" Kevin kept his focus on the girl. "Your name is Michelle? Is that it? Well, what if we walk you downstairs, Michelle, let you go? You go back and tell your people out there, they let us leave, we'll go. They pull back, we walk away. It's as simple as that. Otherwise this is not going to go well for your side."

"It's as simple as that," Bruce watched the men and women on the ground.

"You'll do no such thing, 'chelle!"

"Shut up!" Riley yelled at the man.

Someone was screaming down below.

"What happened, Bruce?" Kevin asked, unruffled.

"One of them got bit."

Kitty was eyeing the door to the apartment.

"Don't get any ideas," Riley warned him.

"Come on, Michelle," Kevin said to the girl, "let's go on down there, you tell them what we said. We'll even let Kitty go once we're clear."

"Yeah, right."

"What do you think," Riley asked Kitty, "we want to keep you?"

Before the girl could make a decision and answer, music blared up to them.

"What are they doing now?" Kevin and Riley stood with Bruce on the balcony.

"They think they're softening us up," Bruce smirked. "Psychological warfare."

"They're going to make us listen to this for how many hours?"

"Exactly."

"What is this crap anyway?"

"I think its Richard Prior."

"No," Riley corrected him. "Eddie Murphy." She knew the song from the 80s-themed parties popular in New Harmony.

My girl wants to party all the time, party all the time, party all the time.

"Look down there," Bruce pointed. "Another one of them got bit."

"Is Dee all right?" asked Riley.

"Dee's fine," Kevin reassured her. "Anyone who tries to come in through that lobby isn't."

"We can't stay here all day." Bruce selected targets through the scope. When the shooting started, he'd decided, the Napoleon-guy or whatever he was died first.

"Why not?" Riley thought maybe that was what they should do. "Let them deal with things."

Dozens of zombies were milling around about the raiders below as more staggered in from the road.

"Bruce is right. When those things are done dealing with them, we have to deal with those things."

Riley looked at the mobile artillery piece mounted on the flat bed. She imagined a weapon like that could blow holes like Swiss cheese in this building. The Howitzer's barrel remained pointing back up the road. "They're not too bright, are they?"

The giant with the oversized hammer was braining zombies, screeching at a near falsetto as he did so.

"No," Kevin agreed. "They're not."

The music suddenly cut off.

"Get ready." Bruce crouched down, lining up his shot.

"What should I do?" Riley looked for direction.

"They go to move that cannon, waste them."

The short, wigged man barked into his microphone. "Burning Man, hear me!" The men and women that comprised Burning Man Tribe let out a cheer. "Burning man charge!" They broke off from the zombies they fought, running towards the apartment building. "Burning Man onward!" The giant was in the forefront of the rush, screeching his own shrill battle cry.

"Okay," Bruce centered his crosshairs on the leader's epaulettes. "Here we go." His first shot knocked the wig off the man's head in an explosion of red. Bruce worked the bolt on the rifle and chambered a fresh round. He looked through his scope. "Next."

★ ★ ★

Dee sat in the dark, looking down into the lobby below. There was enough ambient light from outdoors that he could see down into there better than anyone there was going to be able to see up to where he was. He would have rather been waiting with Riley, but he knew she was safe upstairs with Kevin and Bruce.

Muffled shotgun blasts reached his ears. He chalked those up to the people outside tangling with Zed. If something was going on upstairs he needed to know about, someone would come down and tell him. With his limited mobility and the FN FAL .63, he thought his current position the best place for him. Anybody who wanted to get up inside the building had to come by him. The other entrances were blocked with rubble. He could imagine that this was not the first time the perch he manned had served a purpose similar to his own.

When the music started, Dee figured they were getting *really* stupid outside. If they'd played it smart they would have circled the tower, kept quiet, and waited them out. They'd have still had to deal with the zombies coming in off the road, the ones drawn by wounds like his own. But now they were out there blasting some bullshit tunes that could probably be heard for a mile around. And before that they'd been making a racket, attracting who knew how many scads of the undead.

Dee sat where he was, his legs out in front of him, the barrel of the FN covering the hole. He was used to waiting. Waiting didn't bother him. Soon enough the music stopped and the real shooting started.

He listened to the gunfire, imagining Bruce selecting a target, firing, racking the bolt, choosing his neck target, firing. Kevin fired short, controlled bursts from his AK-47. Riley's AR chimed in less frequently. She'd be keeping an eye on their captives. He knew he wouldn't hear the cannon fire as long as Kevin and Bruce were alive on the balcony. If he heard the cannon fire they'd all be in some real trouble and there wasn't much he could do about it here.

They weren't trying to be quiet when they came through the lobby. It sounded like Kevin was on a full auto tear and then there were voices beneath, excited and scared, jostling into the lobby. He looked down his barrel and waited until they showed themselves, their footwear scraping across the floor. They came into view bunched up like he'd hoped they'd be, like they shouldn't have been, completely unaware of his presence. He mowed them down, the Belgian rifle booming in the hallway, echoing through the lobby. One or two managed to look up and the last thing they saw were muzzle flashes licking down from the dark.

They were lying there, unmoving, when Dee heard a quad start up and race out of the lobby. Dummy was trying to take their ride. Bruce's rifle cracked and the sound of the quad died.

Frantic screaming and yelling drifted in from outside now. Kevin and Bruce were putting out a lot of lead. Sounded like they had things under control. Men and women were dying out there. Dee knew it wasn't all because of his friends, either. Zed would be having a field day. The spaces between the cracks from Bruce's rifle lengthened. Dee chalked that up to a dwindling supply of live targets.

He sat where he was, awaiting anyone who rushed the lobby. No more did.

★ ★ ★

"Dee, let's go."

"Help me up, Riley."

She half-lifted, half-supported him as he pulled himself to a standing position, using her as leverage. Bruce and Kevin were waiting downstairs with the fox girl at the door that led out into the lobby.

"Only the one?" inquired Dee.

"Gwen Stefani's backup singer ran." Kevin grinned at Bruce's wisecrack because he was the sole person among them who got it.

"She didn't run my way."

"No. He ran down to the fifth floor." It was the way Riley said it, like the fifth floor should mean something to Dee.

"The fifth floor?"

"The baby," Riley reminded him.

"Right." Dee remembered. "*He?*"

"We'll tell you about it later," promised Kevin.

"Take me with you," their hostage pled.

Bruce told her to be quiet.

They fanned out through the lobby, past the crumpled, pulverized forms Dee had shot down. They looked out the doors and took in a landscape marred by death and devastation. A pile of bodies were strewn almost at the doors where Kevin had strafed them, zombies sitting and kneeling, gorging themselves on the wounded.

A couple of pick-up trucks—all that were left—were disappearing down the road, a few survivors cringing in the beds. A wave of zombies followed the departing vehicles. Between the apartment building and the road the landscape was littered with the injured and the dead, vehicles with their tires shot out, others with steam rising from perforated engine blocks. The Howitzer still aimed at the road, the wheels of its flatbed sunk, the interior of the cab splashed red.

At first glance it was impossible to tell which among the unmoving were zombies and which were recently living. Of the ambulatory, the zombies were easy to distinguish, assailing the aggrieved marauders. At some point in the fracas, Bruce had adjusted his aim, shooting to wound and not to kill.

Riley spotted the big man with the rubber bands in his beard. He was bleeding from numerous bites but still swinging his hammer, keeping a circle of ghouls at bay.

Shotgun fire boomed rare and sporadic, the marauders hopelessly outnumbered and routed. Enough of a commotion existed to provide cover for their escape.

"Let's get out of here," Kevin suggested. "Bruce, you ride with me." The third quad was overturned beyond the beer truck and did not warrant the risk of retrieving.

"Take me with you—*please*!"

"Get out of here," Bruce told Michelle.

"*Please*!"

"Get out of here!" Bruce booted the girl out the door into the open. She looked back at Riley before bolting. Several of the zombies feasting on the nearest of the fallen rose and followed after her.

Bruce and Dee stood guarding either side of the door while Riley and Kevin rolled the remaining quads to the front of the lobby.

"You want to drive?" Riley asked Dee.

"No, you better."

Kevin and Bruce were the first out of the building. The roar of their quad drew the attention of the living and the dead alike. Only one of the former came forward to challenge them, the camisole clad companion to the leader of the Burning Man Tribe. He ran towards them, firing the pistol he had taken from his dead commander. Kevin put him down with a savage burst from his AK, the flesh of the man's upper thighs exploding.

Riley accelerated after them, Dee holding on to her. None of the few shots being fired were intended for anyone on the four wheelers. They bounced over a fresh body and swerved around the corroded chassis of a Ford Mustang, relic of a bygone era. Kevin and Bruce made the trees first, lifting off the ground and sailing through the air before plunging into the woods.

Riley circled the quad once at the forest, sparing a last look at the slaughter. A zombie staggered away from its pack, clutching a blood-stained camisole. The giant was down, screeching in that strange high-pitched timbre. The fox girl had pulled herself up on top of the beer truck, a crowd of undead circling it.

"Drive," Dee suggested, and she did.

THE FORGOTTEN MAN

Though the bullet he had taken to the back of his skull years before had rendered his eyes useless for sight, his other senses remained sharp. The wrinkled man heard their approach from his cave, what he perceived as a tremble upon the ground, the vibrations of motors. Mechanical buzzes filled the air as they neared. He roused himself and took up his habiliments before their arrival, placing himself at the entrance to his cave, a wizened, unseeing watchman.

When the quad she rode on halted, Riley swung her leg around and dismounted it, stepping to firm ground. The figure that awaited them was a strange site to behold. Short and thin, he wore a welding helmet that encased his entire head in black and silver. His face was hidden behind the tinted glass of the window. In one hand, the man gripped a Caduceus staff, two serpents entwined, surmounted by wings. The staff was taller than the man himself. His other hand was wrapped around a handgun. He stood before an aphotic maw that let onto the earth, as though guarding untold subterranean treasures. The man's appearance coupled with that morning's run-in with the Burning Man Tribe left Riley momentarily nonplussed.

The engine of Kevin and Bruce's quad cut off. Riley noticed how Dee left the big FN scabbarded on their own four-wheeler.

"Fuck those other guys." Bruce's delivered his verdict. "*He's* scary looking."

"Is he supposed to scare us?" Kevin asked.

"Who has come to this place?" The man called to their group, his voice high and raspy.

"It's me, Moriarity. Dee. You remember me? I come by here every year. I brought some friends with me."

"I've many memories in this old head. You call me Moriarity, you must have known me as I once was."

"What name do you go by now?" Dee glanced from Riley to Bruce and Kevin. *Humor the guy*, his seemed to say.

"I was Moriarity. Now I'm Mallory."

"Come on, man. I know you can't see me, but don't act like you don't know me. I come by this way every year, eat with you, sleep here."

"What is it you seek?"

"A place to spend the night, Moriarity. Nothing else."

"I told you, my name is Mallory."

"Come on, Moriarity, I'm not just going to start calling you Mallory. We been through this crap last year and I told you *then* Moriarity was it from now on."

"I warn you…" He raised the caduceus towards them. "I wield terrible magic."

The men and the woman looked at one another. Dee shrugged.

"We've got coffee," offered Kevin.

"Coffee." Moriarity popped the window on his welding helmet and squinted at the visitors. "You don't say." They were indistinguishable to him, blurred shapes against the light of day.

"He's pretty out there," Riley remarked to Bruce. Hearing her, Dee muttered, "Just a little bit."

"Coffee." Moriarity lifted the welding helmet free of his head, grinning as he did so, his cheeks stubbled white. "Come on over, friends, and let's partake in some libation and something of a more solid nature. Let me check my traps."

"We already checked them for you." Bruce held a dead rabbit up in each hand.

* * *

The old man who was known as Moriarity but wished to be called Mallory was very pleased with the food they brought him, both gathered from his traps and what they bore. They cooked fresh game over a fire under the crisp autumn sky, the hermit's cave like a mouth in the earth behind them.

They ate and Moriarity bore a look somewhat akin to euphoria as the sugar from a tin of mixed fruit they'd imparted to him hit his system. He used his fingers to spoon it into his mouth until he grew impatient with this method and upended the tin, guzzling its contents, its syrupy juices dribbling down his chin. Kevin looked from the old man licking the syrup from his fingers to Dee and blew out his breath, like *You brought us here? To this?*

"Moriarity?"

"Mallory."

"I'm not calling you that," Dee reminded him. "You ever hear of an outfit calls themselves Burning Man Tribe?"

Moriarity laughed in confirmation.

"What do you know about them?"

"They fear me. They fear the magic." He chewed a maraschino cherry. "Why? What do you know of them?"

"They're pretty much defunct by now."

The old man laughed.

★ ★ ★

Several tins of fruit and peaches later, his appetite sated, Moriarity began to speak. He told them tales of life as it had been. Kevin and Bruce listened with mild interest because they had known some of the things of which he spoke to be true. Having heard the stories before, Dee considered the remains of the meal before them and the lengthening shadows of the day's end.

Riley weighed the parallels between this blind old man and Krieger, the tracker guide who had delivered herself and her friends to these Outlands. Both had carried staffs. They had that in common. Krieger had put on a good act, like he was disinterested, with no stake in society or civilization. And though Riley and her brother and Evan had found Krieger seated by himself in a bar, he had been social enough that he sought out New Harmony. Unlike this man Moriarity before them with his caduceus and his hole in the earth.

Krieger had died, though his death—Riley was certain—had been premeditated. Still, their tracker guide had not wanted to die alone. Moriarity was out here on his own, separate and apart, blind and alive.

They listened to him talk and watched the night descend about them, wondering if the gloom itself or anything in it was looking back. There was no indication. Bruce stood with the M40 in his arms, a wary eye on the encroaching dark. *Maybe*, Riley thought, Bruce had been right when he'd asked if there couldn't be another explanation for what they had seen, for what had happened to her brother's body, to the old man's. Yet she didn't think so. And it didn't look to her like Bruce—standing there eyeing the dark—thought so either.

Moriarity did not invite them into his cave, and even if he had, they probably would not have entered. They most definitely would not have spent the night in it, preferring the open sky and vast plains spread out about them. Only Burning Man's ineptness had kept them from being trapped in the apartment building.

Kevin asked what he had in his cave, to which Moriarity replied "chotskies, bric-a-brac and books." Bruce, alone among them standing, asked what kind of books and the old man replied with names none of them had ever heard—Friedman and Hayek and Nozick. When Kevin disregarded Dee's waved-palm warning—

Don't get him started! Don't get him started!

—and asked the old man what the books were about, the hermit launched into an exegesis.

He spoke of ideas and beliefs long forgotten, his speech erudite, rife with esoteric references. Moriarity spoke of the divine right and feudalism and other antiquated human relationships, of the rise of classical liberalism with its emphasis on freedom as the ultimate goal, of the individual human being as the decisive entity in society.

Kevin yawned.

Moriarity said that the state was never meant to get involved in the economy the way it had. Its existence, he assured them, was meant to ensure the freedom of markets at home, free trade among nations, and the protection of individual liberties. But the individualist tradition underlying classical liberalism itself was betrayed, he related sadly, and liberalism went from being the revolutionary doctrine of the free man—*and woman*, he added, with a nod towards Riley though he could not see her—to a mask for coercive, centralized state power.

Kevin had completely tuned him out.

Above them, the stars began to wink into life as the old man waxed poetically about what he and the men whose books he cherished saw as the magic of something he referred to as "the market". Riley was familiar with markets in New Harmony where she purchased items she needed, but quickly caught on that the market this man spoke to was a larger, all encompassing entity. Moriarity spoke of the "equilibrium" of this market and how individuals were protected in it because sellers always had more buyers and buyers always had more sellers, or that a worker could always find another boss and a boss another worker.

Moriarity pointed out that this was Friedman's example and not his own, and then he offered another that he posited to Friedman, noting, "When you buy a loaf of bread you don't know if the wheat it was made out of was grown by a Commie or a Republican, a constitutionalist or a Fascist, a Negro or a white." Riley would have laughed at the antiquated terms—Negro, Republican, constitutionalist—but the thought of spending a night with this mentally ill man did nothing for her somber mien or spirits.

Dee had risen and wandered over to where Bruce stood and the two men conferred in quiet tones. Moriarity never stopped speaking, explicating the benefits and drawbacks of monetary policy.

Riley again found herself wishing Anthony were here. Her brother would have loved this conversation, would have relished challenging the man. Or perhaps he wouldn't have. Anthony had known people, and maybe he would have been content to let the old man speak his piece. Anthony would have seen him as an old, lonely person out here by himself in the middle of what was basically nowhere. These were the rantings of an abandoned, friendless soul, one who clung to an archaic faith, desperate to believe.

When Moriarity stopped speaking and took a breath, Riley interrupted him. "So what are you then, out here?"

"I'm a free market liberal. In the classical sense."

"In the classical sense."

Moriarity nodded. "I am the forgotten man."

"The forgotten man."

"Yes. All of my life, my own labor—my own self-denial—were taken from me to benefit others."

"Well…" Riley gazed past the man to the outline of his cave in the night. "No one's taking your labor from you now, are they?"

"No, they most certainly are not." Moriarity shook the caduceus. "And I challenge any man to."

Riley looked at the man, studying him, considering his existence. "Do you ever get lonely out here, by yourself?"

"No one tells me what to do or how to do it."

"But you're all alone."

"I've got my books."

"Which you can't read any more."

"I've read them enough. I know what they say."

"Wouldn't you like to be able to read them again?"

"What do you mean?"

"Why don't you come with us?" Riley invited him, not sure why she did. An image—the fox girl on top of the beer truck, surrounded by the undead—had flashed in her mind. "Come back to where I'm from. They'd fix your vision."

The old man laughed. "I'm better off out here by myself." He touched the back of his head. "And how would I pay to fix my sight anyway?"

"You wouldn't."

"I wouldn't. Who would?"

"New Harmony. Where I'm from. The state would."

"Government. The state." The old man rubbed his forehead. "What good was the state when the zombies came? Do you know that most countries collapsed within a few months? Individuals stood against the zombies. Individuals."

"Yes," Riley granted him. "But they stood together."

"And the ones that didn't, fell." Kevin spoke up from where he lay near the fire. "We know, Moriarity. We were there."

"I'm nothing but an old man with big ideas in a world that isn't listening anymore."

He was an old man, Riley granted, an old, lonesome man whose ideas were fantasy. She yawned. "I'm getting tired."

"None of you were planning to murder me in my sleep, were you?"

They all ignored him.

"I'll take the first watch," Bruce announced, he and Dee rejoining them.

"Someone needs to warn him," Riley told the men she travelled with.

"Warn me about what?" Moriarity asked suspiciously.

Dee told him. "We might be being followed."

"*Might* be?"

"We're not sure."

"And who might it be following you? Burning Man Tribe? They couldn't follow you if you left bread crumbs."

"Not them," Riley admitted. "We don't know."

"Whoever it is," continued Dee, "I don't think it'll mess with you. But you might want to stick close to your cave for a day or two after we leave."

"I'm intrigued."

"I'm serious here, Moriarity."

"Just like strangers to show up and throw a man's routine off."

"Just be careful is what we're saying," said Bruce.

"The end's chased me I don't know how many times. I'm through running."

"Too old?" Kevin inquired.

"Got nothing to do with age."

"Just be careful, okay?" Dee echoed Bruce's words.

In reply, Moriarity hefted his handgun, the light from the fire glinting off the slide. "I wield powerful magic."

"No argument there." Kevin yawned.

Dee nodded. "Okay."

∗ ∗ ∗

By mid-morning of the day they had left Moriarity to his cave, they came to a river. It flowed fast and wide, dark with sediment. They kept the water in sight, their quads revving beneath them, each all too aware that the gas in their tanks was ebbing ever closer to empty with no hope of refueling.

Riley watched the country pass from Dee's back. They rolled by the shells of vehicles overgrown with plant life, their chassis melded with the undergrowth. There had been highways under these cars and trucks, but the roadways had long disappeared. Stone chimneys stood as tall as the winds and salts eroding them allowed. The sky was clear except for some innocuous white clouds, while a chill breeze stirred the grasses of the plains.

She spotted a groundhog on its hind feet in the wild flowers, standing stock still, observing their passage.

They reached the remains of a bridge, long fallen into the river on their side and the other. Passing the derelict span, they came upon overgrown mounds, greater and lesser piles of rubble and wreckage. Scattered among these were relatively intact blocks of two- and three-story buildings, all of it constituting the ruins of an abandoned town. The structures were largely swallowed by greenery, roots having expanded into crevices, forcing mortar and stone aside, entire facades crumbled and crumpled. Gutters hung from buildings, their leaders peeled off, stirring in the autumn breeze. Segments of paved roads were visible in spots through a covering of moss and lichen.

They halted the quads, killing the engines.

"Are those mannequins in the windows?" Kevin had the stock of his AK pressed to his shoulder, the muzzle somewhere between the ground and parallel to the ground.

Riley looked through the vines and bushes overgrowing openings that once fronted stores behind long-removed panes of glass. From window to window it was as Kevin had thought, figures propped in several, many of them mere shadowy forms in the murk of buildings.

"Looks like it," confirmed Bruce.

"Why would someone put them like that?" Riley pondered.

"A warning. Like scarecrows."

"A warning?" She looked at Bruce and again thought that he didn't look good. He was sweating. His shoulder must be infected.

"To scare off other humans."

The stillness in the ghost town was palpable. It brought to mind the abandoned city Riley had travelled through earlier. Unlike those streets, this place showed no signs of life. Riley didn't feel that anyone was observing their passage here. In fact, it seemed to her that nothing had passed through this place in years.

"You don't look too good, Bruce."

"Since when are you a doctor?" The other man waved off Dee's assessment. "I'll be okay."

"I'm going to take a look around," said Dee. "See what I can find."

"With that leg and foot?" Kevin looked at Dee. "You wait here. I'll be right back."

"I'll go with you." Riley unslung her AR-15.

As they walked they spoke to one another, neither Riley nor Kevin concerned that anyone would hear their conversation.

"I'm thinking we can follow the river to the sea," he said to her. The water had disappeared behind the ruins. "The quads aren't going to make it much further."

"Bruce doesn't look good."

"Nope."

"I cleaned out his shoulder as best as I could this morning again. He must have some bullet fragments or something in there."

They stopped to study a mannequin leaning halfway out of a window frame.

"Riley, we're not going to make it if we have to get there on foot."

"We can carry Dee if we have to."

The mannequin had been white once but exposure and weathering had stained it a different color.

"Let's see if we can find what I'm looking for."

"What *are* you looking for?"

The dark eyed man didn't answer.

They stepped through tall grasses between what had been two blocks of buildings. One had nearly disappeared completely, the wood-framed structures long since razed and devoured, termites feasting on the lumber's cellulose. The other block of houses and stores was still recognizable. Its roofs sagged, beams having given way and collapsed. Mortar and rock still rose, crumbled in sections. The process of quiet decay proceeded uninterrupted. Rust accumulated on exposed metal, concrete buildings deteriorated, and vegetation tore masonry asunder. Nature was slowly, inexorably, but certainly swallowing it all back up.

"Who was—" Riley squinted, trying to read the sun faded name on the former museum sign "—Ava Gardner?"

"An actress or something, I think."

Riley guessed the woman must have come from this place. "Who do you think set up the mannequins?"

"Whoever they were," Kevin looked around, "I think they're gone a long time now." He consulted his dosimeter. "Let me ask you, Riley. Why'd you go and invite him along last night?"

"Who? Moriarity?" Riley shrugged. "I felt bad."

"Did you think he'd say yes?"

She thought about it. "No."

"You felt bad about that girl, the one who thought she was a fox or something, didn't you?"

"I did. What'd you do before all this, Kevin? What was your job?"

"I was a therapist. School psychologist."

"That makes sense."

"Glad you think so." The dosimeter wasn't telling him anything they needed to worry about. "And I'm glad he didn't come along. Moriarity. You know, Bear would have killed him."

"Why would he have done that?"

"Call it philosophical differences." An owl inspected them from a window. "Dee wouldn't tell you that."

"Why not?" asked Riley.

As they walked by, the owl turned its head without moving its body.

"He wouldn't want you to think bad about him. About Bear."

Lifeless telephone and electrical wires snaked across the ground, disappearing into the soil and grass.

"When they saved me…" Kevin stopped where he was, resting the muzzle of the AK-47 against his thigh, the shoulder stock on the ground. "I was in a town a lot like this. I heard them. At first I thought it was just some people passing by, bit off more than they could chew. There were thousands of zombies where I was."

"Thousands?"

"Thousands. No way out. It was bad. I listened to them fight, the two of them—Bear and Nadjia. Nadjia," Kevin sighed the name. "Now there was a sight for sore eyes." He whispered this last sentence nostalgically. "She was from San Diego. You ever hear of San Diego?"

"No."

"That woman was *tough*. She could fight. You should have seen her. No Tris, but who is? You know, you kind of remind me of her though, come to think of it. A little bit."

"Of …?"

"Tris."

Riley didn't see how. "Why are you telling me all this?" she asked him, not because she wasn't interested or didn't want to listen. She hadn't expected his forthcomingness.

"I guess I'm just worried."

"We have something to worry about," Riley gestured to the dosimeter.

"Lots of things to worry about," granted Kevin, "But no, not the radiation. Not here."

"Worried about what then?"

"That if a person dies, whatever they know, whatever they've experienced, lived—what if it all dies with them?"

"And you're expecting…?"

"No." Kevin looked around the ghost town. "It's just this place. Brings back bad memories."

"I don't want to spend the night here."

"We're not. Let's keep looking. River should be over that way a bit."

They passed the hollowed hull of a personal computer left outdoors to weather the elements. A wren bolted from the hard drive casing and into the air. They tread across greened-over embankments and piles. The shells of cars rested on their undercarriages. Many were windowless, tendrils of vines and creepers twining around door and roof posts.

Riley spied a gap between two stone facades. "I have to go to the bathroom."

"You going to be awhile?"

"A minute."

"Okay. I'll wait up ahead."

She stepped into the space between the buildings, soil and human artifacts crunching under her feet. A chipmunk bounded from her. Riley worked her way through the narrow passage, advancing no further when the passage ended in a wall of vegetation. She undid her pants and squatted, going about her business. As she urinated, she considered the slate shingles underfoot, realizing she was now on top of what had once been a roof.

When she had finished, Riley stood and fixed her pants. She was about to head back the way she'd come, towards Kevin and what was left of the street. Before she did, she turned and considered the wall of green behind her. Riley found herself face to face with a mighty horned head. It was turned slightly in her direction, munching on plants, one wrinkle-hooded eye regarding her disinterestedly. She gasped before it registered in her mind that she was in no true danger.

Riley watched the ungulate as it browsed, stripping leaves off branches. When it had denuded a final branch, it backed up and trundled off.

Kevin came running when Riley called. Before he could ask, she told him. "I just saw a rhinoceros. A *rhinoceros.* Where'd that come from?"

"Probably escaped from a zoo."

"I've never seen one in real life."

"Like running into a dinosaur, huh?" Kevin pushed through the vegetation where the rhino had fed. "Yeah. Here we go."

Riley parted the branches and followed him. The rhinoceros had its back to them, wallowing in the river. Kevin wasn't looking at the rhino. His attention was captivated by a flat bottomed skiff washed up on the shore nearest them. "*That's* what I'm talking about," he told Riley.

✶ ✶ ✶

The snores accompanying Moriarity's mid-day nap, echoing through the cavern, ended suddenly as he opened an unseeing eye. The .45 was in his hand on his lap. Someone was outside his cave. He could *feel* the other's presence. Moriarity donned his welding helmet, masking his wrinkled face. He retrieved his caduceus, which served double duty as a talisman to ward off evil and as a cane. Padding to the mouth of his cave barefoot, he supported himself on the staff. He kept the pistol close in against his side, the business end of the .45 aimed outside towards the world and its inhabitants.

"I know you're out there." He called to whatever was there.

"And I know you're *in* there," it called back.

"I know why you're here."

"And I know where you're going."

The voice had answered from a different position. Whoever he was—and judging from the voice, it was a *he*—he was moving around out there.

"Oh yeah?" Moriarity asked from the safety of his cave, "And where's that?"

"Let me ask you a question…" When the query arrived, the voice had shifted again. "How long you been out here by yourself in this cave?"

"They told me you'd be by."

"Yeah. I figured they knew I was on their trail. What surprised me is they led me here to you."

It felt to Moriarity like the middle of the day, the way the sun fell on his face in the cave. "Why does that surprise you?"

"You can't see, can you?"

"I can see fine enough." The old man circled the pistol in the air, his attempt to menace. "Aren't you going to ask me where they're going?"

"Why? So you *won't* tell me?"

"That's right." Moriarity took a step closer to the mouth of his cave, confident.

"The same way I know where you're going, I know where they're going."

"I don't like your attitude, mister-whoever-you-are. I want you off this property. Posthaste. Which means *now*."

"Don't need to get so testy about it." The voice moved off, fading. "My curiosity is satisfied. I'll be on my way."

"You best be." Believing the other to be retreating, Moriarity grew bold and stepped forward, out of the cave. "I wield terrible magic."

The voice, when it answered, was behind him, nearer than it should have been. "I wield this."

The first blow knocked the welding helmet off the old man and put him down.

"And I know where you're going."

"Where would that be?" Moriarity asked from his hands and knees, his head swimming, still defiant.

"To sleep." The man stood above him. "Now go to sleep."

The second blow rendered him insensate.

When Moriarity came to, the sun was warm on his bare feet. He lifted his aching head from the ground and listened.

"You out there?"

When no one answered, he knew he was alone. Alive. He couldn't believe it. Alive. The old man sat up and felt around the earth about him, finding his staff, finding his pistol. He checked the handgun by feel and memory. All was as it should be. The man had clobbered him over the head and left him there with his gun loaded and his staff intact.

For whatever reason, Moriarity had been spared. His head ached and he suspected it would for some time. Should have stayed down the first time, he reprimanded himself. Could have had his melon split open. Moriarity got to his feet unsteadily, bracing himself on the caduceus. Had to find his welding helmet.

JUST BEFORE DAWN

It took little discussion for Kevin to convince them to continue to the coast on the river. Their quads would have sputtered out empty long before they'd reached their destination, leaving them to complete their trek on foot. With Dee's splinted leg and shot foot and Bruce growing feverish, that wasn't an option. Though he was sweating profusely, Bruce persisted in downplaying his physical state, insisting all was well.

They clambered aboard the skiff with their guns and packs, weighing the boat down in the water. They had taken boards from the town and used these as oars when necessary, the river's current taking them downstream. Bruce sat at the bow, the barrel of the M40A3 sniper rifle resting on the portside gunwale. Riley was next to him, their backs resting against the backpacks they'd propped against the bench seat. Dee and Kevin sat towards the stern of the small boat, Kevin with a plank of wood—a makeshift oar—directly behind Bruce because Bruce was not rowing. Dee's FN-FAL jutted out over the transom, above the water.

The river had carved its channel from the earth for some two million years. Catfish, shad and bass darted beneath them. Occasionally a sunken kayak or canoe poked out of the water they moved through. Aside from a skeleton in the river, they saw no sign of the living or the dead. The sun was warm, the air was cool, and Riley found herself nodding off.

When she opened her eyes, Dee's oilskin Drover covered her and Bruce like a blanket. She sat up, straightening her legs. Turning, she thanked Dee, who smiled. The river had changed, empting into an estuary. The water was slower moving and brackish, wide enough that details from either shore were difficult to make out. The sun had begun its descent.

They saw the dilapidated span long before they floated under it. A series of highways connected to either end of the bridge, wishbone interchanges no car had travelled in many years. More than three kilometers in length, the eighty-meter main span under which they passed looked intact. Twenty meters above them, sea birds rested amid the structural steel plate girders and thousands of X crossframes. The birds remained in place, noting their passage, unperturbed.

Some distance after the bridge they put ashore for the evening.

"Bruce. You okay?"

"Yeah, I'll be all right," he told Riley. He was sweating but he was standing.

She handed him more antibiotics. "Take these, okay?"

He took what she gave him and swallowed the pills, chasing them down with a long draught from his canteen.

The following morning they woke to a visitor.

"How long has it been standing there?" Dee asked Kevin, who was on watch.

"The last hour or so. It wandered over, been standing there ever since."

The zombie stood in place on the border of their camp. Its pants, reduced to rags, hung off its bony hips, low slung. A blackened, cruddy shirt covered its torso. Flies circled and alighted upon its sallow frame. It stared at them with blank eyes set back in darkened sockets, its low moans barely audible.

"Why hasn't it attacked?" Dee questioned its inactivity.

"Maybe it's shy."

"What do you think it's thinking?"

"It doesn't think like we do." Bruce had sat up, soaked in sweat. "Why didn't anyone wake me up for my watch?"

"Hard to believe they were human once." Dee slipped into his coat.

"They were," confirmed Kevin.

"Not any more." Bruce drank from his canteen, emptying it. "Why didn't anyone wake me, I asked."

"Bruce, look at you." Kevin never took his eyes off the zombie, holding the dosimeter out in its direction.

"Let's wake Riley." Dee patted the Colt he wore. "Don't want to scare her."

Bruce peeled back the bandage on his shoulder, under his shirt, eyeing his wound. "It could smell us a mile off."

"Speak for yourself," said Kevin. "I'm not ripe."

* * *

After Dee had set a pot to boil, he roused Riley. She saw the thing on the periphery of their camp and immediately asked how long it'd been there.

"About an hour or so now," Kevin repeated for her benefit. "I didn't want to alarm any of you guys," he spoke to them all, "and I still don't, but listen—Bruce was right—we *are* being followed."

The others looked expectantly at him.

"Here." Kevin handed Dee the single lens field glasses. "Over that way." Dee glassed the scene, *harrumphed*, and went to hand the minocular to Bruce, who had not gotten up off the ground yet and waved it away. Dee passed the tool to Riley. She scanned the horizon to their northwest, the sky there dark enough with the retreating night that a campfire showed clearly. She thought she saw one figure seated next to its flame. It was hard to tell, because even with the magnifying lens the distance between their two camps was great.

"Who do you think it is?" Riley asked the men. "Burning Man?"

"It's one of those mutants." Bruce hadn't even looked.

"Couldn't be those people who were following you, Riley," Dee agreed. "They're all dead."

"Riley, the little red head," Kevin tried to make out what details he could through the minocular, "you saw her dead?"

"Well, no, that bomb pretty much..."

"She's dead, Kev." Bruce coughed.

The zombie loitering outside their camp lowed plaintively.

"Could be anybody out here." Kevin lowered the minocular. "Whoever they are—*whatever* they are—they're not trying to hide themselves any longer."

"No they are not." Dee furrowed his brow.

"We could walk over there," said Riley.

"And?"

"See who they are," she told Dee. "See what they want. Kill them."

"We could wait here," Kevin built on her suggestion. "Ambush them."

"I think we should keep going," Dee said, the water in the kettle simmering. "If we ever want to catch up to the others. We're already three days behind them. Taking this river was great, but it took us south of where we need to be."

Bruce still hadn't risen. "Hope the hermit is okay."

"Come on, Kevin," Riley said. "You and I will go. It'll take us most of the morning to get there, but whoever it is, they'll be on the move soon."

"Riley—"

"Dee. You or Bruce are in no condition—"

"Riley."

"—it's got to be me and Kevin."

"No, Riley, listen to me for a minute, okay? We have to assume that whoever that is back there, he's dangerous. Very dangerous. Think: how'd he survive the battle with Tris and the bomb?"

"Maybe he wasn't at the battle," Riley countered. "Maybe he hid. Maybe he's not as tough as we're afraid he is. We do think he was hiding, right? That he heard every word we said on that riverbank?"

"*Think*, Riley. How has he managed to follow us as far as he has? And why is he showing himself now?"

"Who cares why—"

"*We* have to care why. *Think*, I said. We split up. You and Kevin head back there. It makes it easier for him—for it. Then me and Bruce, what have we got? We're left alone here, and—it's like you said yourself a minute ago—look at us."

"I like Riley's idea, go back there and kill whoever it is," acknowledged Kevin. "But Riley, Dee is right. We have to stick together."

"What do we do? Wait for him to attack us first?"

"That thing wants to provoke a confrontation," Kevin smacked his hands together like he was squashing a fly, "we give it to him."

"Whoever he is, he's smart." Dee peered through the minocular. "He waited all this time before letting us see him. He wants us to see him. He's got a fire going. Believe me, Riley, if I could, I'd walk back there with you and Kevin—"

"Hey," Bruce griped, "what about me?"

"—and we'd take care of business. But something's not right here." Dee lowered the field glasses. "Yeah, something's not right about this."

The zombie groaned, bringing their attention back to it.

"Hey!" Dee hailed the dead thing. "Hey, you!"

It moaned back at him.

"I think it's talking to you, Bruce," said Kevin. "Yeah. It's like," he lowered his voice, drawing out his words, "Bruuuuuu-sssssss, where's myyyyy cooooooough-fee?" Bruce managed a weak smile.

The water in the kettle started to warble, a low, shrill sound that gave to a whistle, like a wind picking up steam. Dee handed the minocular to Riley and limped from the fire, towards the zombie, half-hopping on his injured foot and leg. His lower limb was splinted straight with a length of PVC piping they'd found along the way. The undead watched him come, cocking its head inquisitively at the man.

It whined and parted its jaws, revealing a mouthful of broken and jagged teeth.

Dee fired his revolver once and the zombie went down. He limped back to the others, holstering the Python in its belly band, the kettle whistling sharply. Back at the fire, he donned an oven mitt and removed the kettle from the flame, the whistle trailing off.

"Get over here, Bruce. Let's clean out that shoulder."

The mouth of the river widened as it flowed out into the sound. They resorted to their improvised oars to a greater degree than previously, steering their small vessel near enough to shore to keep land in sight. The fish here lived out in the sea but migrated up the river to spawn.

By mid-morning they spied a pier projecting into the water. They glassed the scene with the minocular. A boat not much larger than their own puttered out into the open water of the sound, away from them, its outboard motor inaudible to them from this distance. Wispy vapors touched the sky from beyond the trees fronting the pier. Smoke.

"That's what we need," Kevin remarked of the vessel.

"I'm not feeling so hot…" Bruce finally admitted, and he didn't look it either. "…so let me make sure I have this right. We're further south than where we need to be, right? Because we took the river?"

Dee told him that he was correct.

"Are we still serious about this Africa bullshit?"

No one answered him.

"Okay, good. I thought it was just me."

"We need to find someone who can help us help you, Bruce."

"If we can get to New Harmony," Riley reminded them all, "that won't be a problem."

"So we need that boat," explained Kevin. "It'll get us where we need to go a lot faster than this thing."

"You think they're just going to give us their boat?"

"Let's go talk to them," Dee suggested.

None of them particularly liked the idea. There were four of them, and although it appeared there was only one man on the boat, there was no telling how many people there were where the smoke emanated from. Riley knew that if the men she travelled with were a different kind of people, they would have all waited at the pier, hidden, letting the boat come back and taking it from its pilot, forcefully if need be. Instead they beached their own small skiff and went ashore.

They proceeded guardedly and, from necessity, slowly. There were no signs of life at the pier, a wooden dock that overhung the water beneath by half a meter. A few barrels of diesel fuel were stacked where the wooden structure met the beach. A short strip of sand gave to trees where a clear path had been trampled through the underbrush. They moved through the trees together, Kevin supporting Dee, Riley with an eye on Bruce—"I got it"—the wind rustling the branches about them.

A short distance later they looked out from the trees onto the remains of a society. A dilapidated strip mall faced a simple house across a distance of twenty meters. The strip mall was barely recognizable. Like many of the abandoned structures they had passed along the way, this one was largely given to corrosion and disrepair. Parts of its walls had come down and the last two stores had collapsed into heaps of building materials.

The house looked better kept, solid save where one part of its roof had been boarded over. Further in the distance, a water tower stood against the sky.

Three children played in what had been the street between the house and the strip mall. The lush grasses had long before retaken the territory, but someone had cleared a space for the kids. They kicked a ball back and forth between the weeds and the wild grasses; a girl no more than eleven, another girl younger than the first, and a boy younger than both .

The older of the girls saw them first: Riley supporting Dee, Kevin helping Bruce stay on his feet, crossing from the trees. She grabbed her sister's arm and ran with her and the boy to the house, calling for someone inside. A young man came out of the house, armed with a rifle.

"This guy tries anything," Dee had one arm over Riley, his other hand helping to balance himself as he hopped forward, "you guys take him out."

They kept their muzzles down at the ground. The guy from the house kept his up towards the sky. When they got close enough to him, they could see he was little more than a kid himself, a young man grown tall and awkward, thin. "What do you all want?" He tried to sound tough, but there was no mistaking the look of worry on his face.

Kevin answered. "We want to talk to you about the boat we saw down at the dock."

"You'd need to talk to my uncle about that."

"Can we? Can you go get him?"

"Nope."

"Why not?"

"He's gone. Won't be back."

"That was him on the boat, wasn't it?"

The kid didn't answer.

"He left you here with the kids, didn't he?"

The young man took a step back, lowering the barrel of his rifle.

"Stop!" Riley stepped forward, dropping her assault rifle, putting herself between the kid and the three men of Bear's Army. She turned to them first. "Do you guys have any idea how threatening you sound and look to him?" To the young man she said, "And you, what'd you even come out of the house for?"

"What do you mean?"

"Four people show up at your house with guns, so why'd you come outside?"

"I wanted to see what you all wanted."

"What if we were bad people? You came out of that house, anything could have happened to you."

"Maybe."

"*Maybe?* And then what would happen to those kids?"

"Who's to say you're not?" There was a blackened tooth in the guy's mouth. "Bad people, I mean?"

"Lucky for you, we're not." Riley thought about meeting Dee days earlier. She thought about the family she and Anthony and their friends had spied on their first day out of New Harmony, how they hadn't made contact with them because they hadn't wanted to alarm them.

150

How they'd wanted to avoid a situation just like this one. "You're just going to have to believe us."

"Your uncle," asked Dee, "he won't be back at all, or won't be back until later?"

"Why?" The kid still looked suspicious. "What do you want?"

"We want to find out about renting your boat."

"Why?"

"We want to get out of here," explained Kevin. "Our friend is hurt."

"He don't look so good," the kid said of Bruce, who looked like he was going to fall over where he stood.

"We'll pay," Kevin assured him.

The kid looked at them, puzzled. "Where do you want to go?"

"Out onto the water. The ocean."

"Why would you want to do that?"

"We'll pay," Kevin told him again.

"You said that. I told you, you're gonna have to talk to my uncle."

"When's he getting back?" Dee asked.

"Tonight sometime."

"Then we'll wait for him," said Kevin.

"Well, shit," the kid said, "don't think I'm going to invite you all into the house."

"We'll wait over there," Riley pointed. "In those buildings."

"Nothing in there but junk and some mice."

"Yeah, well we've got some people here who are pretty badly banged up. We can't go far."

"Maybe you're not bad people," the kid weighed the situation. "But be honest with you, I'm not so comfortable with you this close to my sisters and brother."

"Look." Riley laid it out for him. "There's four of us and there's one of you and some little kids. We're not going to hurt any of you. We're not bad people."

"We aren't either."

"My name is Riley. And this is Bruce, that's Kevin and the big, bald guy is Dee."

"I'm Elmore. You scared my sister Melissa something bad."

"We're sorry about that."

"What's that on your head, mister?" Elmore asked Dee.

"It's an Oakley Medusa headpiece."

"A what?"

"It's kind of like my hat."

"Makes you look somethin' fierce."

"That's the idea."

"Like a gorgon or somethin'."

As she had the day before, Riley turned to the three men she travelled with. "Someone's got to tell him."

"Tell me what?" Elmore's suspicion—recently abated—returned.

"We're being followed."

The kid waited for an explanation.

"This person following us," Dee warned, "he isn't going to be friendly."

"And you're telling me this because?"

"Because of Melissa," Riley said quickly. "Because of those other little kids you've got in there. Because of you, Elmore."

"If you're so worried that you're putting us in danger, why don't you get out of here then?" Elmore nodded to Dee's foot and the stained bandages above Bruce's chest. "We're already gonna have zombies dropping by."

"We're sorry about that." Dee meant it. "We really are. We're going to put someone up in that water tower over there. Keep an eye on things until we leave. You have food for those kids?" He asked Elmore. "For yourself?"

"Yeah. Why?"

Dee gestured to Kevin. "Give him some."

Kevin knelt down on one knee, placing his AK-47 on the ground by his side. He opened his backpack and retrieved some freeze-dried packages. He held them out to Elmore. The kid made no move forward.

"Just put them down," Riley told Kevin. "Like I said, we're going to wait inside over there. And you're right, Elmore. If there are any zombies around here, they're going to be showing up sometime soon. We'd rather not be out here in the open with them when they do. And that's just one more thing for you to look out for with those kids."

"When your uncle gets in," Dee requested, "can you tell him we'd like to speak to him?"

"You bet I will."

"Okay, listen, Elmore," Riley told him sincerely. "I'm sorry we got off the way...I'm sorry this played out the way it did. We really are not bad people."

He nodded.

"Okay, Elmore," she smiled at him. "You know where we'll be when your uncle gets in."

* * *

"Bruce," said Dee. "This doesn't feel right, us leaving you here." Dee leaned on Riley while Kevin, bent over with his hands on his knees, caught his breath. Kevin had lent Dee a hand hopping from the buildings to the base of the water tower, a task that—with the distance and their assorted injuries—took them the better part of an hour.

"Yeah, well," Bruce rasped. He'd volunteered to climb the tower. Dee's leg and foot wouldn't allow him to do it. Kevin was the only one among them who, if he had to, could pilot the boat. Without speaking to it, each man felt for Riley and what she had gone through these past weeks. They didn't want to put her up on the tower by herself. So Bruce had said he'd go, that he was the best shot, that he had the sniper rifle, that the rest up top would do him good.

"Wait." Kevin straightened, sliding out of his pack. "I've got something for you."

"Your side bothering you, Kevin?" Riley asked.

"Only when I breathe. Here, Bruce." Kevin pulled two milky, twenty-centimeter tubes from his bag. "Glow sticks," he explained as he handed them to Bruce. "Bend them to make them light up. You need help, place one where we can see it up there."

"You'll be able to see this?" Bruce sounded skeptical.

"With Dee's minocular. They stay lit for six to eight hours."

"Whoever that is following us," Bruce stared up the ladder to the catwalk that circled the water drum. "I'll see him from up there a long time before he sees me."

"If he's still following us," Riley said, though she had no doubt whoever was on their trail would still be.

"Stay alert up there." Kevin looked up at his friend, who was drenched in sweat.

"I'm planning on it."

"Bruce," Dee told him. "It's something you can't handle, fire a shot."

"Believe me, I will," The hint of a smile passed over Bruce's worn face.

"Here, take another canteen." Riley handed him another.

"Thanks."

"Whether the uncle is back or not," Kevin promised, "by morning one of us is going to come and get you."

"Well, I'll see you when I see you then."

"Bruce?"

"Yeah, Dee?"

"You see that thing following us? Just shoot it."

Bruce raised the sniper rifle before slinging it over his back for the ascent. "That's what I was thinking."

* * *

They watched Bruce climb and when he reached the catwalk he waved down to them that he was okay. Leaving him to his perch, Kevin and Riley supported Dee and the three headed back to the erstwhile strip mall. It took them another hour and by this time the sun was well into its descent. They spent the remainder of the daylight finding a suitable place to sleep amid the mess that constituted the interior of the tumbledown stores, settling on a suite of rooms on the second floor. The stairwell creaked and protested under their feet and parts of the roof and corridor wall were open to the elements, but the floors of the rooms they chose were solid.

They prepared a meal and ate it. Kevin borrowed Dee's minocular several times, focusing on the water tower, squinting against the glare as the sun sank on the horizon. Bruce's figure was lost to them on the other side of the structure. No glow sticks shone.

When Kevin gave him back his minocular, Dee swept it from the tower to the house across the grass from them. A little kid's face loomed large in the eyepiece. Dee lowered the field glasses, the child clear to him from this distance. He waved to the boy, who raised a hand tentatively in return before disappearing inside the house.

Riley asked the question that was on all their minds. "What are we going to do if the uncle doesn't want to let us use his boat?"

"We're going to have to take it," replied Dee.

"I'd hate to have to do that to Elmore."

"We can always ask them to come with us."

"You two," scoffed Kevin. "Inviting everyone along. What is that about?" Then, soberly, "We need to get Bruce looked at. He's not doing well."

"We will," Riley vowed.

Shortly after the moon rose, the first zombies appeared. Dee, seated at the window, eyeing the terrain, spotted them first.

"I'm going downstairs." Kevin picked up a section of pipe discarded on the floor. "Take care of this."

"Don't go alone." Riley stood to join him.

"You sure?"

When she nodded, Kevin held out another length of piping to her. She took it, noting it was the longer of the two, which meant she wouldn't have to get as close to the things as he would. She thanked him.

"Be careful," Dee told them.

"You sure you're up to this?" Kevin asked her as the rickety staircase creaked under them. Riley assured him she was.

They stepped out into the night with the dead things in it. The zombies were clearly visible, the moon showing all. Kevin raised the pipe and pointed with his index finger, indicating the zombies he would dispatch.

Riley crouched down in the grass and approached the two undead she had been allotted. Neither seemed aware. The closest of the two was looking elsewhere and she thought about calling out but did not. It wore a barber shop's backward cape. Riley's pipe connected with the back of its skull. It staggered forward a step and began to turn towards her, obviously bothered. Now she had its attention. The other's, too.

Riley swung harder, knocking the zombie to the ground.

She walked to the next beast, which was doddering towards her, its arms extended. Side stepping its reach, she cracked it in the face. Its nose caved into its head and it hit its knees, an undead penitent. Riley struck it once more, leaving a visible dent in its skull. The zombie slumped over in the grass and shuddered. Riley prodded it with the pipe. It shook but did not rise.

Kevin joined her. He'd taken out his three targets and was breathing heavy, holding his side.

"You okay?" she asked him.

The creature Riley had first laid out was crawling towards her on its elbows and forearms. Kevin bee-lined to it and braced a foot on either side of its torso, bringing his pipe up over his head. "Sometimes—" *whack* "—these things—" *whack* "—are pretty tough—" he bludgeoned it a third time and it lay motionless. "There."

Riley looked away from its demolished head.

"No wonder," Kevin remarked, staring into the mess atop its neck. "Thing had a steel plate in its skull."

Riley's second zombie had stopped trembling.

"It's dead," she said as Kevin put his foot on the back of its neck.

"Better safe than sorry." He crushed its skull as he had the first. "While we're out here," Kevin said as he stepped away from the corpse, "I'd like to talk to Elmore."

Riley called out to the house, hailing the boy. He came out into the night with his rifle.

"What you want?" It was a question, not a threat.

"They're coming now," Kevin warned him. "Thought we should tell you."

"Yeah, I saw."

"You stay inside with your sisters and brother," said Riley. "Don't go outside for anything, okay?"

"You don't have to worry about me."

"We might have to come out here once in awhile," Kevin added, "deal with these things." When the boy nodded, Kevin asked him, "What's out there? On the water?"

"Some islands a ways out. Nothing between here and there but a bunch of wrecks."

"Any of the islands inhabited?"

"You mean do they have people living on them?"

"That's what I mean."

"There's one, old woman lives on it with her dogs."

"An old woman and her dogs? She all alone?"

"For years now. Her family's all gone. My uncle used to go out there, check on her once in awhile. Make sure she was okay."

"No zombies out there on that island?"

The kid didn't answer immediately and when he did—"She's an old lady, but she knows what she's doing"—his answer didn't seem to address Kevin's question.

Riley asked him if there were zombies out on the islands.

"Not that I know of."

"Then how come you guys stay here? Why wouldn't you have moved out to one of the islands by now?"

"My uncle prefers the mainland. Zombies ain't so bad when you know how to deal with them."

"Hey, Elmore, listen up," Kevin's voice grew very serious. "You remember what I said about someone following us, right? You keeping an eye on those kids?"

"Yeah. And thank you for that food. They enjoyed it."

"You're welcome." Kevin unfastened his pack and retrieved several more freeze-dried pouches. "Here," he offered. Elmore stepped forward this time, accepting the packages from Kevin's hands.

"I thank you again," Elmore said. "My uncle should be back in soon. He never stays out past dark too long."

"Well, we'll talk to him later on then. Or tomorrow. Goodnight."

"Goodnight." His blackened tooth clear in the moonlight, Elmore smiled before returning to his house and his wards.

* * *

Dee observed their melee with the undead and their conference with the kid from the window. He had not been able to hear the conversation so they related the salient points mentioned. When they told him about the island and the old lady, Dee said, "Her dogs, huh?"

"The kid's all right." Kevin dismissed what had earlier posed itself as a possible threat.

"I believe he is, Kev. But if the uncle doesn't want to work with us, we're still going to have to take the boat."

"Dee, if we just take their boat, these people are screwed."

"So hopefully the uncle will be willing to work with us, Riley.""Wonder how Bruce is doing." Kevin stood looking out the window. "Better view of the water tower in the room next door."

"There many Zed under the water tower?" Riley found herself wondering if the undead could climb.

"Can't really tell from this distance." Dee motioned futilely with the minocular. "Even with this."

"Better view in the other room."

"You want to move to the other room, Kev?"

"Yeah. Let's move over there. Have a better bead on Bruce, still be able to see the house."

"Somebody give me a hand?" Dee asked. "Please?" Riley went over to him, reaching down and helping him up. He braced himself against his FN-FAL until he could stand, then propped the rifle with its under-barrel chainsaw against the wall near the window, toothed blade up. He draped his arm around Riley's shoulder, his other hand around his minocular and hobbled along on one leg as she supported him from the room.

Kevin gathered up their packs and rifles but was unable to lug Dee's assault rifle on top of all he already carted. He left the room, thinking he'd come right back and get it.

The store they moved into occupied a corner of the strip mall and—as Kevin had promised—provided a better view of the water tower while the house across from them remained easily seen. They placed their gear down and spent some time at the windows, scrutinizing the night.

* * *

Kevin was snoring quietly and Riley found herself entertaining morbid thoughts. Her mind wandered back to the first city she had visited here in the Outlands, the numbers marked on each façade speaking to the corpses within. The adult skeletons on either side of the child's bones, all in the bed. The man or woman alone in the port-a-potty. The barn. *The barn.* She sat up, banishing that show of horrors from her mind.

Moonlight shafted over Dee's features at the window where he kept watch.

"What is it?" Riley asked him, aware that it was later than she had thought.

"The uncle came back," he responded quietly.

She looked over at Kevin on his back.

"Don't wake him, Riley."

She joined Dee at the window. His voice was hushed. "He stood there talking to Elmore, looking this way."

"How's he look?"

"He doesn't look like trouble, if that's what you're asking."

"Aren't those the ones you've got to watch?"

"Yeah. Like you."

She brushed aside the compliment. "How long were they out there?"

"A few minutes. We've got Zed on the premises."

"Do they know we're in here?"

"They know we're around here somewhere. They're not going anywhere."

"Dee, what do you think Bruce is thinking?"

He handed her the minocular and she moved to the next window, set in the wall at a ninety-degree angle to the first.

"He's probably spooked," Dee guessed as Riley glassed the water tower. Even on a night as well lit as this one, the tower was an indistinct outline against the dark blue sky. "I would be. Wouldn't you be?"

"I would be, too."

"I think they'll come over in the morning," Dee said of Elmore and his uncle.

"Do you think Bruce is cold up there?"

"I think Bruce is all right. Bruce is a tough son of a gun. We'll get him somewhere where someone can take a better look at that shoulder tomorrow. Go and get yourself back to sleep, Riley."

"I don't know if I can. You want to lie down? I'll stay up."

"Nah, I'm tweaked."

Dee listened to her settle back down on the floor. In a few minutes her breathing had changed, deeper, rhythmic. Riley was asleep.

The smell of the ocean was strong here, salt and brine. A zombie sounded outside, a lugubrious cry. Dee glanced from the dark shadows in the room about them, to the house across the way, silent and still.

He studied the water tower.

He'd told Riley that Bruce would be okay, that they'd get him the attention he needed. And he'd meant it. They'd *take* the boat if the uncle wasn't accommodating. Dee wouldn't want to have to, but he would if he needed to.

For Bruce. For them.

* * *

"Dee. Wake up."

Kevin hailed him out from the dream realm.

"W-what is it, Kev?"

Kevin beckoned. Dee got up on his one good leg and limped across the room, joining him at the window. "Look." Kevin passed him the minocular.

Dee scrunched his eye shut before affixing it to his face. He almost immediately removed it, wiping sleep from his eyes. Through the lens, the sky to the east was lightening, a blue-ish tint foretelling the day. Stars dotted the sky to the west. Even with the magnification device, the water tower remained an outline in the distance.

"What am I looking for?"

"I thought I heard something, Dee."

"What'd you think you heard?"

"A scream."

Dee studied the water tower, a tenebrous shadow against a darker night.

"Can't see much," he remarked.

"What is it?" Riley was sitting up, blinking.

"It's nothing." Dee watched the volume of his reply. There were many things outside now. "Get your stuff ready."

He panned the vast stretch of grassland, dusky in the moonlight. He scanned the strip of land between the water tower and the street above which they took refuge, forbidding umbrae faltering about in the gloom.

Screams sounded from across the way. Three children ran out of Elmore's house. Melissa, gripping the little girl's arm, ran in one direction. The third child, the boy Dee had seen through the window, ran off in the opposite direction, towards the pier and the boat.

"Oh no," Riley whispered.

"It's here," stated Dee.

Kevin was looking out another window.

"Kev."

The other man did not reply, lost in his reverie of the water tower.

"*Kev!*"

"Right, Dee," his attention returned to their room. "You're right."

"Riley. Kev. You guys get out of here. Get down to the dock. Get the boat ready."

"What about Bruce?" demanded Riley.

"I need you guys to go, *now*." He looked at Kevin, a look that said it all. "I'll get Bruce."

Riley gave him a look. How was he going to get Bruce?

"Have that boat ready to go," Dee adjured, "and wait for us. Anyone gives you a hard time—" Dee nodded across the road towards the darkened home "—or tries to stop you, you kill them."

"I think we should stick together," protested Riley.

"I'm getting along easier on my leg than you are on yours," Kevin pointed out. "I can go get Bruce."

Dee could have smacked his own forehead. They weren't getting it, neither of them. "We can't argue about this—not now! Kev," he reminded him, wasting valuable time, "you're the only one who knows how to pilot that boat." Dee stared out the window towards the house the children had fled from, the Python in one big hand. "Go do it!"

Riley and Kevin gathered together their packs, taking Dee's as well. "Hey—" Kevin patted him on his bald head "—thanks," before he left the room.

"Dee."

He turned from the window. Riley was standing in the doorway to the next room.

"Come back to us fast."

"I will, Riley. You go."

He listened to them, the sounds of the stairs beneath their retreating feet. Dee waited with the iodine stink wafting in from the water, with the soft cries of the undead below. He waited, listening for the sounds of his friends making off in what remained of the night, but their getaway was silent. He waited as he had waited above the murder hole, peering down for Burning Man. He strained his ears for any noise Bruce might make tramping through the grass—"Get to the boat! Get to the boat!"—but no one called out, no one came. The tower stood where it had, unchanged.

Dee swallowed a lump in his throat. Bruce wasn't coming because Bruce was done. He knew it. The sky to the east was lightening as the day encroached, banishing the murk. The zombies below took on detail and form: a hideous congregation, most of them standing in place, a few wandering about. He eyed the house across from him, knowing it was there, the thing that had followed them all these days, whatever it was.

He thought he heard a noise from the other room, through the wall. The room, it dawned on him, where he'd left his rifle. *Shit.* Dee hung the minocular around his neck and steadied the Python. Behind him, in the caliginous gloom of the rooms Riley and Kevin had left through, nothing stirred. He believed he was alone.

Dee caught a whiff of something but couldn't place it.

With mounting anxiety, he retrieved the minocular and glassed the water tower. Its shape was more distinct to him now. He could make out the railing that ringed the tank. There was still no sign of Bruce, no green glow, nothing he hoped to see. A rafter cracked once somewhere in the building.

Bruce. Where are you, Bruce? Come on, Bruce.

Dee feared he had seen the last of his friend. Zombies stumbled through the no-man's land between the tower and these buildings. He wondered how many were crawling through the grasses unseen.

He didn't understand why he was as scared as he was. He hadn't felt this in the apartment building, manning the hole in the floor. He glanced out the window to the ground immediately beneath, to a large rhododendron.

Bruce. Why, Bruce, why?

Dee's nose warned him of a new scent, something acrid in the air, masking the briny sea. The zombies below were stirred up, obviously excited, louder. Excited by what?

The windows in Elmore's house glowed.

Fire. Dee pressed his back to the wall beside the window and breathed, listening. He risked quick glances through the windowless frame, spotting the flames as they licked their yellowish orange tongues above the sills. Those people. They were all dead, Dee knew. Bruce, too.

And then, as if to confirm his worst suspicions, a voice came from the dark, carrying through the wall of the room next to his.

"You hear me?" It sounded like a man.

Dee wrapped one hand around the other—

"Yeah, I know you can hear me."

—and straightened the .357 at the wall.

"You killed all my family."

The thing was in the room next to his. *The fucking room next to his!* The room with his rifle, Dee reminded himself. *Fuck.* How it had gotten there, he had no idea.

"Nothing to say about that?"

"I didn't." Dee called back, weaker than he'd intended. *Keep talking.* He tried again, more forcefully. "*We* didn't." If he could keep it talking, he could center the thing, get a good bead on its location. These walls were shit for stopping acoustics and conceivably wouldn't do much to slow a bullet. "You're talking about those other people. And they're all dead now."

"Them."

Dee eased the Python's firing pin back—

"You."

—locking it in place.

"All the same to me." Its tone, dipped in acrimony, brimmed with contempt.

"How have you been following us?" Dee's initial fright was giving to curiosity, to something else.

"Wouldn't you like to know." The voice came from another part of the room beyond. It wasn't standing still in there. "Wouldn't your friend in the water tower have liked to have known?"

Dee almost cursed at the thing, almost fired. But he forced himself to hold his tongue and check his trigger finger. There was a chance—a very slim chance—that the thing in the next room was bluffing him. Sneaking up on a hardened soldier like Bruce, even when he was wounded, sneaking up on him when he was on the alert and the only access to him was a climb up a steel ladder—*that* would have been no easy task.

Bruce might still be sitting up there, greeting the dawn. Or so Dee wished to hope. And because there was this minute chance, he decided to play it and replied, "Was that her who screamed?"

The thing laughed at that. "Yeah. *He* screamed." It had corrected Dee's choice of pronouns, letting Dee know without a doubt that Bruce was done for. "He screamed all the way down."

"Mother—" Dee lost his cool and fired the big revolver, blowing a hole in the wall. The cylinder rotated as the hammer dropped, plaster dust wafting into the room. He fired out the Python and reloaded, waiting for it to speak, and when it didn't he started to think that *maybe*, just maybe he had gotten lucky and wounded or killed it.

"You done?" It called to him from the fresh holes in the wall. No such luck. "If it's any consolation, I didn't hurt the old man."

Dee wondered why he believed it.

"What your family was doing to people," Dee tracked the wall with the revolver. "It wasn't right."

"Want me to tell you what they said when they saw me?"

Dee paused. Who was it referring to now? He squeezed his eyes shut against his anger and opened them. *Can't think that way.* Kevin and Riley would have made the boat long before this thing showed up.

"I didn't kill the kids," it said, and Dee knew it spoke of the family across from them, the family's whose house was burning freely now. "I could have, maybe even should have, but I didn't. And I wouldn't have hurt the younger guy, either..." They knew it meant Elmore. "...except he wanted to play hero. You know what happens to heroes? That what you want to play?" It goaded him. "*Hero?*"

Dee pressed his back to the wall behind him and as silently as he could with his bad leg and foot, he worked his way across the wall, away from his place by the window. Adrenaline was rushing through his body. There was a chance he was going to have to run from here, run

Tony Monchinski

on a broken foot and a broken leg, and he thought he could do it if he had to.

"Actually, I didn't kill him, either." The voice was somewhere else in the other room. "Just smacked him around, trussed him up a bit. Set their place on fire…"

Dee took his eyes off the wall and glanced out to the house. Thick, black smoke billowed from the windows into the paling sky.

"Don't see how he's getting out of that."

"Is there any chance we can talk this out?" Dee called. "You and me?"

"No chance."

"You got a name?"

"Chase."

"Chase." Dee shook his head. "That's appropriate. I'm Dee. Like the fourth letter in the alphabet."

"I wasn't asking."

Dee centered the front sight of the revolver on the exact spot in the wall from which the voice had emanated, sighting over the red insert.

"I'm going to kill you," said Chase, "and then I'm going to kill the other guy and the woman." The voice hadn't moved. "Save her for last."

Dee refused to answer.

"Hey. Bet I know something you don't know."

"Oh yeah?" He shouldn't answer, Dee knew, but he did. "What's that?"

"Bet *you* didn't know *I* know how to use one—of—these!"

Dee threw himself to the side as the wall separating their rooms came apart, chunks of plaster dust and Gypsum board exploding outwards. The hammering of his FN-FAL violated the early morning silence. As the wall above his head burst apart, Dee fired a round from the Python, the revolver close to his body. He extended his arm and continuing to drop the hammer. 7.62mm and .357 rounds tore through the wall in opposite directions.

Firing out the revolver, Dee rolled over the chunks of drywall and through the dust coating the floor. Chase adjusted his aim and the full metal jacketed rounds geysered floorboards and tiles around Dee, who lay flat on his back, dumping the empties from his Python. The rifle silenced.

"Still want to know how I followed you, *hero?*"

A severed head came through the wall, Chase's hand gripping it by its hair. The zombie's eyes blinked against the debris and dust clouding the room. The head dropped and Chase's hand withdrew as quickly as it had appeared.

The head lay there, fixated on Dee. He recognized the tribal art tattoo on the side of its face from the battlefield.

Dee snapped a freshly loaded cylinder back into place and sat up, his splinted leg straight out in front of him, quickly firing three rounds into the wall. Chase came back at him, the heavy booming of the FN-FAL cutting through the rooms. Dee rolled and fired a fourth time.

The head on the floor rested on its cheek and temple, jawing at him. Dee put a round into the zombie's face, sending the head spinning into a dark corner of the room. He braced the muzzle of the .357 on the floor, rising to a standing position.

The perforations pocking the barrier between the rooms smoked.

Dee knew there were no more magazines for the FN, so Chase couldn't be reloading. He popped the cylinder on a live round, extracted the five spent casings, reloaded, and paused. What the hell was it waiting for?

"*Uhhhhhhhhhh*—" The zombie staggered into the room. It wore denim cut off shorts, the pockets hanging out of them over its blue-veined thighs. The white socks it wore to its knees had somehow kept their elasticity and stayed in place. Debris crunched under its work boots. Dee turned and faced it, realizing that Chase would have left the door open to the undead, that their commotion would bring the things up the stairs to them. The Colt boomed, the zombie slumping to the floor, head-shot.

"You didn't shoot my zombie, did you?" Chase demanded. Dee replaced the spent shell. "You shot my zombie. Now I'm mad."

There was a mechanical roar from the other side of the wall, a deafening buzz, and the chainsaw ripped through the partition, bobbing in and out. The blade pressed down, gouging a ragged line to the floor, spewing dust particles. Dee stared incredulously—did Chase think he was going to saw his way into the room? He did. And he was. Dee put all six rounds into the wall, above and to either side of the blade. The chainsaw withdrew but revved on the other side, reappearing perpendicular to the initial incision. It drew across lengthwise, an inverted L perforating the wall.

Dee hastily reloaded and emptied the Python, a succession of booms. The chainsaw blade disappeared and the racket subsided as the engine sputtered out, replaced by an "*ahhh—ahhh—ahhh*," the sound of someone hurt.

"...*ahhh, ahhh, ahhh*, you got me," Chase spoke through the wall. "Oh fuck, you got me good," he coughed—"I guess...I guess it's over"—the cough melodramatic, transitioning from a faux-death rattle—"it's over"—to a brittle titter—"It's over!"—followed by a full throated chuckle—"Over!" The wall burst asunder as Chase came through it like a wrecking ball—

"It's never over, motherfucker!"

—and into the room, wielding a truncheon.

Though he was neither as tall nor as malformed as his brothers and sister, Chase's ontogeny had not proceeded unmarred. Bent through the trunk, his torso was warped and scoliotic, detracting from his true height. Wide through the shoulder, he was clad in a flannel, checkered shirt and canvas pants cut off below the knee. His eyes were wide set in a face masked by stringy, sparse hair that draped down the top of his liver spotted skull, fine hairs like the silk on corn. Chase's face was off-center upon an asymmetrical head, his lower jaw protruding above a pronounced chin, his ears tiny.

"Never over!"

Anyone in the room would have gotten a good look at him, but the room Chase stepped into was vacant. Spent shell casings glinted on the floor. A cloud of building materials wafted through the air. Dee had fled.

"Never."

Chase looked around the room, spotting his zombie head and the other dead zombie. The decapitated skull looked like it was spewing stuffing out onto the floor. He heard the undead out on the stairs, their moans intensifying. The bald black guy was trying to escape.

"Run all you want, motherfucker," Chase muttered. "That's right!" He roared at the top of his lungs. "Run, you motherfucker! *Run*!"

* * *

Having torn the splint off his wounded limb, Dee raced along as fast as his one good leg allowed. Each time he stepped down on his shot, broken foot, the pain fired like lightening up his leg into his spine and brain. He could feel his boot filling with fresh blood. He hopped through the grasses, following the green glow lights Kevin and Riley had left. Chase was screaming bloody murder at him from the building.

He'd dropped from the window into the rhododendron beneath, the bush breaking his fall. He wondered if Chase would think to do that. He was betting the munt wouldn't. He was betting that Chase would think *he'd* come down the stairs, and that Chase would come down the stairs. Let Chase deal with all those dead things coming *up* the stairs.

As the night died and the morning sun rose, Dee spied a little boy in the grass. It was the child he had seen stealing from the house, running away by himself, in the opposite direction of his sisters. The little boy Dee had waved to in the window. He sat there, listless, his head down.

"Kid, come on!"

The child raised its head, fixing Dee with its baleful gaze. Dee saw the wound in the boy's throat, the blood sopping the kid's clothes, the grass under him blacker than the grass around him. As the zombie opened its mouth and cawed at him, Dee gave it a wide berth. Shocked and saddened, he didn't even think to shoot it.

Lest Dee lose sight of them in the grass, the chemical light sticks were spaced two to three meters apart. Dee knew their chemiluminescence would lead the mutant to the boat just as easily as they were leading him. The thing—Dee had trouble thinking of Chase as a man—was not screaming at him any longer, which could only mean it was out here in the ebbing dark, after him.

He thought of picking up the chem lights and scattering them but dismissed the idea. Dee couldn't physically bend down and retrieve each light, not with his leg and foot, which were already slowing him down enough. And doing so wouldn't put Chase off his trail.

Chase, Dee didn't fool himself, already knew exactly where he was going.

A zombie was standing with a glow stick in hand and Dee bypassed it, noting the creature's flat, broad face and heavy brow, its round shape and short stature. The undead cocked its head and watched Dee pass, its tongue protruding from its mouth. Its life had been marked by Down syndrome, its afterlife by an olid-debasement.

Dee followed the illuminated trail into the trees, brushing low-lying limbs aside, rushing under indistinct trunks in the opaque shadows. The ocean smell was stronger here, and under it, something else. A moan from nearby gave him a start. Dee turned in the direction of the sound, shuffling ahead sideways, tracking with the revolver. He saw nothing in the dark and wasn't going to wait for it to materialize.

Breaking from the trees, Dee hopped across the sand to the pier. The boat had already pulled away, idling out past the dock. Riley yelled his name when she saw him. Dee made the pier and started across it, stumbling and falling, the wood surface slippery and stinking. He landed on his back, unharmed, amid the stench of diesel fumes, realizing Kevin and Riley had doused the pier with fuel. He regained his feet as quickly as he could, lurching past the upturned fifty-five gallon drums, one still seeping fluid.

"*You!*"

The cry brought Dee up short in the center of the dock, the diesel stink nearly overpowering. He looked past the edge of the pier to the boat waiting in the water. Riley beckoned him—a flare gun in one hand—her eyes wide at whatever sight she beheld behind Dee.

Dee turned to face Chase, the outside of his Drover coat sopping with diesel from his spill.

Chase had stepped from the trees, dragging a zombie with him. One arm was under the zombie's chin, the other across its forehead. The undead gripped a drumstick in either hand and its arms flailed wildly as Chase manhandled it. In the hand that pinned its forehead, Chase gripped a side-handle baton.

"You!" Chase looked down at the zombie in his hold, as if he had forgotten about it, and, spotting Dee, could not be bothered with the dead thing any longer. He wrenched its head with a grunt, snapping its neck, pushing the undead away from himself.

Chase trudged to the foot of the pier and halted, his face wrinkling in repugnance at the diesel stink. Craniofacial malformation had left his eyes wider spaced than normal while radiation had wreaked havoc with his thoracic curvature. One clubbed foot trailed along behind him.

"You."

"What?!" Dee yelled back a challenge. When Chase had been an unnamed presence *out there*—something Dee and the others feared was following them—an aura had accompanied his presence. A nightmare quality attended his being, an ascription of dread on the part of Dee, a fear that they faced something insurmountable. Out on the pier, revealed for all to see, Chase was big and nasty, *yes*, but facing his awfulness in the certainty of dawn, any trepidation Dee may have felt melted away, replaced by anger.

This was the thing that had killed his friend, had *told him* it'd killed Bruce.

"Come on, munt!"

A demoniac look stole over Chase's malformed visage as he raced forward, dragging his clubbed foot. Riley was screaming at Dee from the boat as he straightened the Python, firing—

"What munt!?"

—and missing, the recoil jerking his arm up, throwing off his aim as—

Chase crossed the space between them, a wild, barbarous glare on his face

—Dee firing a second round, Chase jerking to the side as the bullet tore through his shoulder—

"What you gonna do, munt?"

—the revolver's hammer striking an empty chamber following the third discharge, the final round errant.

Dee holstered the weapon, infuriated. "*What you—*" He limped at Chase, his jaw set. Chase had the truncheon overhead, bellowing. They collided, a tangle of arms and animosity, muttered curses and slipped boots seeking a secure foothold on the slick deck. Chase brought the baton down, Dee blocking his arm, hugging it, dragging the limb across his body, putting his hip into Chase and flipping him over onto his back amid the diesel. He leaned down and delivered a devastating right hook to Chase's macrognathiac chin, Chase's head rebounding off the wood.

A glow shone in the distance behind them, the buildings they'd vacated engulfed in flames.

Dee drew his fist back to land a second blow but Chase's leg snaked out, snapping into Dee's wounded limb, taking him off his feet. Lying on his side, his jacket soaking up more of the diesel, Dee lashed out like a mule, his boot catching Chase in the chest and torso. Each time Dee's foot connected, Chase grunted and tried to get a hold of it, and each time Dee ripped his boot free to deliver another kick.

Riley sighted down the barrel of her AR-15.

Chase finally managed to latch onto Dee's injured foot. He squeezed and blood welled from the eyelets of Dee's combat boot. Dee screamed and flopped over onto his back. Chase pulled Dee's wounded foot and leg into his stomach and used it to steady himself as he rose, one leg slipping out from under him in the fuel, until he stood, towering over his supine opponent.

Riley fired and the zombie that had stepped onto the dock behind the two combatants dropped.

Chase looked out past Dee towards the woman on the boat, the woman lining him up in the front iron sight post of the carbine. He flicked his tongue in and out of his mouth at her as he crouched down behind Dee's raised leg, presenting less of a target. Riley fired and the air near Chase's head snapped as the round broke the sound barrier. Satisfied that the woman couldn't shoot him without risking injury to her friend, Chase turned his attention to the man stretched out beneath him—

Just in time to catch the butt of the Python between his eyes. Chase blinked, stunned.

"Keep—"

Dee let him have it again, clutching the revolver by its barrel.

"—your tongue—"

Chase tried to react, tried to squeeze Dee's foot, but Dee's next blows disoriented him further.

"—in your—"

Chase's grip on Dee's boot loosened and Dee pulled his foot free.

"—fucking mouth—"

Sitting up, Dee continued to hammer away at Chase's face and head—

"—you rude motherfucker!"

—until the other fell away from him, draped over the dock, moaning dazedly.

"Dee!" A rifle cracked and Dee looked up in time to see a zombie pitch from the dock to the water below. "Come on!"

He got up, glancing back once at the thing lying there, one of its arms covering its face, a purely defensive measure. Dee turned his back on the grotesquery, on the undead lurching onto the dock behind them, several slipping and falling, littering the pier. He limped ahead. Each time he set his foot down, waves of agony gripped him and he felt blood squish between his foot and the boot sole.

Riley screamed something at him that he couldn't understand and a blow from behind knocked Dee down. He hit the drenched wood and slid forward a short distance. Instinctively he scrambled to get up, slipping on his bad foot, looking back towards whatever had taken him off his feet.

Chase brandished one of the partially emptied fifty-five gallon drums like a battering ram. He had the drum at his knees and then jerked, his whole body into it, momentum and his own brute strength cleaning the barrel to his shoulders. He took a step towards Dee, pressing the barrel overhead, intent on crushing the bald man with it. Chase caught the streak of the flame as it rocketed towards him and managed to drop the barrel back down to chest level, shielding himself. The flare the woman on the boat had fired lodged in the drum and sputtered like a sparkler. Chase guffawed before heaving the barrel overhead once more, triumphantly.

The diesel pouring out of the barrel ignited from the sparking flare, cascading down Chase's arms, chest and torso. He dropped the barrel and howled, wind-milling his flaming arms in opposite directions.

Dee lunged towards the end of the dock, going for the boat, using his hands and feet. He saw the orange rescue float on the water, connected to the boat with a nylon cord. The diesel burned slowly, igniting the dock and advancing after him. Chase writhed in the flames, beating at the fire devouring his body, bellowing incoherently at the top of his lungs.

"Jump, Dee! Jump!"

His Drover coat afire, Dee launched himself from the lip of the dock towards the boat and Riley, towards the float. He fell short of all, hitting the water and sinking like a stone.

Riley yanked off her boots, ignoring the blazing forms careening about the dock, enkindled zombies screeching in agony. She pulled her shirt off over her head, not concerned for the withering forms that pitched from the pier to sizzle and smoke in the waters below. Riley pulled herself up onto the gunwale using the grab rail.

"Kevin!" She yelled before diving off the boat.

She opened her eyes but could see little in the murky waters, a faint glow where the deck burned above. Riley kicked her legs and parted the waters with her hands. She found Dee where she had seen him go under, bubbles rising from his mouth and nose as he struggled. The weight of his coat had sunk him, the duster open and floating above him like some cape. She helped him free his arms of its sleeves and they broke the surface of the water together, Dee sputtering, "I can't—I can't swim!"

Riley had her arms under and around him, keeping his head out of the water. She found the orange float and drew it over.

"Dee—hold this! Hold this!"

"I've got it—I've got it!"

"You've got it?"

"I've got—"

A hand took her ankle and yanked Riley under the surface.

She twisted her body to face it but couldn't see what it was. Her foot recoiled and the thing would not let her go, dragging them both towards the seabed. She feared it was a zombie seeking to bring its teeth to her flesh and she kicked out with her free foot, impacting something. Whatever the thing was, it released her and Riley shot to the surface with a few powerful kicks, breaking from the water, gasping for air, nearly landing on Dee's back.

"Riley!"

"Dee!" She raised her feet under her, refusing to let them trail in the water. "There's something down there!" The raging red flames of the pier gave off toxic black clouds. Zombies wobbled on the beach, wrapped in flame, pitching to the sand. Others stood about, looking vaguely disturbed, watching their brothers and sisters burn.

Riley held on to Dee while Dee held fast to the float, Kevin drawing them to the boat.

They left the dock burning behind them in the early morning light, the wooden structure partially collapsed and submerged. Great rollicking flames licked up from the exposed surface, its smoke marring the first blush of morning, joining that of the blazing house.

"I hope he burns until there's nothing left." Riley's loathing was apparent from her tone, from the way she nearly spit the words out of her mouth.

"Riley." Dee's tone was calmer, his wounded leg and foot throbbing. They'd stripped him of his soggy pants and boots and he sat there in his underwear.

"I hope he lived long enough…" the vindictiveness left her inflection "…to *feel* it."

"Its okay, Riley."

"There's no chance, is there?" Kevin asked from the boat's controls. "About Bruce?"

Dee considered all they had experienced this morning, what he had seen and what had been said to him by the creature now cremated. They could go back and look for Bruce—for what remained of their friend—and they would not like what they found. They could go back and look for the two little girls, but he doubted they were alive, and if they were, he didn't think they'd let themselves be found. They could go back and see how many zombies were on the beach, outside the strip mall, under the water tower. They could do all this, but Dee knew they shouldn't and they wouldn't, so he simply answered Kevin's question with a no.

"Fuck." There were tears in Kevin's eyes as he turned his full attention to the throttle. "That fucker."

"Kev, we need you alert on the tiller there."

"It's the helm, Dee." He pushed the throttle wide open. "The fucking helm."

Riley stared silently back at their wake.

The motorboat glided through the sound, a lagoon prodigious and wide. They could see no sign of land on the other side, though Elmore had told them it was there. The tide subsided with the new day, revealing expansive shoals, gravel bars upon which mis-piloted and abandoned vessels had wrecked themselves. They passed capsized hulls, holed and rusted, vessels half sunken. In the deeper, clearer water a catamaran was plainly visible, submerged beneath their path. Empty life jackets floated on the water, faded from the merciless sun.

The dock and land were lost to them, and as they journeyed east an object loomed on the horizon, a contraption of immense size and voluminous girth. A cruise ship, somehow misplaced here in the sound, its deep draught effectively anchoring it in place. Kevin steered their boat closer for a look at the passenger liner. Its flat transom canted lower in the water than the bow, the retractable dome over an aft pool cracked and vented. A waterslide was visible on the deck, the bridge long abandoned by the living.

"I knew there couldn't be people on it." Kevin looked away from the cruise liner. About the wraparound promenade, the undead tottered on their sea legs, motioning towards the passing voyagers. Reaching out to the smaller boat, one after another they crested the deck-side railing and flopped from the cruise liner to the blue waters below, disappearing with splashes. They followed one upon the other, mindless, deadened lemmings.

Riley and Dee stood transfixed, watching them plunge one after the next. "There's got to be..." Riley thought about it in her head. "The sea floor is probably carpeted with those things."

Dee looked down into the water and wondered as to the secrets enfolded in its depths.

When he looked back, he saw nothing he recognized. He thought about the thing that had chased him to the dock, the thing that had blasted through walls to get to him, the thing that had killed Bruce.

He mulled over the manner in which Bruce had perished. Alone on a water tower, watching and waiting. Dee envisioned the thing climbing up, rung after rung, its movements stealthy and noiseless, catching

Bruce unawares. Bruce had been feverish from his shoulder wound. He would have been easier to dupe than ever before, easier to sneak up on. Could he have been asleep?

Dee wouldn't countenance that Bruce had nodded off—not up there, not even in the condition he was in. They'd all known they were being followed. And they knew whoever was on their trail was not a friend, that whoever was pursuing them was either related to the little redhead and her troupe, to the munts, or to an unknown and potentially hostile third party. Whoever it was—out here—they wouldn't have been coming in peace. There was no way Dee could believe Bruce would have slept on such a threat, metaphorically or literally.

He considered Bruce's last thoughts. Had he seen the thing that called itself Chase? If he had, was Bruce shocked by its appearance? Had it pushed him or had it grabbed him and thrown him from the tower? Images of the beast haunted Dee. The wispy hair sprouting in patches from its head. The curve of its body, its spine warped. The size of its chin, its lower jaw sticking out like that. Dee had seen it clearly on the dock, seen it as the flames licked over its body, consuming it. Maybe it wasn't as disturbing as its brethren they'd faced on the battlefield—*definitely* not—but it was a sight to behold.

He reflected on the earlier battle, on the way those things had stood there with their father, one of them toting Fred's stuffed cat. They'd lined up, relishing the task at hand, the carnage they were about to visit on Dee and Riley and Kevin. And then Bruce had stepped up and obliterated them with the grenade launcher.

I should have been up on that tower, Dee thought, not for the first time. *Not him.* Yes, a part of Dee's foot was nearly blown off and his leg might be broken, but he could have made it up the ladder. Two arms and a leg, he could have pulled himself up. The thing was, Dee hadn't wanted to let Riley out of his sight. He hadn't wanted to be away from the woman. When Bruce had volunteered to man the tower, Dee hadn't argued too strongly against it. His own selfishness had resulted in his friends' demise.

As Bruce had fallen, as he'd plummeted to the ground—the image almost sickened Dee—had his last thoughts swirled about the monstrosity that had pitched him towards his end? Or had Bruce thought of his family twenty-five years ago, before the world changed? Were his thoughts with Tris? Dee wondered if Bruce's concern would have been with them—with himself, with Riley and Kevin—knowing the mutant was upon them. Bruce and Kevin went way back. Bruce and

Dee too, but Dee had been a boy when he'd met Bruce, whereas Bruce and Kevin had been men when Bear brought them together in his army.

Yes, Dee berated himself, Bruce would have been thinking about them. And all he'd been able to think about was Riley and his own bullshit romantic stirrings.

Chase had said—

Dee corrected himself. *The munt* had said Bruce screamed all the way down, and Dee believed it. He couldn't imagine that Bruce's yell was one of terror. He conceived of Bruce's final cry as a shout of defiance, the battle cry of a warrior who expected to get up and continue the fight. So while Dee believed the mutant when it said Bruce had been screaming, he refused to accept its connotation. He believed what it said about Bruce because he believed what it said about Moriarity. If Chase had killed the hermit—

If it *had* killed the hermit, it would have tried to rub it in, like it had with Bruce.

All these dark thoughts weighed heavily on Bear's son. He knew it wasn't good. He had to get his mind elsewhere. He turned and looked out across the water, turning his back on a dock he could no longer see, on Bruce and Tris, on Fred and Victor and all the others. On Chase. *Chase.* The thing—so inhuman—with a human name. Just a name, a regular name you'd give to anybody. Yet Dee couldn't think of it as human, and not because of its appearance. He'd encountered deformed men and women before; Tris had been quite a sight for almost all of the time he'd known her.

He couldn't conceive of the mutant as human because humans didn't do what Chase and his family had done, what Riley had told them she had seen in the barn. Actually, Dee corrected himself, he knew all too well what human beings could do. He remembered his father. He'd seen his father make *how many* kills? Too many to count, too many to remember. Zed *and* human beings. Dee believed his father had only killed the people that deserved to die, those that had it coming to them. People who had threatened Dee or their own group, those who attacked them first, the ones who refused to come back into the fold of civilization, content in their savagery. A savagery which spelt misfortune for others, a misfortune Dee's father would never allow.

And yet, Chase—*the mutant*—had spared the hermit.

Would an animal have done that?

When he was a little boy, they'd come to a town. Their army was much smaller then and what there was of it needed to recover after New

York City. Bear had thought it prudent to put up for a fortnight in an abandoned house where the injured could begin the process of healing.

His father had come one morning, waking him, walking Dee through the house, around inert forms cast in sleep. He'd taken Dee to what had been a kitchen, the floor covered with loose tiles. Pointing out the window above the sink, Bear indicated a tree immediately outside, its branches pressed against the kitchen. A bird sat in a nest. Dee couldn't remember what kind of bird it was, what coloring or markings it bore. All he could recall clearly was thinking then that it was small, so small. *She's going to have her babies in that nest*, his father told him. Dee couldn't imagine it. If the bird was so small herself, how was she going to have babies?

He watched the nest carefully and closely that first day, there being little else to do inside the house. Fighting sounded throughout the day outdoors and the bird did not leave its nest once.

Each morning, Dee looked out the window, checking on her. And then one morning she was gone. She was gone, but three little orbs swayed within the nest. Their necks impossibly thin, eyes slitted, yellowed triangular beaks opening and closing silently. He'd stood at the window, fascinated, until their mother flew back to the nest, the little blind orbs bobbing up and down as she fed them.

What can I do for them, dad, he'd asked his father. *Nothin'*, his father had told him. Dee wanted to touch them, to hold them in his hand. *You do that, your scent will be all over them, their mother will abandon them.* Abandon them. As Dee himself had been abandoned. Knowing what it was like to be forsaken in a blighted land, Dee would never wish such on another living creature. He refrained from touching them, opting to observe from the kitchen.

They grew quickly in the two weeks he watched, their eyes opening, down appearing. Their little voices protested in shared hunger whenever their mother disappeared. They fascinated Dee. He noted the way their mother doted on them, sitting with them, keeping them warm. As her babies grew, she spent less time in the nest and more on its lip, until Dee worried she would be pushed off or one of the babies itself pushed out.

There came a morning when Dee stole to the window to find the nest bare. He went outside, to the back of the house. The gun his father had given him was in his hand, because theirs was not a safe world. He rounded the house to the tree beside the kitchen window, searching the ground.

They're gone. His father spoke from behind him. He'd followed Dee outside. *Yes. The nest is empty.* His father squatted down and studied under the tree with his one good eye. *They flew off, with their mother.* Dee remembered how sad he'd felt. He wasn't going to see the birds again. There were tears in his eyes.

The boy Dee had seen untold zombies and innumerable humans die. His eyes welled up over the departure of the fledglings, over the course of nature. Dee had seen enough in his short life up till then to know that not everyone who left had the chance to say goodbye. *Why?* He looked up into his father's face, at the teardrop tattoo. *Because they were ready,* Bear wrapped one mighty arm around his bony shoulders and held him for a long time.

Dee remembered being that boy, sitting there outside that house on his father's leg, wondering what the little birds had felt when it was their turn to fly. Had they been scared? Had they leapt eagerly from the nest, or did their mother have to prod them?

An image of Bruce—hurtling screaming through the void— occurred to him.

A seagull screeched as it passed by the stern of their boat and he jerked his head from his reverie. The bird dropped down towards the water, its wings held steady, floating on a current. Had the others seen it? The others in Bear's Army, on their way to Africa? The bird flapped its wings and rose gracefully.

"Dee. You okay?"

"I'll be fine, Riley."

"Then can I ask you," her voice turned stern, "what you were thinking?"

"What do you mean?"

"On the dock. Turning around and going after him like that?"

"I was thinking of how scared I was." That was the truth. The bird flew away from them, getting smaller. "I was thinking of Bruce." That was also true. He looked at her. "I was thinking of how bad I wanted to mess that thing up."

"Was that some kind of *he's-a-man, he-can-bleed* crap?"

"It wasn't a man," Dee shook his head disdainfully, "but, yeah, it could bleed."

"He was a man, Dee. Human."

"No. Not him."

"I saw it back there," Kevin said from under the awning. "I think 'humanoid' is the word. It didn't look as bad as the other ones. That one with the foot growing out of its head? I can't get *that* out of *my* head."

"I just got tired of running, Riley."

"Now you sound like Moriarity."

"Why should I run? My dad never ran. Tris never ran."

"What did you think was going to happen?"

"I wasn't thinking. Either it was going to kill me, or I was going to kill it."

"Yeah, well," Kevin concluded, "we Kentucky-fried its ass."

"When you guys left...It was talking to me. It sounded...like us. Like a person."

Riley asked him what it had said.

"It said it didn't hurt the hermit."

"Probably lying," asserted Kevin.

Dee looked down at the back of his hand. "I don't think it was lying about that."

"Why not?"

"It was honest about other things."

"You're either very brave," Riley looked at him sitting there in his underwear, "or very stupid."

"Look who's talking."

She grinned at that.

DOG ISLAND

They reached the barrier islands. Many had long washed away, erosion and a lack of upkeep leaving entire islets disconnected one from the next. Hurricanes had come through and halved still more, rending tears and washing out fresh channels. Others were reduced to dunes and piles of driftwood sprouting from the blue. Tides from what had been known as the Atlantic Ocean rushed out, sucking the waters of the sound to sea.

Among the smaller islands they spotted one larger landmass, carpeted in green. Kevin brought the motorboat in closer. Ringed by beach and plant life, the vegetation grew dense towards the middle of the island, which was wooded and hilly. If there was anything there it was masked from their eyes at this distance, from this vantage point.

"Think this is our island?" asked Riley.

Kevin squinted towards the shore. "Could be."

"Let's see what this brings." Dee fired a round from Kevin's AK-47 into the air, the crack reverberating across the sea to the shore. He fired another shot for good measure.

Riley was laughing quietly.

"What are you laughing at?"

"You should see yourself."

Dee sat there in his damp underwear, his injured leg and foot stretched out ahead of him, the AK pointed skyward in one hand, his back against the side of the boat. His revolver was snug against his midsection in its bellyband. He put his free arm on the gunwale and looked down on his legs. The flesh was goose-bumped from the damp and chill.

"I look ludicrous, don't I?"

"You look ridiculous."

"I'm cold."

* * *

Some time later the sun was directly overhead. There was a nippy bite to the air out on the water. The heavy nylon of a sea anchor kept them in place as they waited to see if their earlier gunfire would draw any zombies to the shore. Kevin had an arm over his eyes, flat on his back on the deck, assault rifle across his stomach. One of the two thin blankets Riley had found was draped over her shoulders, her clothes still wet from their earlier plunge. Dee wore the other blanket over his lap.

Much time had passed silently between them like this until Dee saw the look on Riley's face. "You're thinking about Anthony again?"

"No." She could have let it go at that and he would have let her, but she felt the need to answer this man. It wasn't because she had to or felt she owed it to him. Riley *wanted* to talk to Dee, his leg extended out over the side of the boat, his foot re-bandaged. "I was thinking about Lim."

"Who's Lim?"

"He was my *Sabum-nim*. My taekwondo teacher."

"Yeah, I see how you move. How you hold yourself. Like when I first met you at the bomb. You got into this stance, holding your arms..." Dee tried to physically replicate what he remembered from his seated position but couldn't. Both he and Riley laughed at his effort. "You looked like you were going to mess me up."

"I work in a *dojang* back home."

"What's a *dojang*?"

"A gym. I teach taekwondo."

"You teach?"

"Yeah."

"So you're a master?"

"Not quite." Riley thought about her own training, about her sixth *dan*. "Not technically. In taekwondo, there's belts, right? When you get your fourth degree black belt, you're *sabum-nim*—you can teach."

"*Sabum-nim* isn't master?"

"Not in the sense that you're thinking. You've mastered the art well enough to teach it to others, but true mastery—*Sahyun*—is rewarded with the seventh and eighth black belts."

180

"So you're...*sabum-nim*. What are you, like fourth or fifth degree?"

"Fifth. Working towards my sixth."

"Man, seventh or eighth sound like they can take forever."

"They can. And they should."

"Lot of hard work and suffering for anything desirable, huh? That it?"

"Well, look at you guys," Riley answered him. "Out here fighting zombies for decades. But taekwondo isn't about suffering. It's about discipline."

"Lim was your *sabum-nim*?"

"Yes, until I was fourteen."

"What happened at fourteen?"

"He died."

"Oh. Sorry."

"He had cancer." The boat rose and lowered on the swells. "He taught right up to the end. I went and saw him before he died. He was so weak. He smiled this little smile for me and lifted his fingers from the bed. He was waving at me. I didn't let him see me cry."

"Sounds like you were a tough girl. And Lim was a tough man. *Mentally,* I mean."

"He was. I always thought— *that's* how I'd want to die. Like he did. I mean—when the time comes, and you know there's no way out of it—quietly. Bravely. He didn't whine. He didn't say, *why me?*"

"You think that's what you're doing, is that it? Whining about Anthony? About your friends?"

"In *my* head I am. I don't know why, I can't explain it. I just have this feeling that things are going to get so much worse before they get better. *If* they get better."

"It's going to get better." He tried to reassure her. "The last few days? They were about as bad as it can get for someone. For you, for me. But, personally Riley—and I only met you not too long ago, right?—I don't know how you're holding up as strong as you are."

"Thanks, Dee."

"And it is going to get better."

"When?"

"From this moment on."

"You promise?"

He didn't hesitate. "Yes, I do."

She favored him with a winsome grin and he paused to savor it. When she looked away he asked her, "What happened after Lim died?"

"My dad found me another *sabum-nim*. I trained with him." She moved her hand around in the air before her, balled fist opening to a knife hand. "Took over his *dojang* when he thought I was ready, when he felt he couldn't continue."

"He couldn't continue?"

"Cancer." She pushed back at the atmosphere with her palm. "Again."

"Yeah, there is a lot of that." Dee looked into the blue sky. "Damn this world of ours."

"He's not dead. Not yet. He's still alive and doing okay. I saw him a few weeks ago, actually."

"Well, that's good then."

"You know," she lowered her hand, "I've never talked to anyone about this."

"Why not?"

"I don't know. I never thought it would be interesting to anyone."

"I think it's interesting, Riley. I think you're interesting."

She blushed and looked away.

"Sorry, Riley."

"No, it's—"

"No, you know what it is? I *get you*, Riley."

"You get me, huh."

"Yes I do."

"Yeah." She thought about it. "Maybe you do."

"We've still got a few hours left of daylight." Kevin had risen from his nap, joining them. "You guys want to take a chance, go check it out?"

They scanned the shore with Dee's minocular. No zombies were in sight.

"I don't think we should get off the boat." Riley sounded hesitant.

"And I agree with you." Kevin nodded. "But we don't have enough fuel to get anywhere else."

"You guys took the time to douse the pier with fuel, but you didn't bring any extra for the boat?"

"Those drums were heavy, Dee."

"So," Riley hadn't taken her eyes from the island, "we either go and explore it, or…?"

"Or we sit here and wait," Kevin laid out the other option, "for whatever, whenever."

"Let's take our chances on land," suggested Dee. "Riley." She looked over at him. "What'd I tell you?" The towel covered his bare legs. "From this point on—it gets better." His bandaged foot. "I promise."

Riley couldn't help it.

She started to laugh again.

* * *

As they approached the shore, Kevin trimmed up the motor, pointed the bow towards the beach and let the engine idle. The boat glided forward until they all felt the first touch of sand under the hull, at which point Kevin gave the boat a little fuel, effectively beaching it without damage. Riley leapt from the deck to the shore. Her AR-15 was in hand but no suitable targets presented themselves.

"Do we need to tie it up or anything?" Dee asked as Kevin and Riley helped him over the side of the boat.

"We can anchor it later on." Kevin didn't add that, depending on what they found here on the island, they might be in a rush to get back out onto the open water. "Tie that blanket around yourself, Dee."

"I'm not embarrassed." Dee looked down at his underwear, at his naked legs.

"We are."

"Oh, that was a good one, Riley."

"Glad you think so, Dee."

A dog's bark brought them up short halfway between the surf and the tree line. She came out of the trees raising a racket, a medium-sized, mixed-breed collie-whippet.

"Riley, wait," Kevin said. She had raised the AR to her shoulder.

The dog launched itself into a sprint towards them.

Riley was sighting along the barrel when Kevin—"Wait!"—stepped in front of her. The dog reached the three and began to circle them, its hind legs shaking, tail between its legs, tongue hanging out of its mouth. It looked wary but happy to see them, its face just about smiling.

"You're not gonna hurt us, are you, boy?" Kevin took a knee, placing his assault rifle in the sand, leaving Dee to stand in his towel on one leg. The dog came in close and smelled the hand Kevin held out before licking it. "There, there you go…" She leapt up, her front paws on Kevin's shoulders, licking his face furiously. "Hey, there you go, okay!" Kevin turned his face from the onslaught, sputtering happily.

"Glad you made a friend." Dee had his hands out at his sides, one filled with the Python, trying to balance himself.

"There's a dog, there's no zombies, right?" It made sense to Riley.

"Hopefully not," Dee agreed.

"What about it, girl—" Kevin had gotten a look under her tail "—there anything on this island we need to worry about?"

The dog prostrated herself on her back, twisting her body and offering Kevin her tummy.

"That's cute." Riley had to grin, lowering her AR, returning to Dee, who thanked her as he placed an arm around her shoulders.

Kevin stroked the dog's belly. "Yeah, you're a good girl, I can tell. You're looking a little skinny, girl." Kevin tore open a sealed package and found something edible for the dog. "Here you go, here you go. You came out to meet me and my friends, didn't you?"

"Feeling better about leaving the boat?" Dee asked Riley.

"We'll see."

Kevin was feeding the dog out of his hand, stroking her flanks, talking to her.

"Hey, Kev? Maybe we can get a move on?"

"Yeah." Riley glanced towards Dee leaning on her. "This guy is heavy."

Their new companion accompanied them as they trekked through the sand, circling small dunes, leaving the lap of water on the shore behind them. The beach grasses transitioned to eastern prickly pear, the low growing perennial cactus bearing red fruit. They stepped into the first of the trees, Pindo palms with thick, strong trunks. As they progressed, the land rose slightly, and the palms grew taller. The going was slow with Dee and his foot, but the afternoon was sunny and cool, the palm fronds swaying in a slight breeze. The dog ran ahead of them and then returned, dancing around the trio, leaping into the air, excited, joyful.

A wail froze them where they were.

"Zombie?" Riley crouched, bringing the AR-15 up.

"You have to ask." Dee was doing his balancing act again, the hand with the .357 raised.

"The dog doesn't look bothered," Kevin noted. Surely enough, their four legged companion continued to bound ahead and back, circling them, a happy look on her face.

"Let's be *real* careful," Dee cautioned unnecessarily. The blanket he had wrapped around his midsection came undone and fell to the ground.

No one found it funny.

"Kev—" Dee looked down at his towel. "Help me!"

They spied the house's roof through the palms before they reached it. The wail of the undead sounded once more, no closer than previously. The trees around the house had been cut back years before, clearing an area about the grounds. Some of the palms around the property were six meters tall.

The home was elaborate and multi-storied, reflecting the Queen Anne style of the Victorian era. A shingle-covered, multi-gabled roof boasted tall chimneys and both shed and gable-roofed dormers. It bristled with turrets and a round corner tower. Stone banding and decorative brickwork sided the house. There were no signs of movement through the several bay windows, nor any signs of life past the tall, narrow panes with decorative stone arches. A lattice-work skirted lower portions of the house.

Much of the outside was encircled by a veranda.

The three humans and the canine emerged from the trees near the front entrance, which boasted a heavy double-leaf door with sidelights and fan. The windows looked down on them, empty.

Together they worked their way around the home, marveling at its size, wary lest it were occupied. The dog ran off, lost to their sight around the side of the house.

They found an overgrown vegetable garden, weeds encroaching upon eggplants, squash and herbs. Cellar doors abutted the home. Kevin gave them a try before stepping back, shaking his head. "Locked."

The veranda and grounds appeared well kept, wicker furniture and a swing in place. In the back of the house, the roofed gallery ended. An elaborate patio took over, constructed of paved concrete and decorative stone. Upon it rested a cast iron fireplace, a barbecue grill with side burners, an assortment of chairs, a sofa and table. One of the chairs had been knocked over. A stone walkway connected the patio to a door in the house.

From the outside, the house itself appeared intact. Only minor signs of disrepair were evident, as though whoever lived here had maintained it for some time until recently.

The zombie cried out again.

They found a pen set up in the shade where the palms met the patio. A hodgepodge of bars and mesh, tied and soldered together, the cage enclosed five undead. There was a blur within as one rushed to the side nearest them, peering intently through the bars.

"Well," Kevin noted curtly, "*that's* going to be an issue."

They neared the pen, weapons at the ready. A tall, thin male zombie stood pressed against the bars, looking out at them. It wore a suit with vest and tie, its dress shoes crusted with dried mud. A young female zombie in a soiled sundress sat in the dirt behind the first, legs splayed before it. A checkered bonnet was tied in place under its chin.

The fast-moving zombie bore a flagitious look on its face that perfectly matched its corrupted body. It darted from one section of the enclosure to the next in an attempt to get a better view of the three human beings. In the back of the pen, keeping to itself but watching their every move, a yellow-toothed ghoul crouched, its eyes darting about furtively, its gaze astute, missing nothing. Its two-pocketed Guaybera had once been white.

The fifth zombie stood in place off to the side, watching them with forlorn eyes. Twigs and clumps of earth clung to its beard. The ripped t-shirt it wore rode up over its blue veined pot-belly. The shirt bore a single word: *COLLEGE*.

The suited zombie opened its mouth, emitting a low rasp. Riley shuddered.

"That look like somebody to you," Kevin asked, "up at that window?"

A Palladian window faced them from the second story of the house. Divided into three parts, a figure was pressed against the largest, center pane, under the arch.

"Hello!" Dee waved. "Hi!"

"What are you doing?" Riley remembered when she'd been with Anthony and Troi and Evan, when they'd hailed the farmhouse. What had come out...

Dee continued to wave at the figure in the window, which remained unresponsive.

"I don't think it's alive." Kevin lowered his AK-47. "Whoever it is."

The fast moving zombie screamed, startling them.

"Son of a—" Dee lifted his arm off Riley and hopped closer to the pen, losing his blanket again.

"Wait." Riley looked from the window to the caged zombies. "Dee, wait."

The wicked-looking zombie that had bellowed at them was straining to press its head between two bars. The Python boomed as Dee shot it in the head.

The zombie in the sundress looked up at that.

"Dee, wait—" Dee had cocked back the hammer on the revolver and was lining up the suited zombie. "*Wait!*"

"What?" He looked at Riley.

"Later, okay?"

He saw the look in her eyes. For some reason this was important to her. "Okay."

The zombie squatting in the back of the enclosure in its Mexican wedding shirt stared bitterly at him.

"What?" Dee demanded of it. The thing cracked its mouth open, a periodontal nightmare of rotted gums and carious teeth, hissing at him.

"Hey, girl!"

The boom from the revolver had brought the dog back. She sought Kevin's hand, and when he petted her head she lathered his fingers with her tongue before bounding away again.

Dee, Kevin and Riley continued their perambulation of the grounds, checking the one side they had yet to see. A concrete birdbath and its pedestal had fallen to the ground. It was a quarter full of water and their canine friend was lapping from it as they rounded the house. She saw them and trotted off to the shade where another dog lay. This second animal was old, its dark coat shot through with white hair.

"Looks like your friend has a friend," said Riley. The old dog brushed its tail against the ground but made no move to rise.

"Hey there," Kevin called. "What's your name?"

A sizable keg with a spigot towards its bottom was next to the house, near the dogs. A downspout from the roof leader emptied into the barrel, which was sealed with a screened lid. A wooden bucket with a ladle was set beneath the spigot. Kevin tapped on the barrel with the muzzle of his AK. When nothing stirred within he crouched and loosed the spigot, discolored water emptying into the bucket. He let it flow for a few seconds until it cleared and then he cupped his hands, the AK hanging by its strap from his shoulder.

He sipped at the water tentatively and then wholeheartedly, lathing handfuls over his face and neck. "Damn, that's good."

"You get the runs in a couple hours," Dee warned him, "don't blame anyone except yourself."

Riley had approached a blue tarp pulled over a woodpile. Two axes were embedded in a stump set next to the stack. One axe was solid steel, no more than fourteen inches from wedge to heel. The other was significantly larger, a yellow handle leading from a woodchopper's maul with two ends, one for splitting wood and one for driving wedges.

She wrapped her hand around the larger axe and pulled, but it did not budge. The smaller axe came right out of the wood. "What do you guys think?"

"Nice axe," said Dee.

"No, I mean the house."

"I think they're all dead." Kevin walked over to the woodpile and tried his hand at the larger axe. "I think, those things in the pen—" he grunted, trying to pull the axe from the stump "—used to live here." He strained again before giving up. "Man, that thing is in there good."

"What's up in the window, then?" Dee leaned against the side of the house on one hand, his other brushing the top of the old dog's head with his knuckles.

"Let's go find out." Riley didn't replace the smaller axe.

They stood on the veranda, considering the front double doors. Kevin had cupped his hands to the glass of the side window and scanned the interior of the home. "I can't see anything." He stepped back. "Riley, can you kick the door open?"

"And what?" She reached out and tried the door handle. "Break my foot like this guy?" The door opened inwards, noiselessly.

They stepped into a roomy, wood-floored foyer. An umbrella rack flanked one side of the doors, a coat and hat rack the other. Openings led to rooms on their left and right. A staircase rose to a second floor, lost around a bend at an intermediate landing. The banister, handrail and railing atop the vertical balusters were of finely crafted woodwork.

"Dee," Kevin looked at Riley and nodded to the right, "you wait here."

She handed Dee the axe. "Hold this for me."

Riley stepped into the library. Though the house felt empty, her assault rifle was ready. Bookcases covered two of the four walls in the library, each lined with a variety of tomes. The metal scuttle next to the fireplace brimmed with wood. An enormous desk took up most of the wall underneath a curtained window.

As she entered each room, Riley noted how spacious and high-ceilinged each was. Together the rooms comprised a curious, decorative mix of period furnishings and arrangements and would have been considered contemporary twenty-five years prior. Fully draped windows boasted cornices at the ceiling, heavy curtains tied back with ornamental ropes. A variety of rugs and oilcloths decorated the hardwood floors.

"Living room is clear." Kevin's voice was distant in the large home.

The dining room featured a sideboard with mirrors and a rounded-edged table under a chandelier. A floor-length cloth covered the table. The parlor was taken up with balloon-backed wooden chairs, a plush-covered round table, and a velvet, upholstered sofa.

"Kitchen clear," called Kevin.

Riley stared up at the elaborately detailed ceiling molding before stepping into the mud room where she met Kevin again. "All clear on my side," she said.

The mud room featured a variety of appliances, including a washing machine and dryer rendered useless due to the lack of electricity. Unlike the rest of the house, its floor was tiled. One door gave onto the backyard patio and the zombie pen. A second door led to a basement. A flight of steep stairs took them down to a wood burning stove, concrete double washbasin and rows of wine cabinets.

"Whoa." Kevin selected a bottle from the rack and blew the dust off the label. "Nice."

Riley crossed the basement to the cellar doors and unlatched them. She opened them to the afternoon light and stood there on the stairs, half in the ground, looking at the palm trees swaying in the breeze.

After she closed and locked the cellar doors, they returned to the mud room, splitting up once more. Riley went the way Kevin had come, entering a kitchen shining with stainless steel appliances. Pots and pans hung from a rack above a sizeable, granite-topped kitchen island. She ran her index finger across the handles of a block of knives next to the double-bowl sink and looked out the window above the basins. It offered an unobstructed view of the zombies in their corral.

Paint-stained drop cloths covered the walls and floors of the next room. An aluminum folding ladder was open in the middle of the floor.

Unopened cans of paint lined one wall. The next room was a modern living room with a leather sectional couch and a fully stocked entertainment center that led out onto the vestibule where Riley found Dee waiting, revolver in one hand, axe in the other.

"How's it look?"

"Empty," she told him.

"Kevin's upstairs already."

She let him put his arm around her shoulders and helped him to the stairs. The staircase reached a small landing and turned before continuing, ending at a narrow, door-lined corridor. The hallway stretched from one side of the house to the other, a window at the end granting access to the late afternoon sunlight. As they reached the top of the stairs, Kevin stepped from a bedroom.

"This place is beautiful," he said. "These people must have been loaded."

Doors off either side of the passage led to bedrooms connected by adjoining baths. Dark woods composed the floors, walls and doors of this second story. Each room contained a bed and a variety of antique armoires, dressers and dressing tables. One bathroom contained a shower-curtained claw foot tub, while another featured a shower/bath stall with sliding glass doors.

They found her in the master bedroom.

Larger than the other bedrooms, its canopy bed was neatly made. Dust ruffles masked the gap between the box spring and the wood floor. A window seat was set at a Palladian window, the same one they had seen from outside. A body rested there, clad in a house dress, its partially skelefied head resting against the glass.

One by one they stepped to the body and looked out the window. She'd been sitting there, looking out at the zombies in the pen. Even now the Guayabera-clad undead was staring back up at them.

A stain, marking the wood of the wall and floor beneath the window seat, spoke to the liquefaction of bodily tissue, to the disintegration of the body upon death. Whatever stink had accompanied her decomposition was long dissipated, the windows in the bedroom open.

Riley gazed down on the caged zombies. "They were her family."

"What do you think happened to her?" asked Dee.

"She died."

"Well," Kevin said as he looked the corpse over, "she wasn't bit." He said what they were all thinking. "If she'd been bit, she'd be roaming the house, not slumped over here at the window."

Who had she been, Riley wondered. A mother? Wife? Daughter? What were her hopes, what were her dreams? Staring out at her family... Had she borne hope for them, or were her last moments given to despair?

"Riley." Kevin was talking to her. "Give me a hand." He'd pulled a floorcloth over. Riley rifled through her pack, looking for something to cover her hands with before they touched her. She dropped a speedloader for her Taurus and it rolled across the wooden floor.

"I've got it," said Kevin.

"Here." Dee had stripped cases from the pillows on the bed and tossed them across to Kevin and Riley. They pulled them over their hands and forearms and took the corpse from the window, placing it gently on the oilcloth. They wrapped her up in it and carried the carpet down the stairs.

* * *

"What is this again?" Dee looked at the liquor in his glass, the evening air on the island crisp.

"Mint Juleps." Kevin had found a sealed bottle of bourbon in the basement and mint leaf in the garden on the side of the house. "Minus the ice, minus the sugar." They'd settled on wicker chairs on the veranda. Draped with a thin blanket, Kevin had a dog on either side of him, a tall glass in his hand and a very satisfied look on his face. His AK-47 lay across his lap.

"This stuff tastes like..." Dee set the glass down on the table his freshly dressed leg rested on. Earlier, Riley had found a pair of men's grey sweat pants in a bedroom dresser. Kevin had helped Dee change into them.

"That good?"

"No."

Kevin chuckled. The old dog looked like it was sleeping. The younger one glanced up at him and then at the full moon, apparently very pleased with the situation.

"What kind of whiskey is in this, Kev?"

"Bourbon."

"Did it go bad or something?"

"Nah." Kevin sipped his drink. "This stuff will last forever."

Dee eyed his glass suspiciously. People used to enjoy this stuff? "Kev?"

"Mmmm."

"How important is Africa to you, really?"

"Really?" Kevin touched the fresh mint sprig garnishing his glass. "Not at all. Up until about now, I was just thinking we'd catch up to the others, get some help for Bruce."

"They're long gone by now."

"What about you? What about your foot, Dee?"

"Oh, I'll be all right."

Riley and Kevin had carted water from the cistern and heated it on a fire. Kevin helped Riley carry water into the house to fill one of the tubs. A bath, Kevin had to admit, sounded like a great idea, but he was exhausted. He'd washed his side and crotch and under his arms.

"Hey, Kev." Dee fingered the crutch he'd put together out of a mop, a sofa pillow and duct tape.

"I'm here, Dee."

"Maybe we can stay right here."

"Right here?"

"Yeah, why not?"

"And what?"

"And heal up. My foot. Your side. Then get Riley back to where she's from."

"What about you and me, Dee?"

"I don't know. Maybe we can check it out ourselves."

"Check what out?"

"Where Riley's from."

"What about where Riley's from?" She stepped around the veranda, a towel on her head, her hair wet. She was wearing thin cotton pants and a t-shirt she'd found somewhere in the house and had placed a blanket across her shoulders.

"Dee was just saying, maybe we should stay here for awhile, lick our wounds. Then see about getting you back to New Harmony."

"I was just thinking," said Dee.

Riley sat down on the couch next to Dee. She inspected the bandages on his foot before picking up his glass, eyeing its contents. "What is this?"

"Bourbon," answered Kevin.

"Tastes like crap, Riley."

She sipped from the glass. "It does." She took another sip. "Is this how it's supposed to taste?"

Dee looked towards Kevin. "He says it is."

"It needs ice," Kevin hastened to add. "And sugar."

They sat around on the veranda, listening to the night, for a few minutes until Riley said, "You guys have given up on finding the rest of your friends?"

"I wouldn't say 'given up,'" explained Kevin. "It just doesn't seem like the most important thing right now. Crossing the ocean to—where was it again, Dee?"

"Africa."

"Yeah." Kevin scoffed. "Africa."

"I think we should all get a good night's sleep," offered Riley, "and talk about what we're going to do tomorrow. Personally? I'm in no hurry to leave here."

"Sounds good to me." Kevin was agreeable. "How are we doing as far as our ammo goes?"

"I've got six in my Python and eighteen loose rounds."

"I've got a full mag in the AR. Five in my revolver."

"And I've got this magazine," Kevin tapped the banana clip in his AK, "and one other. Oh yeah, Riley, I put your speedloader up on the bureau in my room."

"Thanks, Kevin. I'll get it later."

"You're welcome." It took Kevin a little longer than usual to get up out of his chair. The drink. The fatigue. "I'm going to go sit down over there." He nodded towards a rocker on the far end of the veranda. The young dog rolled off its back and onto its feet, rubbing its head against his side. "Sleep for a little while out here, I'm thinking." Kevin slung his AK over one shoulder and reached down with the hand that wasn't holding his glass, petting the dog between her ears.

"Don't freeze out here," Dee told him.

"I won't freeze." Kevin had his blanket and his dogs.

Riley wished him a good night. Kevin walked off with the younger dog at his side. The old dog did not stir beside the chair he'd vacated.

Riley sipped at the cocktail before holding the glass up for Dee. He took a drink and turned his head so she wouldn't see him blanch.

"You really like that stuff?" he asked her.

"Not one bit."

"Then why are you drinking it?"

"It's chilly."

"Come here."

She was already sitting next to him. She scooted under the arm he lifted. Dee held her and she felt good. She offered him the mint julep and he took a sip. It didn't taste nearly as awful this time.

"Doesn't this feel right to you, Dee?"

"What—this place?"

"Yeah. *Us*, being here."

He knew exactly what she meant and it did.

"Riley, this is the closest I've ever felt to home, whatever that means. You. Me. Kevin. This place. You had a house in New Harmony you grew up in?"

She told him she had.

"I didn't. We were always on the move. Always."

"Can we stay here forever, Dee?"

He looked pleased. They sat together and shared the drink, Kevin's back to them in the rocker, the chair swaying back and forth slightly.

Dee looked down at Riley and she was looking back up at him. "Not tired?"

"No, I am. But I can't sleep." He waited for her to offer a reason and she did. "I see her in my dreams."

"Who?"

"The red-haired one."

"She's dead, Riley."

"I know." Her head was on his shoulder.

"So. Glad we got off the boat?"

"Would you quit?"

"This moment…" He smiled at her. "If I could keep this and preserve it, just like it is, I would. Forever."

"Forever?"

When he leaned down and kissed her, she kissed him back.

"Forever," he said, lowering his head to hers again.

Sometime later they pulled their mouths away from one another, both looking towards Kevin at the end of the veranda. His back was still to them and his chair was still. The old dog had opened an eye and was watching them interestedly, swishing its tail slowly across the veranda floor.

Dee looked at his home-made crutch.

"Help me inside?" he asked Riley.

"Get up, you!"

★ ★ ★

The first sheen of dawn was paling the windows when Dee stirred. Riley slept faithfully at his side, and he leaned over, kissing her on her forehead. He got out of bed as quietly as he could with his injured foot and dressed. Riley had found more clothes in some drawers elsewhere in the house, leaving them for him on the three-drawer dresser next to the bed they'd shared.

He pulled on a long-sleeved fleece pajama top and bottom, glad for the warmth this fall morning. The pajama top smelled old going on over his head and he supposed it was. He would see about washing it later on today, about finding some more clothes. He had the sweatpants from the night before for a second pair, but taking them on and off involved two people with his leg splinted. Dee wrapped the belly-band around his midsection, outside his pajama top, fastening the Velcro. He checked the cylinder on his revolver out of habit before stuffing it deep into the elastic.

He took the Oakley Medusa from the table with the arch mirror and fit it to his head. He knew he looked outrageous in the thing, but it brought him comfort.

Pausing before he left the room, Dee looked at Riley. She was so pretty there, her head on the pillow, the butt of her own revolver poking out from under the cushion. Dee grinned and told himself what a lucky man he was.

In the hallway, on his makeshift crutch, Dee saw that the door to Kevin's bedroom was open. No one appeared to be in there. The stairs creaked under Dee's feet and crutch. He paused to balance himself on the intermediate landing. At the bottom of the stairwell, dull light seeped into the house through the side windows that flanked the front double doors.

He found Kevin standing on the veranda, next to the chair he'd originally sat in last night. The butt of his AK was on the seat of the chair and his hand was on the foregrip. On the table was the bottle of bourbon, half empty. The rocking chair faced away from them at the end of the veranda, into the rising sun. The young dog was nowhere to be seen, but the older one sat sheepishly at Kevin's side, obviously bothered.

"You're up early." Dee carried Riley's AR, taken from the umbrella stand.

"Thought I heard something." Concern hovered in Kevin's voice. "Heard something again." He appeared relieved to see Dee; they both knew what had happened the last time Kevin thought he'd heard something. "Maybe I'm just paranoid."

"Where's the other dog?"

"That's what I was wondering."

"The zombies?"

"Still there." Kev gestured towards that side of the house. "First thing I checked."

"You sleep out here last night?" Dee crossed his arms over his chest.

"I did." The lone dog glanced up and licked Kevin's hand. "Almost froze my ass off, too. Nice jammies, by the way."

"Thanks. Think I'll take a walk. Go check things out."

"I'll go with you."

"No. Stay here. Riley's still asleep."

"You're in no shape with that foot, Dee. Stick around."

"No. I want to check it out."

"It feels different, Dee. You feel it?"

"Yeah. That's why I want to take a look."

"Dee."

"Kevin?"

"Think."

"About?"

"The battle with Tris. Burning Man. Yesterday with that thing. What do they all have in common?"

"I don't know. We killed a lot of motherfuckers?"

"Morning, Dee. Each happened in the morning."

"Which means?"

"Probably nothing, but..."

"If I stand here any longer you just might freak me out, Kev. I'm going to go, take a look. I need you I'll let you know."

Dee hobbled off the porch on his crutch, grimacing anew each time he put his weight on his foot. At the bottom of the stairs, Kevin hailed him.

"What's that, Kev?"

"Dee. Be careful out there. Something ain't right."

"Okay." Dee looked ahead to the palms and the beach past them. "Hey. That thing on the dock... There's no way it could have survived, is there?"

Kevin kind've laughed. "Now we both sound paranoid."

"Nothing wrong being careful." Dee drew the Python, held it up and dipped the barrel, the AR across his back.

Kevin waved as Dee disappeared into the trees. He reached down—"That's a good girl"—and patted the old dog on her head. "You're okay."

After a while Kevin decided to go have another look at the zombies around back. He left the old dog where she was, taking his AK.

He found the pen much as he had earlier: locked and secure. The zombie with the beard and gut was standing closest to the bars, watching him. Kevin stepped nearer and looked in on it and the other dead things inside. The little girl one had shifted position, sitting somewhere other than where it had been before. The suited zombie had its back to him, its attention drawn to the palm trees.

Kevin didn't see the yellow-toothed monstrosity at first, then spied it crouching in the shadows in its Guayabera.

The bearded zombie groaned, reaching between the bars, trying to touch him.

"You poor bastard." Kevin wanted to reach in and pull the thing's t-shirt over its stomach but thought better of it. That would be a good way to get his hand bitten off. And dignity, he reflected, didn't mean anything to these things.

Its forearms resting on its knees, its hands upturned, the Guayabera-clad zombie studied Kevin intently, peering out at him from behind its bearded relation. "You're a smart one, aren't you?" He took a step away from the cage. The thing gave him the creeps. "Bet you're fast, too."

He looked around the grounds, his eyes passing over the bare stump, the blue tarp pulled over the fire wood, up to the window where the woman had sat for who knew how long, back to the thing lurking in the rear of the cage, still watching him.

"Yeah, I bet you are."

Satisfied yet still unsettled, Kevin returned to the wicker chair. The old dog had her head down on her paws. He sat back, the assault rifle across his upper thighs, listening. This island wasn't *that* big. If Dee fired his pistol or rifle he'd hear it. Hell, if Dee *yelled* he'd probably hear it.

When she loosed a low growl at his side, Kevin looked from the old dog to the trees.

"What is it, girl?"

The dog whined and sat up, her tail sweeping the veranda floor.

Kevin leaned forward in the chair.

She raised herself as quickly as her old bones allowed and stepped daintily from the porch to the steps and the ground below.

"Hey." Kevin stood.

She disappeared in the trees, her tail going the whole time.

"*Hey!*"

Kevin waited but the dog did not come back. He looked around the veranda, the rising sun flooding the pillared gallery above the rocker, his hand rising to his eyes against the glare.

"Yeah." He said it aloud. "Something ain't right." The next few words he whispered to himself. "Come on back, Dee."

In the house, he checked the windows on the ground floor. He drew back the curtains and opened the blinds, making sure each window was locked. Although he tied back the curtains, there were still shadows. Another hour and it would be fully light. Kevin thought about waking Riley but decided against it. Chances were he *was* being paranoid. It was understandable. Let Riley enjoy her sleep.

And then it hit him. A detail he hadn't first noticed outside, one that now stood out crystal clear in his mind. The axe in the stump. Was the axe still outside? Kevin went to the window in the kitchen—there was the smaller axe on the granite-topped island where Riley or Dee had left it—went to look and see if he was really being cuckoo.

And when he looked out the window he could not believe what he saw.

Kevin flicked the safety off the AK-47 as he exited the house through the vestibule. Rounding the veranda, he scrunched up his eyes against the sun.

Dee had returned, settling his large, dark frame in the rocker. As Kevin neared—

"Dee, you're not going to believe this."

—something in his mind noted that Dee was a black man, and that this thing in the rocker rising and turning to face him wasn't black.

It was burnt.

★ ★ ★

It took him awhile to get to the beach, but when he did Dee found the boat a few meters from where he found the dog.

There wasn't much left of the dog. So little in fact that it was hard to tell that this was Kevin's new friend. But Dee knew it was. Parts of her spotted the dunes, strewn over the cabbage palmetto and cacti.

Unlike the dog, the boat was immediately recognizable. They'd rode in it together, the four of them: Dee, Riley, Kevin and Bruce. They'd taken it down the river, all the way to Elmore and his uncle's place. And here it was drawn up on the sand. Why here?

Dee knew *exactly* what it was doing here.

"Damn."

He turned and hopped away on his crutch, cursing himself for leaving Riley asleep, for leaving Kevin by himself. He made for the palm trees and thought he should fire a shot and warn them.

He'd almost cleared the revolver of the band when a monster leapt up from the sand dune—a flash of yellowed teeth and dirtied Guayabera—and was on him.

★ ★ ★

She walked in a cold and threatening place, surrounded by the night. She walked towards a light. At first it appeared to her a star, the way it shone, its intensity, a pinpoint against the dusk. As she neared it, a figure stepped from the effulgence, a form beckoning.

Anthony.

Not grown Anthony. Not Anthony as she had last seen him, but Anthony as a kid, the way she remembered him as a kid. He wore his beanie, the strings hanging down either side of his face.

He was speaking to her but she could not understand his words. The darkness followed, close on her heels, threatening to absorb her at any moment. Almost to her brother, she saw the concern writ on his face and heard him as he pointed behind her, into the dark, the Cimmerian shade imperiling the light.

Heard him clearly: *Sis, wake up.*

She heard something mechanical in the distance, through the black. She turned—

Wake up, sis.

—and it was coming for her, through the night, through her dreams. Short and mean, backlit crimson. A blade in either hand, chopsticks in its hair. Blood coursed out of its mouth and ran down off its chin. And it was smiling as it came for her—

Riley sat up with a gasp. Morning light streamed through the slats over the window in the bedroom. She reached out but the bed beside her was empty, though still somewhat warm.

Dee.

The house was silent around her. He must have risen sometime earlier. She yawned and wiped her eyes. Riley found the Taurus under her pillow and placed the revolver on the three-draw bureau with the arched mirror while she made the bed. She folded the top sheet down over the top edge of the blanket. She retrieved the pillows from the floor—knocked there last night—and fluffed them, replacing the shams before adjusting them on the bed.

Satisfied, Riley placed her five-shot revolver on top of the pillow and stood back to admire her handiwork.

She padded across the hardwood floor sockless, the grain cool beneath the balls of her feet. Outside the bedroom, the long hallway was deserted, the stairwell yawning at the end of the corridor. A powerful shaft of light beamed in through the window above the curio table and she held up her forearm, squinting against the glare. The door to Kevin's bedroom was closed. Riley figured he might still be asleep. She would have been, if Dee were next to her still.

In the bathroom with the door closed, she urinated in a pan. Looking at herself in the mirror, her eyes swollen from a good night's sleep, her hair in disarray, Riley smiled. She ran a brush through her hair several times, trying not to think that it had once belonged to the dead woman in the chair, knowing it had. She was going to have to do something about her hair.

When she stepped back into the hallway, the door to Kevin's bedroom was cracked open and there was something in the air, an odor. Maybe Kevin was up. The sun continued to flood the corridor and Riley thought about closing the blinds. She decided she'd get it later, her back to the brilliant light as she descended the stairs. They creaked under her bare feet.

"Dee?" Riley stepped into the vestibule. "Kevin?" It smelled like someone was cooking something, and it hadn't necessarily turned out well. Men in the kitchen, Riley thought and smirked. She'd heard people used to joke about that. The rifles were absent the umbrella stand and no one answered her, which led Riley to believe they were outside where they couldn't hear her.

She was going to open the door and step out onto the veranda when her curiosity got the better of her and she decided to see what was cooking in the kitchen. Riley passed through the living room, through the sheeted room with the ladder and paint cans, and into the kitchen. The stink hung heavy in this room, yet there was no evidence of a meal's preparation.

Everything was as it had been the day before, their few supplies neatly stacked, the vegetables they'd taken from the garden atop the kitchen island next to a pitcher of water. She'd left the axe here, too, she thought, but wasn't certain. It wasn't here now, so Dee or Kevin had probably snagged it.

Riley considered the veggies and chose a zucchini. She bit into it and found it wasn't all that bad raw. Not all that good either, but it was fresh food. The kitchen was cooler than the rest of the house, like it had a draft. It's autumn, Riley told herself. Winter would be here before she knew it. She wondered what winter on an island was like.

Filling a glass from the pitcher, Riley sipped her water. She circled the granite-topped island, taking another bite from her green squash. The stove and burners looked unused, but still that smell persisted. Looking out the window, Riley almost choked on the vegetable in her mouth.

The zombie pen was open and empty.

She forced herself to chew the food in her mouth and swallowed, setting the remainder of the zucchini next to the sink. She'd parted the blinds with her index and middle fingers. As she stared at the pen, her hand reached out to the knives set in the wooden block beside the sink. She moved from handle to handle, seeking out the largest knife in the set, and when her finger brushed against the glass she'd set down and knocked it to the floor the noise it made shattering startled her.

She yanked her hand back and touched her chest, breathing fast. "Wow."

Riley laughed at her fear, how easily she'd frightened herself. Dee. He'd *really* wanted to get rid of all those zombies yesterday. She guessed she hadn't understood just how much. The largest knife was missing—see, she told herself, Kevin and Dee *had* cooked something for breakfast—but Riley drew another blade from the block. Just in case.

She'd asked Dee to wait for her, that they could do it together. After all, he was wounded. How was he going to finish off the remaining four undead? Riley hadn't heard any shots, which was unusual. *Something* had woken her, some noise. Not gunshots. Dee *was* crazy, she decided, if he was out there finishing them off without a gun. Riley almost put the knife back but didn't.

"Ow, shit!" She lifted one foot and stepped daintily from the broken glass and pooled water, stepping clear of the mess. She looked down at the sole of her foot. No blood. She hadn't cut herself. She looked back at the water and shards of glass. She was going to have to clean that up, but first she wanted—*needed*—to say hello to the two men. She sought reassurance. Gripping the five-and-a-half-inch boning knife, Riley crossed the kitchen, retracing her steps through the empty room that was being refurbished and then the living room.

She opened the door to the vestibule and the suited zombie was standing *right* there. It raised its hand, index finger extended, as if accusingly. Riley slammed the door in its face. She pressed her back to the wood, her heart hammering in her chest. The thing outside moaned and pawed at the doors. She set the lock and stepped back, staring at the doors, wide-eyed. The undead had its face pressed against the side window, looking in on her.

Dee. Kevin.

Riley trotted back through the rooms into the kitchen, pausing briefly to look out the window on what appeared an otherwise calm, cheery morning. She stepped over the shattered glass and around the island, out of the kitchen.

In the mud room, the back door was ajar.

The draft in the kitchen.

A trail of blood—smeared across the floor—led into the darkened parlor. The door to the basement was shut. Riley approached the back door slowly, the boning knife raised defensively.

She stepped out of the house. The porch swing hung still in the fall air.

"Dee…" She called out weakly, then once more, louder, stronger. "*Dee!*"

The zombie came around the corner of the house, hell-bent on devouring her. It ran in its dirtied sundress, arms and legs akimbo, a mix of hunger and animosity writ on its rotted face. It gained the porch and rammed its bonneted-head into the door, which Riley had thrown closed behind her. It bounced back and faced the locked door. Frustrated, it wailed.

* * *

Riley stood stock still in the center of the mud room, her hand clenched around the handle of the boning knife. Where was Dee? Where was Kevin? *What do I do? What do I do?* The zombie outside protested, circling the rear of the house, crying out.

She looked down at the thick, red blood disappearing into the drawing room. It was dark in there, the curtains drawn against the day. Riley stood in place and concentrated on getting her breathing back under control, listening to the sounds of the house, for any sounds *within* the house.

Okay. She had one outside the front door, a slow one. And one outside this door, a fast one. *Okay.* That accounted for two. But how many zombies were there? Five. There were five, she told herself. *No,* there *had* been five, and then yesterday Dee had shot the one. So there were four. There would be four left out there.

Where were Dee and Kevin?

Remembering the cellar entrance on the side of the house, Riley turned to the basement door. If she could get out through the basement she could run or at least get into the open and put some distance between herself and the fast little one.

When she opened the door to the basement the dead thing in its COLLEGE t-shirt was standing on the stairs. It cracked its mouth open through its beard, showing Riley its teeth. *Holy shit.* Riley latched the door. *Holy shit.*

She listened to it climb the stairs and try the door. The knob turned but the door wouldn't open and then there were no more sounds from the basement stairs. It was standing there, she knew, waiting for her to open the door again.

The thing outside cawed.

When she had steadied herself, Riley made her way from the mud room, back through the kitchen into the sheeted room and the living room after that, aware of each room in a way she hadn't been earlier.

In the vestibule, she peeked through the side window beside the front door. The undead in its suit and tie was still waiting on the veranda, standing around. It wasn't going anywhere.

Riley thought about her options. She could probably take that thing out with the knife, get past it and get away from the house. Then she'd be outside with at least one booker that she knew about. The staircase above and the rooms on the other side of this entranceway were dark.

The darkened rooms would lead through the house to the mud room, but the blood on the mud room floor had trailed off into those rooms and Riley had no intention of stepping into the black to find its source. What would she do if it were Dee? Or Kevin? What else could it be?

She looked up the stairs. The staircase to the second floor was shrouded in gloom. When she had left her bedroom, the sunlight through the window above the curio had forced her to raise her arm. And when she'd stepped out of the bathroom she'd thought of closing the blinds but hadn't because she'd been walking away from the sun.

Now it was dark up there.

Riley hadn't shut the blinds and it'd only been a few minutes at most since she'd come down the stairs. The sun couldn't have moved that much... which left her realizing that someone else upstairs had closed the blinds after her.

Okay, okay. Have to stay calm.

The details were what would save her now, Riley thought. The details.

Think.

The rifles in the umbrella stand were missing. Her revolver was upstairs on the pillow—*why'd she do that?* She'd left the hand axe on the kitchen island last night and it wasn't there now. The stench, like burnt bacon. The vestibule where she stood reeked. Blood all over the mud room floor—

The second-floor landing creaked and Riley ducked into the darkened library.

She crossed the room, the ambient light from the vestibule guiding her to a place beside a bookshelf. She stood stock-still and forced herself to remain in place. Her eyes were adjusting to the lack of light when another creak sounded, the stairs protesting beneath someone's weight.

She heard scraping on the stairs and held her breath, listening.

It was coming down.

Who...?

She knew without having to be told. That mutant thing. Chase. They'd written it off, believing it had perished in the flame. It had survived. It had survived and it had found them. It had tracked them from the burning pier to this island and was after each of them, exacting its revenge. She'd thought it dead: the zombies, the fire. The fire would explain the stink.

A final stair creaked as it stepped to the vestibule floor. Riley stood in the shadows. If it turned into the doorway, she would see it before it saw her. Maybe, she thought, if she stood perfectly still like she was now, it would walk past her. Riley remembered the boning knife in her sweaty palm and looked down at it. She didn't move, listening, trying to discern anything she could, but only silence came from the vestibule.

The glass in the kitchen *crunched* and Riley forced herself from her hiding spot, back through the darkened library and into the entranceway. Resting on the first stair was the stuffed cat Fred Turner had carried, its hair singed, confirming Riley's suspicions. She refused to allow herself to shriek.

A noise sounded from a room closer than the kitchen and Riley—abandoning stealth and silence—raced headlong up the stairwell, around the landing and up the remaining steps, into the corridor. She passed the first doors on either side, choosing the second door on her right, shutting herself inside a bedroom, locking herself in.

She'd been right. It had closed the window above the curio.

Riley backed away from the bedroom door, thinking of her revolver in the other room across the hall. She crossed the bedroom, searching for a suitable hiding spot. She considered climbing under the bed and pictured being dragged back out into the room by her ankles. Riley stepped into the bathroom that connected this bedroom to the next and pulled back the shower curtain, stepping up into the cast iron tub. She drew the curtain back into place and waited, the boning knife raised, feeling vulnerable in a way she never had before.

Dee and Kev were dead. She had to assume they were dead. The blood on the floor...The thing had killed them.

Now it was going to kill her.

No, it was going to *try* and kill her. It was going to pursue her through this house and find her and when it did...*And when it did*, Riley resolved, she would fight it until either she or it was dead.

Stop thinking of it as an it, she admonished herself. It was a man. A man with a name.

Chase.

Different than other men she'd known, yes. The nature of its birth and its circumstances had elevated it to little more than a wild animal. Yet it was human, like her. It could feel pain. It could die.

She made herself breathe in through her nose and out through her mouth. There were no sounds from the house, though the pounding of her own heart was nearly deafening to her.

Dee had refused to recognize its humanity. For him, Chase was some kind of creature, an *it*. Riley granted that Chase's actions—his family's actions, too—were inhuman. But disallowing Chase's humanity elevated him in an unhealthy way, in a manner that threatened enervation and hopelessness on their part.

No, Chase was human. Tough like his brothers, but human. And, Riley knew, her fear was understandable, so long as it did not paralyze her. She'd been frightened sitting with Anthony's body, frightened when the old man, Thomas, and the other man—Dalton—had walked up to her. Frightened, yes, much as she was frightened now. But she'd killed them both. Like she was going to kill Chase.

The tub was cool under her feet.

* * *

For the moment she had to outthink him, outthink Chase until she had the upper hand. Hiding behind a shower curtain in a claw-footed bathtub, she was painfully aware that she did not command the upper hand. She'd fight him hand to hand if she had to, but she'd rather not.

The boning knife gripped in her palm didn't seem like much.

The shadow passed on the other side of the shower curtain. Riley wasn't breathing. She heard him leave the bathroom, stepping into the connecting bedroom. Riley waited another moment before stepping from the tub, locking the door to the bedroom behind Chase.

The knob turned.

He was on the other side—Riley could picture him—trying the knob, and when he found it locked he started punching the door. She stared in fascinated horror as it shook violently, the stench of burned flesh rank here in the bathroom where the man had passed.

When the blade of the knife—the largest kitchen knife—splintered through the wood, Riley raced from the bathroom to the bedroom and into the hallway. She heard a door open as she darted past and Chase was behind her on the stairs as she tore down to the vestibule. She ran through the house, overturning a lamp and ladder and paint cans, Chase grunting and cursing as he crashed over and through them, after her.

* * *

She put the island between herself and Chase and turned to face him as he came into the kitchen. He was naked, his body singed, charred in places. His face gleamed pink from the heat, all of his hair seared off. Still there was no mistaking him: the size of him, the bend to his torso, one arm larger than the other, the foot crooked beneath him, a club belying the speed of which he was capable.

He gripped the kitchen knife in one hand and Riley's fourteen-inch axe in the other. "You gonna keep runnin'?"

"Go to hell!" She screamed back at him, her voice quavering.

"Run, little girl!" Chase launched himself across the island, swatting at her with the axe, missing. He came close to clearing the island but did not, stranding himself belly-down upon it. Riley waded in, stabbing down on his outstretched form. The five-and-a-half inch boning knife sunk into his back. He cursed and swung at her again with the axe, the back of his hand knocking her clear.

Riley rebounded off the kitchen counter, tearing down the nearest object at hand, a stainless steel pot. She threw it at him and Chase—shimmying back the way he'd come—blocked it with an arm. As the pot clattered across the floor, Chase rolled from the island, regaining his feet. They faced one another with the island between them once more, Riley's hands wrapped around the handle of a fourteen-inch stainless steel frying pan.

"This gonna be fun. You want to play?"

His burnt lips pulled back on raw gums and crooked teeth—he was grinning at her—and Chase vaulted onto the island, windmilling his arms, the axe clanging against the frying pan she brought up, the knife tearing through her shirt and the flesh of her shoulder. Riley took his leg out from under him with the side of her knifed hand and Chase flopped down on the island in a seated position, thrusting the kitchen knife he welded like a rapier.

Riley side stepped and drove the palm of her hand at his throat, but Chase tucked in his chin and took the blow on the face. It laid him out on the island and she leaned in to bludgeon him with the frying pan but he had slid from the granite-top like a snake, the pan bouncing harmlessly off the island's surface.

From the floor where he squatted, Chase lashed out at Riley with the axe. She deflected the blow with the pan and tried to step away, to put some room between herself and the murderous freak, but there was nowhere to go and Riley backed immediately into the kitchen cabinets.

They were stuck here together, between the cabinets and the island.

Chase made to his feet, taller than her, stabbing at Riley's face with the knife. She dodged her head and it buried itself in the cabinet behind them. Riley catapulted her elbow up from its position next to her ribs, catching Chase in the mouth, knocking him back. She hit him with the frying pan and he went down. Before he could recover she was over him, bringing the frying pan up and down repeatedly. Chase tried to block her with his arms, grunting with each blow, his blood spattering the floor, the axe lost from his grip.

Riley crouched over him and raised the frying pan, intent on bringing it down and crushing his head to a—

He punched her squarely in the face and Riley stumbled back a step, tasting blood in her mouth. She threw the frying pan in his general direction and missed, the pan rebounding off the island. Riley ran, putting the kitchen and Chase behind her, hearing him slipping in the water and broken glass, regaining his feet.

She threw the mud room door open and screamed at the top of her lungs, "Come on!"

She had just opened the door to the basement—the slacker zombie stood on the top step waiting, a blank look in its eyes—when the axe blade cleaved the air and lodged itself in the doorframe. Riley screamed and backed away from the blade and the seared hand that clasped its haft, a burnt claw.

"You got me good," Chase admitted, leaving the axe in the wall. The handle of the boning knife jutted from his back. "Yes, you did." He took a step towards her—

"Now it's my turn."

—and then another, his arms raised, hands intent on her throat. "Now it's—"

The booker burst in from outside, barreling into Chase's legs. The two of them hit the floor, wrestling.

Riley did not wait to see what happened next. She ran into the first darkened room—the parlor—and then the dining room, circling the shadow she knew to be the table, aware that something was laid out on it. She pulled a curtain away from the window, flooding the room with daylight.

What was left of Kevin lay on top of the table, inglorious and dead. As she stood there she watched with fascinated horror as his blood dripped from the table to puddle on the hardwood floor below. She clearly heard it *plop*.

Kevin.

The ruckus from the mud room was over. There was movement. Riley looked up, and Chase was standing in the dining room with her. He did not look happy.

She let the curtain go, taking most of the light from the room.

Maybe he was thinking about what had happened to him when he'd come across the kitchen island at her, because instead of rolling over the dining room table towards Riley, Chase disappeared under the floor-length tablecloth. Riley didn't wait to see where he reappeared. She hopped up onto the table, getting to her knees beside Kevin's corpse. Chase stood beneath them, heaving the heavy table onto its side, flinging Riley to the floor.

She landed as she'd been trained, rolling from her shoulder to her feet, sprinting through the darkened rooms, leaving Chase to maneuver around the obstacle he himself had created, the overturned table blocking him from her. The zombie from the basement stepped into the vestibule just as Riley did, reaching for her, arms stretched out from its COLLEGE t-shirt. She deftly side-stepped it and darted up the stairs.

Her gun. She had to get her gun.

She found it in the bedroom on top of her pillow, right where she had left it. The cylinder was open and empty. Where would he have put the bullets? Another room? Somewhere in this one? The window was cracked open a few inches where it hadn't been earlier. Chase had thrown the bullets out the window.

Riley heard him barrel into the entranceway and up the staircase, where he ran into the zombie.

What had Kevin said to her last night?

There was the sound of struggle, grunts and a low moan, a tumbling down the stairs.

He'd said: *Hey, I put your speedloader—*

She hastened to the hall, to the top of the stairs. Riley looked down in time to see Chase straddling the zombie, its bearded head in both his hands. The zombie saw Riley, groaned, and Chase looked up at her. He sneered at her, savagely wrenching the zombie's head, its neck audibly snapping. He continued to twist until he had torqued its head completely around to its back.

* * *

He let it drop and the zombie continued to work its greedy mouth. Ignoring it, Chase mounted the stairs. A door slammed above him. In his hands he welded the woodchopper's maul he'd pulled from the stump outside. The same axe he had finished the man on the veranda with, the man whose body he'd dragged through the house and set on the table.

Chase was breathing hard and he was in agony. She'd been smart to bring the zombies into this the way she had, the way *he* had. He gave her points for that. And she was tough. She'd hit him and hurt him and he could still feel that knife she'd put in his back. He'd asked her if she'd wanted to play and she'd given it to him good. Yeah, she was tough. But now, Chase decided, stepping from the stairs to the hallway, enough of this bullshit. The game was over. It was time for the woman to die.

Ignoring the first doors on either side, Chase trusted his ears. The second door to his right was open. She'd hidden in the bathroom in there before, let him walk right past. That was slick. She wouldn't do it again.

The second door on the left was shut. He tried the knob and found it locked. Yeah, this was where she'd gone. Chase raised the axe before reconsidering. He knocked on the door and waited a moment. When she didn't reply, he called out to her, "You can either let me in"—yeah, she was tough, but he had her running scared, and he pictured her huddled somewhere within, crying and shaking—"or I can let myself in." He punched the door, rocking it on its hinges.

"Let me in!" he demanded, bringing the axe into play, hacking at the door.

"Let—"

The axe broke through the door and he lost it, hearing it hit the floor in the next room.

"—me—"

Chase grasped either side of the frame, his knee rising and falling as he drove the naked, singed sole of his foot into the door

"—in!"

A panel splintered and he found himself stuck in the door thigh-deep.

A woman's cry—more a roar than a scream—and Chase, trapped there, looked up as Riley set upon him, a fireplace poker raised above her head, the door to the connecting bedroom open on the hall. He raised his arm and absorbed most of her first blow, a gash opening up on his forearm. He made to grab the poker and snatch it from her hands but she had already drawn it back a second time and swatted him in the head. Chase grunted and attempted to free his leg from the door, but couldn't.

"Bitch!" he cursed her as she split his scalp open, the poker bouncing off his skull.

"Look at me, you motherfucker!" Riley raised the poker above her ear like a baseball bat. "I'm not running any more."

Before he could reply she brought the poker around and down, the blow shattering his cheekbone and knocking him off his feet, his thigh freed from the door frame. Chase rolled onto his stomach and then his hands and knees, the woman beating him about the head and shoulders the entire time.

He lunged and managed to take her down at the knees, but no sooner had she landed on her back than her bare foot snaked out and caught him in his broken face, dazing him. She tried to stick him in the face with the poker, but luck was on his side and Chase managed to knock the implement from her grasp. It clattered across the hall and down the stairs.

Her counterattack relented. When Chase's head cleared, Riley had disappeared into another bedroom.

"Looks like you're running to me!" Chase shouted after her, back on his feet, unsteady. "Yeah—*run, bitch!*"

Let her run, let her run anywhere she wanted in this house or on this island. He'd find her. He'd find her—

"*Run!*"

He'd find her and he'd—

She came out of the bedroom with the revolver in her hand. He laughed at her until he saw the look on her face. A look she shouldn't have had. He'd thrown her bullets away.

Chase lunged at Riley as the handgun fired, pain searing across his torso. He grabbed her and pushed the Taurus away from his person, the weapon discharging into the wall of the corridor. They struggled close against one another, Chase gripping her wrist, attempting to break it. Riley brought the flat of a hand against the side of his neck and he grunted but would not let go. She snapped her foot into his stomach once, twice. The third time, he scooped her up by her leg and ran her across the hall, the two of them bouncing off the walls. They pitched together down the stairwell, the revolver barking.

Though Riley landed on top, her ankle screamed and she knew it was broken. She rolled off Chase, maintaining her grip on the Taurus. The bearded zombie, immobile, its head twisted around, snapped at them. Riley pushed herself across the entranceway floor, away from the undead, away from Chase. His hand had closed around the handle of the poker and he brought it down—barely missing her—cracking the wood floor, the tool bouncing free of his grip.

Riley straightened the revolver and fired, her bullet tearing through Chase's cheek and teeth, splattering part of his head on the door and umbrella stand behind him.

He wouldn't give up.

Yanking the zombie by its hair, an arm around its waist, Chase brought it up close to his body as he rose and made for the door. Riley tracked him with the pistol but he had the dead thing between them like a shield.

He abandoned the broken zombie on the veranda and bounded down the stairs towards the trees. A round burrowed through the back of his thigh, a spray of bright blood showering the earth ahead of him.

He stopped running because he no longer could run.

Chase turned, panting.

Riley stepped around the zombie Chase had dumped on the veranda, careful of its mouth. He was standing out there, a bloody, burnt mess, facing her. Riley hopped down the veranda stairs on one foot, landing wrong and falling on her ass, banging her back. She kept the revolver on him as she pulled herself back up, his smile a ghastly leer, half his face missing where she'd shot it off.

Riley covered the distance separating them on her one good foot, stopping when she was a good three meters from him.

Chase glowered at her.

"Believe me," Riley said sighted down the barrel of the pistol, "I feel the same way." She squeezed the trigger.

The hammer fell on an empty chamber.

Riley looked at the Taurus in her hand, a five shot revolver. She'd fired it out without being aware.

A scowl on his distorted face, Chase growled at her.

Riley threw the pistol away and growled right back at him.

They'd each taken a step towards the other when the remainder of Chase's head came apart, chunks of his skull disintegrating. The rifle's crack echoed in Riley's ears a moment later before being drowned out in a fusillade of gunfire. Chase's body jerked in place, blood misting the morning air, until gravity drew it down to the dirt.

Riley looked over and couldn't believe it. Her father, her Uncle Brent and Dee walked towards her with a fourth man she vaguely recognized. Brent was lending Dee a hand. Smoke curled up from the barrel of Dee's Python, from the Model 7 Brent tensed on its sling, from the 9mm Beretta in her father's hands.

"Fleshy-headed mutant!" the man Riley hadn't recognized yelled. "Are you friendly?" It was Gary, the autistic guy from the hospital. "No way, eh."

"Daddy? Uncle Brent?" She stared at them in disbelief. "Where'd you…"

"Oh—you hoser!"

Her father embraced her, pressing Riley close to his body so as not to part with her again.

"Daddy!" Riley cried between breaths, overwhelmed. "Daddy— Daddy—*wait*!" She tried to push him back—

"Why did Canadians say *eh*?" Gary rubbed the sides of his head. "What does that mean?"

—but her father held her tight. When he put her at arm's length he still didn't let her go, looking his daughter over from behind his mirrored sunglasses. "You're okay?"

"Daddy—"

"You're okay?"

"I'm okay."

"Thank god." Steve's voice was gentle, encouraging, "Then what is it? What is it, baby?"

"Daddy." She couldn't bring herself to tell him what she needed to.

Brent shot the zombie on the veranda in the head.

"Anthony." She barely managed to say his name.

Steve pulled her close again. "I know, I know, I know," he whispered. "Dee told us. I know—I know all about it." His voice broke.

"This is sad," Gary observed. "Isn't this sad?"

"Yes, it's sad," said Brent. "But it's happy, too."

"Why is it happy?"

"Daddy, you stink!" Riley sniffled and smiled through her tears at her father. "Gosh, do you stink. I don't understand—how did you get here?"

"Your Uncle Brent and I—"

"Uncle Brent!" Riley latched onto her father's best friend and hugged him tight.

"Hey there, Rye girl. It's all going to be okay now."

Riley stepped back from her uncle and held his hand, held her father's in her other hand. "How…?"

Her uncle explained. "We got Grimaldi—the helicopter pilot? Guy who dropped you off in the Outlands? We got Grimaldi to take us. He's on the other side of the island with the chopper—" Riley remembered the feint mechanical noise that she thought she'd dreamed "—and Alex."

"*Alex?*"

"Yeah," her uncle Brent continued. "Fool got it into his head to come looking for you guys. Almost didn't make it."

"Huh?" Riley didn't understand.

"He fell," said her dad. "Hurt his ankle."

"His ankle? Me, too."

"He's okay but he can't get around too well. And he got himself sprayed by a skunk."

"Were Bob and Doug KcKenzie really brothers?" Gary asked no one.

"I still don't…"

"He brought us to this house," Brent said of Dee, who was standing off by himself, observing the reunion.

"Dee."

He smiled at her. "Riley."

"Dee, he got Kevin—" Dee was nodding as though he suspected as much "—he killed Kevin, I'm so—" Riley noted the fresh blood on Dee's arm "You're hurt."

She went to him.

"I am."

"You're…" She took him by the wrist and held his arm out from his body, studying his wound. She looked at him, a question in her eyes.

"I'm bit." He pronounced it with finality.

"You're…" She let his hand free and stood there looking at him.

"I am."

"Oh, Dee." Riley clung to him, nearly bowling him off his good foot, half catching him, helping Dee regain his balance. Despite the situation, he laughed, taking her face in both his hands.

"I just wanted to see you, before…" Dee looked into her eyes. "Make sure you were okay."

"I'm okay." Riley's nod was exaggerated. "I'm okay." She hadn't let go of him.

"Rick Moranis and Dave Thomas were both on SCTV," Gary mused, "weren't they?"

"Hey, I know you just got back with your dad and uncle here," Dee held her gaze, "but you want to take a walk with me?"

Riley looked at her dad, who did not appear too excited about the idea. "Yeah—yeah, okay."

"I always thought Dave Thomas looked like Bill Murray," observed Gary, plucking hairs from the back of his knuckles. "They were both in *Stripes*."

"*Hrrrrrrrrrrrrrrrrrrrrr....*"

The suited zombie shuffled around the veranda, one arm reaching out towards them, fingers splayed.

Dee raised the Python but Brent's M-7 cracked before he could fire. The zombie fell to its knees and then on its face as Gary looked out from between his clasped hands.

"That was the last of them," Dee told Brent and Steve. "He must have killed both of the dogs, too."

"Is *Troll 2* really the worst movie ever made?"

"I don't know, Gary." Brent shook his head like he'd been listening to this for a long time.

"Let me help you." Steve joined his daughter in supporting Dee. Riley gave her father a look. "Daddy."

"What?"

"*Dad.*"

Steve understood, but this guy was bit. "I don't ever want to leave you alone again, little girl."

"Dad!"

"No, it's okay," Dee interceded. "Come on."

Together, father and daughter supported Dee as they walked away from the house toward the beach.

"Why wasn't Torok the Troll in *Troll 2*?" Gary asked rhetorically. "And what did *Troll 2* have to do with *Troll 1*, anyway?"

"I said I don't know."

"*You can't piss on hospitality! I won't allow it!*"

"Now you're just talking nonsense." Brent was standing over Chase's body, the muzzle of his M-7 poking about in the remains of his skull. "Cover your ears," he told Gary.

"Why?"

"Because I know loud noises bother you and I'm going to shoot this thing in the head."

"There's not much left of its head, is there?"

"Just cover your damned ears."

Gary cringed behind clasped fingers as the shots reverberated from the house to the trees. "Is it still dead?"

"Yeah." Brent looked up from the body. "It's deader than shit."

★ ★ ★

"So you knew my dad," Dee was saying to Steve as they walked. "And you knew Tris."

"Yeah. I knew them all."

"She didn't speak too highly of you," Riley told her father.

"I don't suppose she would."

The going was slow but they were together, Dee and Riley, Riley and her dad. Dee requested they journey to the other end of the island, away from the motorboat and the skiff, away from the helicopter where Grimaldi and Alex waited. They made some small talk as they walked, trying to act normal when things were far from.

Chase was dead. He was really dead and the island held no other conceivable dangers. Yet Anthony wasn't with them and Kevin was gone. Bruce hadn't made it, nor had Tris or Evan or Troi or any of the others.

And still the dying wasn't over.

The remainder of Dee's existence stared nakedly back at the man and Riley.

They broke from the trees onto a rise that overlooked the surf and stood looking out upon the boundless blue ocean.

"I'm going to go on ahead here a little." Dee limped forward on his foot.

"I'll catch up in a minute," promised Riley. She stood there with her father and they watched the doomed man totter off away from them, down to the sand, finally lowering himself to a seated position a couple of meters from the surf.

"Riley."

She looked at her father.

"I couldn't leave you out here." Steve took off his sunglasses. "You and your brother. I shouldn't have let you go—"

"You wouldn't have stopped us, dad."

"I should have tried harder."

"No. *I* should have told Anthony there was no way we were going."

"He wouldn't have listened to you. You were always the stubborn one, vocally at least. But Anthony was just as stubborn in his own way."

"You're right." She smiled, thinking of her brother. "I know."

"I'm going to walk back that way." Steve nodded towards the palm trees. "Wait for you there. You need me, you call me, okay?"

"Okay."

"Here, you're going to need…" He extended his pistol to her, butt first.

"Dad!" She looked at him.

"Why do you think he wanted to go for a walk with you, Riley?"

"I can't do that, Dad, not that…"

"It's hard, I know." Tears had welled up in his daughter's eyes. "Look at me, Riley. Look at me. It's hard, but you've got to do it. He wants you to."

Dee was sitting on the sand with his back to them.

She sobbed freely.

"Get it out of you, now. Don't let him see you like that. Be strong for him, Riley. Riley, you're hearing me, right?"

"Yes, Dad." She wiped her forearm across her eyes, sniffed, and took the Beretta. Riley pulled back the slide, chambering a round, checked that the safety was in place and stuck the pistol in the back of her pants.

"You be strong, little girl. For him."

"I will."

"You go." Steve put his sunglasses back on. "I'll be waiting for you when it's over."

"Okay."

She went down to the beach and sat beside Dee.

"Do you know that ocean goes on and on and on?" he asked her.

"It does?" As soon as she got it out she thought it sounded stupid and wished she hadn't opened her mouth. *Of course it does.*

"You're here," Dee remarked.

"Yeah. I'm here."

"I'm glad I'm not alone." Dee reached out and took her hand. "What are you going to do?" He squeezed it and smiled at her. "After this?"

"Go home with my dad. I sound like some kind of kid, don't I?"

Dee smiled a little smile, looking back out over the sea. "You're lucky, you know, to have your dad."

"And you were lucky to have yours. Where I come from, your dad is like a god or something."

"He wouldn't have liked that, but I think it's cool."

He squeezed her hand again before letting go. She thought he was concentrating fully on the ocean until he spoke to her again. "I don't know…if I ever thought I'd actually find him out there. I guess I kind've liked going off and being alone, being able to think. You know?"

"Would you like to be alone now? I can go."

"No—stay, please. I'm glad you're here."

He unfastened the Velcro of his belly-band and tossed it aside. Dee broke the cylinder on the Python and checked the load. Satisfied, he snapped it shut and, gripping it by the barrel, offered it to Riley. "Here."

"I don't need that." Her words sounded cold to her own ears.

Dee gripped the revolver, hefting it in his hand. He looked down on it, considering its history, the solemnity of all those who had held it before him. He nodded and laid it in the sand at his side.

"It's going to be a beautiful day today," he remarked. "Alex seems like a nice enough guy."

"He's nice enough…"

"But?"

"Yeah, *but.*"

"Go easy on him, Riley. The guy came all the way out here to find you. Broke his ankle. Got sprayed by a skunk." They laughed a bit together at that. "That's got to count for something."

"It does. It's noble, but…"

"There's that *but* again."

"But I like *you*, Dee. I want *you*."

He blushed. "You just made my day." He stared into her blue eyes. "You know that?"

"Why'd you…" She quieted for a moment, not wanting to lose it. When she could say it, she said it very fast, wanting to get it out there. "Why'd you have to go and get bit?"

Dee considered her question and a myriad of answers, the paths his life had followed to arrive at this day, his last. "Yeah, it sucks. But," he remarked without hesitation or any sense of irony, "I'm glad it's you."

"How do you feel?"

"I feel great." He was amazingly calm, at ease even, staring out across the water. "I like talking to you, Riley."

"I like talking to you, Dee."

"I always have."

A sea bird winged its way past overhead. *Keee, keee.*

"Well," he looked at Riley one last time, "I'm ready, whenever…"

"Can we just sit here for a little while? You and me?"

"For a little while."

They sat together, neither feeling the need to speak, content with each other's company.

Dee regarded the sun, bright amid the cobalt blue. The surf washed up on the shore and retreated, foamy scum left running behind. The ocean was strong in the air, heavy with salinity. Beach grasses swayed hypnotically in the cool morning wind. Somewhere above them, a bird. *Keee, keee.*

Dee thought of his father. He thought of Riley seated near him, his love.

He didn't hear the shot.

ACKNOWLEDGEMENTS

As I was finishing up *Eden*, a sequel was writing itself in my mind. With *Resurrection*, a trilogy became a quartet. These things happen.

I don't want to say this is it—never say never, right?—but this *is it* for the time being, for the conceivable future. I will say that if I want to revisit the zombie genre again I think I'd do so with another *Eden* book. I mean, why go about reinventing the wheel? (Aside from Nazi zombies, that is; there will be Nazi zombies in the *I Kill Monsters* series).

There are many people to thank. First and foremost, my lovely and loving wife, Myoungmee, and our children, Tony Michael and Honalee. I'd like to thank my parents, who indulged the hours upon hours of reading that marked my youth. I used to write action-horror stories that involved my elementary school friends—Greg Pasquale, Thomas Chodakiewicz, Chris Giardullo and Chris Kozlowski—and then when I was in high school, friends like Mark Fotakis and Octavian David. These stories usually saw each of us rising up at some point to play the hero before being dispatched in some horrific way. Thanks, guys!

Three men have been instrumental to my writing *career* (if we can call it that). Robert Kennedy, for whose *MuscleMag International* I continue to work, cut me the first real paycheck I'd ever received for my writing and took the time to comment on and edit my work. The late, great Joe Kincheloe—and his wife, Shirley Steinberg—is responsible for the publication of my academic works. Joe will never be forgotten. Jacob Kier reissued *Eden* when it was just a self-published book that no other publisher or agent cared to look at. I am grateful to them all.

I appreciate and thank George Romero for providing the template and Robert Kirkman and JL Bourne for growing the genre.

Above all, I thank the readers. We writers don't work in a vacuum. We write to be read, by ourselves and by others. Without readers, our existence would be a meaningless, solipsistic exercise. I really like hearing from the people who take their valuable time and spend their hard-earned money to read one of my yarns; I can't promise we'll become pen pals, but if you take the time to email me at tmonchinski@gmail.com, I promise I will write you back.

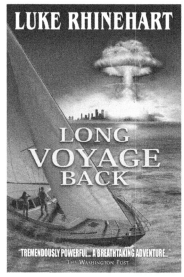
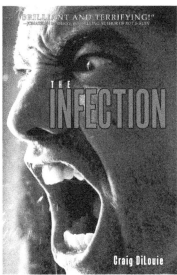

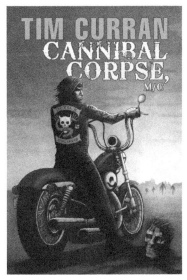
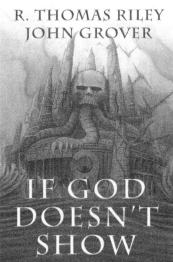
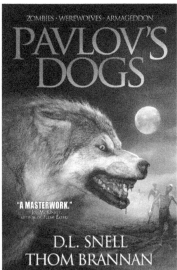

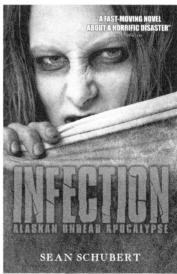

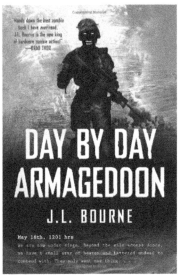
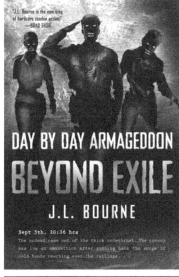

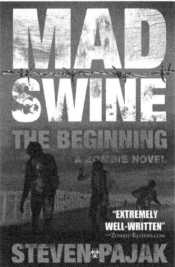

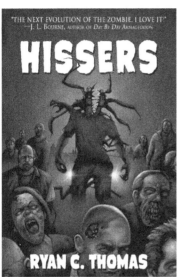

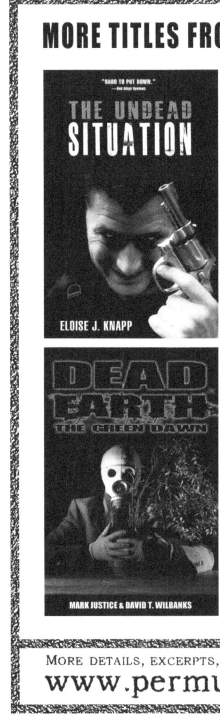

Made in the USA
Las Vegas, NV
09 February 2022

43514452R00135